The Kill List

ALSO BY FREDERICK FORSYTH

The Day of the Jackal
The Odessa File
The Dogs of War
The Shepherd
The Devil's Alternative
No Comebacks
The Fourth Protocol
The Deceiver
The Fist of God
Icon
The Phantom of Manhattan
The Veteran
Avenger
The Afghan
The Cobra

The Kill List

FREDERICK FORSYTH

G. P. PUTNAM'S SONS
NEW YORK

G. P. PUTNAM'S SONS
Publishers Since 1838
Published by the Penguin Group
Penguin Group (USA) Inc., 375 Hudson Street,
New York, New York 10014, USA

USA · Canada · UK · Ireland · Australia
New Zealand · India · South Africa · China

Penguin Books Ltd, Registered Offices:
80 Strand, London WC2R 0RL, England
For more information about the Penguin Group visit penguin.com

Library of Congress Cataloging-in-Publication Data

Forsyth, Frederick, date.
The kill list / Frederick Forsyth.
p.   cm.
ISBN 978-0-399-16527-6
1. Undercover operations—Fiction.   2. Islamic fundamentalism—Fiction.
3. Terrorism—Prevention—Fiction.   I. Title.
PR6056.0699K55   2013   2013015342
823'.914—dc23

Printed in the United States of America
1   3   5   7   9   10   8   6   4   2

BOOK DESIGN BY AMANDA DEWEY

For the United States Marine Corps,
which is a very large unit.
And to the British Pathfinders,
who are a very small one.
To the former, Semper Fi.
And to the latter, rather you than me.

ACKNOWLEDGMENTS

To all those who helped me with the information contained in this book, my grateful thanks. As so often, some half would prefer not to be revealed. But to those who live in the light and to those who work in the shadows, you know who you are, and have my gratitude.

PREFACE

In the dark and secret heart of Washington, there is a short and very covert list. It contains the names of terrorists who have been deemed so dangerous to the United States, her citizens and interests, that they have been condemned to death without any attempt at arrest, trial or any due process. It is called the kill list.

Every Tuesday morning in the Oval Office, the kill list is considered for possible amendment by the President and six men; never more, never less. Among them are the Director of the CIA and the four-star general commanding the world's biggest and most dangerous private army. This is J-SOC, which is supposed not to exist.

On a cold morning one early spring, a new name was added to the kill list. He was so elusive that even his true name was not known, and the huge machine of American counterterrorism had no picture of his face. Like Anwar al-Awlaki, the American/Yemini fanatic who preached hate sermons on the Internet, who had once been on the kill list and who was wiped out by a drone-launched missile in North Yemen in 2011, the new addition also preached online. So powerful were his sermons that young Muslims in the diaspora were converting to ultra-radical Islam and committing murders in its name.

Like Awlaki, the new addition also delivered in perfect English. Without a name, he was known simply as the Preacher.

The assignment was given to J-SOC whose CO passed it down to TOSA, a body so obscure that ninety-eight percent of serving U.S. officers have never heard of it.

In fact, TOSA is the very small department, based in North Virginia, tasked with hunting down those terrorists who seek to hide themselves from American retributive justice.

That afternoon, the director of TOSA, known in all official communications as Gray Fox, walked into the office of his senior manhunter and laid a sheet upon his desk. It simply bore the words "The Preacher. Identify, Locate, Destroy."

Under this was the signature of the commander in chief, the President. That made the paper a Presidential Executive Order, an EXORD.

The man who stared at the order was an enigmatic lieutenant colonel in the U.S. Marine Corps of forty-four who also, inside and outside the building, was known only by a code. He was called the Tracker.

The Kill List

1

If he had been asked, Jerry Dermott could have put his hand on his heart and sworn that he had never knowingly hurt anyone in his life and did not deserve to die. But that did not save him.

It was mid-March, and in Boise, Idaho, winter was grudgingly loosening its grip. But there was snow on the high peaks around the state capital, and the wind that came down from those peaks was still bitter. Those walking on the streets were huddled in warm coats as the state congressman came out of the Legislative Services Office at 700 West Jefferson Street.

He emerged from the Capitol's grand entrance and walked down the steps from the sandstone walls toward the street, where his car was parked in readiness. He nodded in his usual genial way at the police officer atop the steps by the portico door and noted that Joe, his faithful driver of many years, was coming around the limousine to open the rear door. He took no notice of the muffled figure that rose from a bench down the sidewalk and began to move.

The figure was clothed in a long dark overcoat, unbuttoned at the front but held closed by hands inside. There was some kind of fretted skullcap on the head, and the only odd thing, had anyone been looking, which they were not, was that beneath the coat there were no jeans-clad legs but some kind of a white dress. It would later be established the garment was an Arab dishdash.

Jerry Dermott was almost at the open car door when a voice called, "Congressman." He turned to the call. The last thing he saw on Earth was a swarthy face staring at him, eyes somehow vacant as if staring at something else far away. The overcoat fell open and the barrels of the sawed-off shotgun rose from where they had dangled inside the fabric.

The police would later establish that both barrels were fired simultaneously and that the cartridges were loaded with heavy-gauge buckshot, not the tiny granules for birds. The range was around ten feet.

Due to the shortness of the sawn barrels, the shot spread was immediately wide. Some of the steel balls went past the congressman on both sides, and a few hit Joe, causing him to turn and reel back. He had a sidearm under his jacket, but his hands went to his face and he never used it.

The officer atop the steps saw it all, drew his revolver and came running down. The assailant threw both hands in the air, the right hand gripping the shotgun, and screamed something. The officer could not know whether the second barrel had been used and he fired three times. At twenty feet, and practiced with his piece, he could hardly miss.

His three slugs took the shouting man in the center mass of the chest and threw him backward. He hit the trunk of the limousine, bounced off, fell forward and died facedown in the gutter. Figures appeared from the portico doorway, saw the two bodies down, the chauffeur staring at his bleeding hands, the policeman standing over the assailant, gun double-hand-gripped, pointing downward. They ran back inside to call for backup.

Two bodies were removed to the city morgue and Joe to the hospital for attention to the three pellets that had lodged in his face. The congressman was dead, chest penetrated by over twenty steel balls that had entered his heart and lungs. So also the assailant.

The latter, stripped naked on the morgue slab, gave no clue to his identity. There were no personal papers and, oddly, no body hair save his beard. But his face in the evening papers yielded two informants. The dean of a college on the edge of town identified a student of Jordanian parentage and the landlady of a boardinghouse recognized one of her lodgers.

Detectives ransacking the dead man's room took away many books in Arabic and his personal laptop computer. The latter was downloaded in the police technical lab. It revealed something no one in the Boise police headquarters had ever seen before. The hard drive contained a series of lectures, or sermons, by a masked figure, staring at the screen with blazing eyes and preaching in fluent English.

The message was brutal and simple. The True Believer should undergo his own personal conversion from heresy to Muslim truth. He should, within the confines of his own soul, confiding in and trusting no one, convert to Jihad and become a true and loyal soldier of Allah. Then he should seek out some notable person in the service of the Great Satan and send him to hell, then die as a *shahid*, a martyr, and ascend to dwell in Allah's paradise forever. There were a score of these sermons, all with the same message.

The police passed the evidence to the Boise office of the FBI, who passed the entire file to the J. Edgar Hoover Building in Washington. At the national HQ of the Bureau, there was no surprise. They had heard of the Preacher before.

1968

Mrs. Lucy Carson went into labor on 8 November and was taken straight to the natal wing of the Naval Hospital at Camp Pendleton, California, where she and her husband were based. Two days later, her first, and as it turned out only, son was born.

He was named Christopher after his paternal grandfather, but since that senior U.S. Marine officer was always called Chris, and to avoid confusion, the baby was nicknamed Kit, the reference to the old frontiersman being entirely coincidental.

Also fortuitous was the birth date: November 10th, the date of the birth of the United States Marine Corps in 1775.

Captain Alvin Carson was away in Vietnam, where fighting was ferocious and would remain so for a further five years. But his tour was close to its end, so he was permitted

4

home for Christmas to be reunited with his wife and two small daughters and to hold his firstborn son.

He returned to Vietnam after the New Year, finally returning to the sprawling Marine base at Pendleton in 1970. His next posting was no posting, since he remained at Pendleton for three years, seeing his boy grow through toddler stage to four and a half.

Here, far from those lethal jungles, the couple could live a customary "on base" life between the married quarters' home, his office, the social club, the PX commissary and the base church. And he could teach his son to swim in the Del Mar Boat Basin. He sometimes thought back to those Pendleton years as the days of wine and roses.

The year 1973 saw him transferred to another "with family" posting at Quantico, just outside Washington, D.C. Back then, Quantico was just a huge mosquito- and tick-infested wilderness where a small boy could chase squirrels and raccoons through the woods.

The Carson family was still on base when Henry Kissinger and the North Vietnamese Le Duc Tho met outside Paris and hammered out the accords that brought to a formal end the decade of slaughter now called the Vietnam War.

The now-major Carson returned for his third tour in Vietnam, a place still seething with menace as the North Vietnamese army poised itself to break the Paris Accords by invading the south. But he was repatriated early, just before the last mad scramble from the embassy roof to the last aircraft out of the airport.

Through those years, his son, Kit, went through the normal stages of a small American boy—Little League baseball, Cub Scouts and school. In the summer of 1974, Maj. Carson and family were transferred to a third enormous Marine base—Camp Lejeune, North Carolina.

As second in command of his battalion, Maj. Carson worked out of the 8th Marines HQ on C Street and lived with wife and three children in the sprawl of married officers' housing. It was never mentioned what the growing boy might like to be when he grew up. He was born into the heart of two families: the Carsons and the Corps. It was just assumed he would follow his grandfather and father into officer school and wear the uniform.

From 1978 to 1981, Maj. Carson was tasked to a long-overdue sea posting at Norfolk, the great U.S. Navy and Marine base on the south side of Chesapeake Bay in northern Virginia. The family lived on the base, the major went to sea as a Marine officer on the USS *Nimitz*, the pride of the carrier fleet. It was from this vantage point that he witnessed the fiasco of Operation Eagle Claw, also known as Desert One, the forlorn attempt to rescue the U.S. diplomats being held hostage in Tehran by "students" in the thrall of Ayatollah Khomeini.

Major Carson stood with long-range binoculars on the bridge wing of the *Nimitz* and watched the eight huge Sea Stallion helicopters roar away toward the coast to back up the Green Berets and Rangers who would make the snatch and bring the liberated diplomats back to safety offshore.

And he watched most of them limp back. First the two that broke down over the Iranian coast because they had no sand filters and had run into a dust storm. The others carrying the wounded after one of the choppers had flown into the windshield of a Hercules, causing a fireball. He remained bitter about that memory, and the foolish planning that had caused it, for the rest of his days.

From the summer of 1981 to 1984, Maj. Carson was posted with his family to London as the U.S. Marine attaché at the embassy in Grosvenor Square. Kit was enrolled at the American School in St. John's Wood. Later, the boy looked back with affection on his three London years. It was the time of Margaret Thatcher and Ronald Reagan and their remarkable partnership.

Charlie Price was made ambassador and became the most popular American in town. There were parties and balls. The Falklands were invaded and liberated. A week before British paras entered Port Stanley, Ronald Reagan made a state visit to London. In a lineup at the embassy, the Carson family was presented to Queen Elizabeth. And fourteen-year-old Kit Carson had his first crush on a girl. And his father reached his twenty-year mark in the Corps.

Alvin Carson was promoted to command the 2nd Battalion, 3rd Marine Regiment, as a lieutenant colonel, and the family transferred to Kaneohe Bay in the Hawaiian Islands, a considerably different climate from London. For the teenage boy, it was a time of surfing, snorkeling, diving, fishing and taking a more-than-active interest in girls.

By sixteen he was developing as a formidable athlete, but his school grades also showed he hosted a very fast-moving brain. When a year later his father was promoted G3 and sent back to the mainland, Kit Carson was an Eagle Scout and a freshman in the Reserve Officer Training Corps. The presumption made years before was coming true; he was on an unstoppable glide path to follow his father into the ranks of U.S. Marine officers.

Back in the States, a college degree beckoned. He was sent to the College of William and Mary in Williamsburg, Virginia, where he resided on campus for four years, majoring in history and chemistry. And there were three long summer vacations. These were devoted to jump school, scuba school and Officer Candidates School at Quantico.

He graduated in the spring of 1989, aged twenty, and simultaneously got his college degree and his single shoulder bar as a second lieutenant in the Corps. His father, now a one-star general, and his mother, both bursting with pride, were at the ceremony.

His first posting was to Basic School until Christmas, then Infantry Officer Course until March 1990, emerging as the Distinguished Honor Graduate. Ranger School at Fort Benning, Georgia, followed, and with his Ranger tab he was shipped to Twentynine Palms, California.

There he attended the Air/Ground Combat Center, known as the Stumps, and was then posted to the 1st Battalion, 7th Regiment, on the same base. Then, on August 2, 1990, a man named Saddam Hussein invaded Kuwait. The U.S. Marines went back to war, and Lt. Kit Carson went with them.

1990

Once the decision was taken that Saddam Hussein's invasion of Kuwait could not be allowed to stand, a grand coalition was formed, and ranged along the Iraqi/Saudi Arabian desert border from the Arabian Gulf in the east to the Jordanian border in the west.

The U.S. Marines came in the form of the Marine Expeditionary Force under General Walter Bloomer, and this encompassed the 1st Marine Division, commanded by General Mike Myatt. A very long way down the pecking order was 2nd Lt. Kit Carson. The division was posted to the extreme eastern end of the Coalition line, with only the blue waters of the Gulf to its right.

The first month, stupefyingly hot August, was a time of feverish activity. The entire division, with its armor and artillery, had to be disembarked and posted along the sector to be covered. An armada of freight ships arrived at the hitherto sleepy oil port of al-Jubail to discharge the impedimenta required to equip, lodge and keep supplied an entire U.S. division. It was not until September that Kit Carson got his assignment interview. It was with an acid-tongued veteran major, probably passed over at that rank and not happy about it.

Major Dolan read slowly through the new officer's file. Finally, his eye caught something unusual. He looked up.

"You spent time in London as a kid?"

"Yessir."

"Weird bastards." Maj. Dolan completed his perusal of the file and closed it. "Parked next door to our west is the British Seventh Armoured Brigade. They call themselves the Desert Rats. Like I said, weird. They call their own soldiers rats."

"Actually, it's a jerboa, sir."

"A what?"

"A jerboa. A desert animal like a meerkat. They got the tag fighting Rommel in the Libyan desert in World War Two. He was the Desert Fox. The jerboa is smaller but elusive."

Major Dolan was less than impressed.

"Don't get smart with me, Lieutenant. Somehow we have to get along with these Desert Rats. I am proposing General Myatt send you over to them as one of our liaison officers. Dismiss."

The Coalition forces had to spend five more months sweltering in that desert while the combined allied air forces achieved the fifty percent "degrading" of the Iraqi army that Commanding General Norman Schwarzkopf demanded before he would attack. For part of that time, after reporting to the British general Patrick Cordingley, commanding the 7th Armoured, Kit Carson liaised between the two forces.

Very few American soldiers were able to establish either interest in, or empathy with, the native Arab culture of the Saudis. Carson, with his natural curiosity, was an exception. In the ranks of the British, he found two officers who had a smattering of Arabic and from them memorized a handful of phrases. On visits to al-Jubail, he listened to the five daily calls to prayer and watched the robed figures prostrate themselves time and again, forehead to the ground, to complete the ritual.

He made a point of greeting Saudis he had occasion to meet with the formal *"Salaam aleikhem"* (Peace be unto you) and learned to respond with the reply *"Aleikhem as-salaam"* (And unto you be peace). He noted their jolt of surprise that any foreigner should bother and the friendliness that followed.

After three months, the British brigade was increased to a division, and Gen. Schwarzkopf moved the British farther east, to the chagrin of Gen. Myatt. When the ground forces moved at last, the war was short, sharp and brutal. The Iraqi armor was blown away by British Challenger II tanks and the American Abrams. Domination of the air was total, as it had been for months.

Saddam's infantry had been pulverized by carpet bombing in their trenches by U.S. B-52 bombers and threw up their hands in droves. The onslaught for the U.S. Marines was a charge into Kuwait, where they were cheered, and a last run to the Iraqi border, where higher authority ordered that they should stop. The ground war took just five days.

Lieutenant Kit Carson must have done something right. On his return in the summer of 1991 he received the honor of transfer to the 81mm mortar platoon as the best lieutenant in the battalion. Clearly marked out for higher things, he then did something, for the first time but not the last time in his life, unconventional. He applied for and received an Olmsted Scholarship. When asked why, he replied that he wanted to be sent to the Defense Language Institute, located in the Presidio at Monterey, California. Pressed further, he admitted he wanted to master Arabic. It was a decision that would later change his entire life.

His somewhat puzzled superiors conceded his request. With the Olmsted under his belt, he spent his year at Monterey and, for his second and third year, was given a two-year internship at the American University in Cairo. Here he found he was the only U.S. Marine and the only serviceman who had ever seen combat. While he was there, on February 26, 1993, a Pakistani named Ramzi Yousef tried to blow up one of the towers of the World Trade Center, Manhattan. He failed, but, ignored by the American establishment, he had fired the first Fort Sumter shot of the Islamic Jihad against the United States.

There were no electronic newspapers in those days, but Lt. Carson could follow the unfolding investigation across the Atlantic by radio. He was puzzled, intrigued. Eventually, he paid a call upon the wisest man he had come across in Egypt. Professor Khaled Abdulaziz was a don at the al-Azhar University, one of the greatest centers in all Islam for Koranic studies. Occasionally he gave visiting lectures at the American University. He received the young American in his rooms on campus at al-Azhar.

"Why did they do it?" asked Kit Carson.

"Because they hate you," said the old man calmly.

"But why? What have we ever done to them?"

"To them personally? To their countries? To their families? Nothing. Except perhaps distribute dollars. But that is not the point. With terrorism, that is never the point. With terrorists, whether al-Fatah or Black September or the new, supposedly religious breed, the rage and the hatred come first. Then the justification. For IRA patriotism, for Red Brigade politics, for Salafist-Jihadist piety. An assumed piety."

The professor was preparing tea for two on his small spirit stove.

"But they claim to follow the teachings of the Holy Koran. They claim that they are obeying the Prophet Muhammad. They claim they are serving Allah."

The old scholar smiled as the water boiled. He had noticed the insertion of the word "Holy" in front of Koran. A courtesy, but a pleasing one.

"Young man, I am what is called *hafiz*. That is one who has memorized all 6,236 verses of the Holy Koran. Unlike your Bible, which was written by hundreds of authors, our Koran was written—dictated, actually—by one. And yet there are passages that seem to contradict each other.

"What the Jihadists do is to take one or two phrases out of context, distort them a little more and then pretend they have divine justification. They do not. There is nothing in all our Holy Book that decrees we must slaughter women and children to please the one we call Allah the Merciful, the Compassionate. All extremists do that, including Christian and Jewish ones. Do not let our tea go cold. It should be drunk piping hot."

"But, Professor, these contradictions. Have they never been addressed, explained, rationalized?"

The professor served the American more tea with his own hands. He had servants, but it pleased him to make his tea personally.

"Constantly. For thirteen hundred years, scholars have studied and composed commentaries on that one single book. Collectively, they are called the *hadith*. About a hundred thousand of them."

"Have you read them?"

"Not all. It would take ten lifetimes. But many. And I have written two."

"One of the bombers, Sheikh Omar Abdel-Rahman, the one they call the blind cleric, was . . . is . . . a scholar, too."

"And a mistaken one. Nothing new in that in any religion."

"But I must ask again: Why do they hate?"

"Because you are not them. They experience deep rage at what is not themselves. Jews, Christians, those we call the *kuffars*, the unbelievers who will not convert to the one true faith. But also those who are not Muslim enough. In Algeria the Jihadists butcher villages of *fellaghas*, peasants, including women and children, in their Holy War against Algiers. Always remember this, Lieutenant. First comes the rage and the hatred. Then the justification, the pose of deep piety, all a sham."

"And you, Professor?"

The old man sighed.

"I loathe and despise them. Because they take the face of my dear Islam and present it to the world twisted with rage and hatred. But communism is dead, the West weak and self-serving, concerned with pleasure and greed. There will be many who will listen to the new message."

Kit Carson glanced at his watch. It would soon be time for the professor's prayers. He rose. The scholar noticed the gesture and smiled. He, too, rose and accompanied his guest to the door. As the American left, he called after him.

"Lieutenant, I fear my dear Islam is entering a long dark night. You are young, you will see the end of it, *inshallah*. I pray I shall not be forced to witness what is coming."

Three years later, the old scholar died in his bed. But the mass killings had begun with a huge bomb in an apartment block favored by American civilians in Saudi Arabia. A man named Osama bin Laden had quit Sudan and returned to Afghanistan as an honored guest of a new regime, the Taliban, which had swept the country. And the West continued to take no measures to defend itself but continued to enjoy the locust years.

PRESENT DAY

The little market town of Grangecombe in the English county of Somerset attracted a few tourists in the summer to stroll through its cobbled seventeenth-century streets. Otherwise, being off all main roads to the beaches and coves of the Southwest, it was a quiet enough place. But it had a history and a royal charter and a town council and a mayor. In April of that year, he was His Worship Giles Matravers, a retired clothier, entitled to wear the mayoral chain, fur-fringed robe and tricorn hat.

And that was what he was wearing as he opened a new Chamber of Commerce building just behind the High Street when a figure rushed out of the small crowd of onlookers, covered the ten yards between them before any of them could react and plunged a butcher's knife into his chest.

There were two policemen present, but neither was armed with a handgun. The dying mayor was tended by his town clerk and others, but to no avail. The policemen tackled the killer, who made no attempt to flee but repeatedly shouted something no one understood but which experts later recognized as *Allahu-akhbar*, or Allah is great.

One officer took a slash to the hand as he lunged for the knife, then the assailant went down under two blue uniforms. Detectives duly arrived from the county town of Taunton to institute the formal inquiry. The assailant sat dumbly in the police station and refused to answer questions. He was dressed in a full-length dishdash, so an Arabic speaker was summoned from county police HQ, but he had no more success.

The man was identified as a shelf stacker from the local supermarket, living in a one-room bed-sitter in a boarding-house. His landlady revealed he was an Iraqi. At first it was thought his action might have stemmed from rage at what was happening in his country. But the Home Office revealed he had arrived as a refugee and been granted asylum. Youngsters from the town came forward to testify that Farouk, known as Freddy, had until three months earlier been a partygoer, drinker and dater of girls. Then he had seemed to change, becoming withdrawn, silent and contemptuous of his earlier lifestyle.

His bed-sitter revealed little but a laptop, whose contents would have been very familiar to the police of Boise, Idaho. Sermon after sermon by a masked man sitting in front of a sort of backcloth inscribed with Koranic inscriptions urging the devout to destroy the *kuffars*. Bemused Somerset police officers watched a dozen, for the sermonizer was speaking in virtually accentless English.

While the killer, still silent, was being arraigned, the file and the laptop were sent to London. The Metropolitan Police passed the details to the Home Office, who consulted the Security Service, MI5. They had already received a report from their man in the British embassy in Washington about an event in Idaho.

1996

Back in the U.S., Capt. Kit Carson was assigned to Camp Pendleton for three years, the place where he was born and spent the first four years of his life. During those years, his paternal grandfather, a retired colonel of the Corps who had fought at Iwo Jima, died at his retirement home in North Carolina. His father was promoted to general with two stars, a promotion his own father was puffed with pride to witness just before his death.

Kit Carson met and married a Navy nurse from the same hospital where he had been brought into the world. For three years, he and Susan tried for a baby, until tests showed she could not conceive. They agreed to adopt one day, but not just yet. Then, in the summer of 1999, he was assigned to the Command and Staff College back at Quantico and in 2000 was promoted to major. Following graduation, he and his wife were posted again, this time to Okinawa, Japan.

It was there, many time zones west of New York, seeking to catch the late-night newscasts before turning in, that he witnessed, unbelieving, the images that would later simply be designated 9/11 in 2001.

With others in the officers' club, he sat out the night

watching the slow-motion shots of the two airliners plough-ing first into the North Tower and then the South, in silence, over and over again.

Unlike those around him, he knew Arabic, the Arab world and the complexities of the religion of Islam, subscribed to by over a billion of the planet's inhabitants.

He recalled Professor Abdulaziz, gentle, courtly, serving tea and prophesying a long dark night for the world of Islam. And others. He listened to the rising buzz of rage around him as the details came through. Nineteen Arabs, including fif-teen Saudis, had done this. He remembered the beaming smiles of the shopkeepers of al-Jubail when he greeted them in their own tongue. The same people?

At dawn the entire regiment was summoned on parade to listen to the regimental commander. His message was bleak. There was now a war on, and the Corps would, as ever, de-fend the nation whenever, wherever and however it would be called upon.

Major Kit Carson thought bitterly of the wasted years, when attack after attack on the U.S. in Africa and the Middle East had led to one-week-long outrage from the politicians but no radical recognition of the sheer size of the onslaught being prepared in a chain of Afghan caves.

There is simply no way of overestimating the trauma that 9/11 inflicted on the U.S. and her people. Everything changed and would never be the same again. In twenty-four hours, the giant finally woke up.

There would be retribution, Carson knew, and he wanted to be part of that. But he was stuck on a Japanese island with years of the posting yet to serve.

But the event that changed America forever also changed the life of Kit Carson. What he could not know was that back in Washington a very senior officer with the CIA, a veteran of the Cold War named Hank Crumpton, was scouring the records of the Army, Navy, Air Force and Marines for a rare type of man. The operation was called the Scrub, and he was searching for serving officers who knew Arabic.

In his office at the No. 2 Building, CIA compound, Langley, Virginia, the records were fed into the computers, which scanned them far faster than the human eye could read or the human brain digest. Names and careers flashed up, most to be discounted, a few retained.

One name flashed up with a pulsing star in the top corner of the screen. Marine major, Olmsted Scholarship, Monterey Language School, two years Cairo, bilingual in Arabic. Where is he? asked Crumpton. Okinawa, said the computer. Well, we need him here, said Crumpton.

It took time and a bit of shouting. The Corps resisted, but the Agency had the edge. The Director of the CIA answers only to the President, and DCI George Tenet had George Bush's ear. The Oval Office overruled the Marine protests. Maj. Carson was summarily seconded to the CIA. He did not want to swap services, but at least it got him out of Okinawa, and he vowed to return to the Corps when he could.

On September 20, 2001, a Starlifter rose above Okinawa, heading for California. In the rear sat a Marine major. He knew the Corps would take care of Susan, bring her later to accommodations on the Marine base at Quantico, where he could be near her at Langley.

From California, Maj. Carson was shipped on to Andrews

Air Force Base outside Washington and thus presented himself to CIA headquarters, as per orders.

There were interviews, tests in Arabic, a compulsory change into civilian clothes and finally a small office in No. 2 Building, miles from the senior ranks of the Agency on the top floors of the original No. 1 Building.

He was given a pile of intercepts of broadcasts in Arabic to peruse and comment. He chafed. This was a job for the National Security Agency over at Fort Meade on the Baltimore road up in Maryland. They were the listeners, the eavesdroppers, the code breakers. He had not joined the Corps to analyze newscasts from Radio Cairo.

Then a rumor swept the building. Mullah Omar, the weird leader of the Taliban government of Afghanistan, was refusing to give up the culprits of 9/11. Osama bin Laden and his entire al-Qaeda movement would remain safe inside Afghanistan. And the rumor was: We are going to invade.

The details were sparse but accurate on a few points. The Navy would be offshore in strength in the Arabian Gulf, delivering massive air power. Pakistan would cooperate, but grudgingly and with dozens of conditions. The American feet on the ground would be Special Forces only. And their British equivalents would be with them.

The CIA, apart from its spies, agents and analysts, had one division that involved itself in what in the trade is called active measures, a euphemism for the messy business of killing people.

Kit Carson made his pitch and he made it strong. He confronted the head of the Special Activities Division and told him bluntly: You need me. Sir. I am no use sitting in a coop like a battery hen. I may not speak Pashto or Dari, but our real enemies are bin Laden's terrorists—Arabs all. I can listen to them. I can interrogate prisoners, read their written instructions and notes. You need me with you in Afghanistan; no one needs me here.

He had made an ally. He got his transfer. When President Bush made his announcement of invasion on October 7th, the advance units of the SAD were on their way to meet the anti-Taliban Northern Alliance. Kit Carson went with them.

2

The battle of Shah-i-Kot started badly and then went downhill. Maj. Kit Carson of the U.S. Marines, attached to the SAD, should have been on his way home when his unit was summoned to help out.

He had already been at Mazar-e-Sharif when the Taliban prisoners revolted and the Uzbeks and Tajiks of the Northern Alliance mowed them down. He had seen fellow SAD Johnny "Mike" Spann caught by the Talib and beaten to death. From the far side of the vast compound, he had watched the British Special Boat Service men rescue Spann's partner, Dave Tyson, from a similar fate.

Then came the storming surge south to overrun the old Soviet air base at Bagram and take Kabul. He had missed the fighting in the Tora Bora massif when the Americans' paid-for (but not enough) Afghan warlord had betrayed them and let Osama bin Laden and his entourage of guards slip over the border into Pakistan.

Then, in late February, word came from Afghan sources that there were still a few diehards hanging on in the valley of Shah-i-Kot, up in Paktia Province. Once again, the intel was rubbish. There was not a handful; there were hundreds of them.

The defeated Taliban, being Afghans, had somewhere to go: their native villages. They could slip away and disappear. But the al-Qaeda fighters were Arabs, Uzbeks and, fiercest of all, Chechens. They spoke no Pashto, the ordinary Afghans hated them; they could only surrender or die fighting. Almost all chose the second.

The American command responded to the tip with a small-scale project called Operation Anaconda and it went to the Navy SEALs. Three huge Chinooks full of SEALs took off for the valley, which was thought to be empty.

Coming in to land, the leading helicopter was nose up, tail down, with its ramp doors open, a few feet off the ground, when the hidden al-Qaedists opened up. One rocket-propelled grenade was so close, it went straight through the fuselage without exploding. It did not have enough time in the air to arm itself. So it went in one side, missed everyone and went out the other, leaving two windy holes.

What did the damage was the raking burst of machine-gun fire from the nest among the snowy rocks. It also managed to miss everyone inside, but it wrecked the controls as it ripped through the flight deck. With a few minutes of genius flying, the pilot hauled the dying Chinook aloft and nursed it for three miles until he could crash-land it on safer ground. The other two behind him followed.

But one SEAL, Chief Petty Officer Neil Roberts, who

had unhitched his tether line, slipped on a patch of hydraulic fluid and slithered out the back. He landed unhurt in a mass of al-Qaeda. SEALs never leave a mate, dead or alive, on the field. Having landed, they came storming back for CPO Roberts. As they did so, they called for help. The battle of Shah-i-Kot had begun. It lasted four days. It took the lives of Neil Roberts and six other Americans.

Three units were near enough to respond to the call. A troop of British SBS came from one direction and the SAD unit from another. The largest group to come to help was a battalion from the 75th Ranger Regiment.

The weather was freezing, way below zero. Flurries of driven snow stung the eyes. How the Arabs had survived the winter up there was anyone's guess. But they had and they were prepared to die to the last man. They took no prisoners and did not expect to be taken. According to witnesses later, they came out of crevices in the rocks, unseen caves and hidden machine-gun nests.

Any veteran will confirm that battles quickly descend into chaos, and Shah-i-Kot was faster than most. Units became separated from the main body and individuals from the unit. Kit Carson found himself alone with the ice and driven snow.

He saw another American—the headdress, helmet against turban, gave the identity away—about forty yards distant, also alone. A robed figure came out of the ground and fired an RPG at the camouflaged soldier. This time the grenade did go off. It did not hit the American but exploded at his feet, and Carson watched him fall.

He took out the rocketeer with his carbine. Two more

appeared and charged him, screaming, *"Allahu-akhbar."* He dropped them both, the second one barely six feet from the end of his barrel. The American, when he reached him, was alive but in a bad way. A white-hot shard from the rocket casing had sliced into his left ankle, virtually severing it. The foot in its combat boot was hanging by a sinew, tendon and some tendrils of flesh. The bone was gone. The man was in the first no-pain, stunned shock that precedes the agony.

The smocks of both men were crusted with snow, but Carson could make out the flash of a Ranger. He tried to raise someone on his radio but met only static. Easing off the wounded man's backpack, he pulled out the first aid wallet and shoved the entire dose of morphine into the exposed calf.

The Ranger began to feel the pain, and his teeth gritted. Then the morphine hit him and he slumped, semiconscious. Carson knew they were both going to die if they stayed there. Visibility was twenty yards between gusts. He could see no one. Heaving the injured Ranger on his back in a fireman's lift, he began to march.

He was walking over the worst terrain on Earth; football-sized smooth boulders under a foot of snow, every one a leg breaker. He was carrying his own one hundred and eighty pounds, plus his sixty-pound pack. Plus another one hundred and eighty pounds of Ranger—he had left the Ranger's pack behind. Plus carbine, grenades, ammunition and water.

Later, he had no idea how far he slogged out of that lethal valley. At one point the morphine in the Ranger lost effect, so he lowered the man and pumped in his own supply. After an age, he heard the whump-whump of an engine. With fingers that had ceased to feel anything, he pulled out his maroon flare, tore it open with his teeth and held it high, pointing it at the noise.

The crew of the Casevac Black Hawk told him later the flare went so near the cabin they thought they were being shot at. Then they looked down, and in a lull saw two snow-men beneath them, one slumped, the other waving. It was too dangerous to settle. The Black Hawk hovered two feet off the snow as two corpsmen with a gurney strapped the in-jured Ranger down and pulled him aboard. His companion used his last strength to climb aboard, then passed out.

The Black Hawk took them to Kandahar, now a huge U.S. air base, then still a work in progress. But it had a basic hospital. The Ranger was taken away to triage and intensive care. Kit Carson presumed he would never see him again. The next day the Ranger, horizontal and sedated, was on a long haul to USAF Ramstein, Germany, where the base hos-pital is world-class.

As it happened, the Ranger, who was Lieutenant Colonel Dale Curtis, lost his left foot. There was simply no way it could be saved. After a neat amputation, little more than completing the job the grenade had started, he was left with a stump, a prosthetic, a limp, a walking cane and the pros-pect of a looming end to his career as a Ranger. When he was fit to travel, he was flown home to Walter Reed Hospital outside Washington for post-combat therapy and the fitting of the artificial foot.

Major Kit Carson did not see him again for years. The CIA chief at Kandahar sought orders from higher up, and Carson was flown to Dubai, where the Agency has a huge presence. He was the first eyewitness out of the Shah-i-Kot, and there was a lengthy debriefing with a gallery of senior brass. They included Marine, Navy and CIA interrogators.

At the officers' club, he met a man of similar age to himself, a Navy commander on a posting to Dubai, which also has a U.S. naval base. They had dinner. The commander revealed he was from NCIS, the Naval Criminal Investigative Service.

"Why not transfer to us when you get home?" he asked.

"A policeman?" said Carson. "I don't think so. But thanks."

"We're bigger than you think," said the commander. "It's not just sailors overstaying shore leave. I'm talking major crime, tracking down criminals who have stolen millions, ten major Navy bases in Arabic-speaking locations. It would be a challenge."

It was that word which convinced Carson. The Marines come within the ambit of the U.S. Navy. He would only be moving within the larger service. On his return to the U.S. he presumed he would be back to analyzing Arabic material in No. 2 Building at Langley. He applied for NCIS and they snatched him.

It got him out of the CIA and halfway back into the embrace of the Corps. It secured a posting to Portsmouth, Virginia, where its large Naval Medical Center quickly found a position for Susan to join him.

Portsmouth also enabled him to pay frequent visits to his mother, who was in therapy for the breast cancer that took her life three years later. Finally, when his father Gen. Carson retired the same year that he became a widower, he could be close to him as well. The general withdrew to a retirement village outside Virginia Beach, where he could play his beloved golf and attend veterans' evenings with other Marines retired along that stretch of coast.

Carson spent four years with NCIS and was credited with tracking down and bringing to justice ten major runaways with crimes to answer for. In 2006, he secured his transfer back to the Marine Corps with the rank of lieutenant colonel and was posted to Camp Lejeune, North Carolina. It was while motoring across Virginia to join him that Susan, his wife, was killed by a drunk driver who lost control and rammed her head-on.

PRESENT DAY

The third assassination in a month was that of a senior police officer in Orlando, Florida. He was leaving his home on a bright spring morning when he was stabbed through the heart from behind as he stooped to open his car door. Even dying, he drew his sidearm and fired twice, killing his assailant instantly.

The ensuing inquiry identified the young killer as of Somali birth, also a refugee granted asylum on compassionate grounds and working with the city sanitation department.

Fellow workers testified that he had changed over a two-month period, becoming withdrawn and remote, surly and critical of the American lifestyle. He had ended up being ostracized by the crew on his garbage truck, as he had become so difficult to get on with. They put his mood change down to homesickness for his native land.

It was not. It was caused, as the raid on his lodgings revealed, by a conversion to ultra-Jihadism, deriving, so it seemed, from his obsession with a series of online sermons that his landlady heard coming from his room. A full report went to the Orlando FBI office and thence to the Hoover Building.

Here the story had ceased to cause surprise. The same tale, of conversion in privacy after many hours listening to the online sermons of a Mideast preacher speaking impeccable English and an unpredictable, out-of-nowhere murder of a local notable citizen, had been reported four times in the U.S. and, to the Bureau's knowledge, twice in the United Kingdom.

Checks had already been made with the CIA, the Counter-Terrorism Center and the Department of Homeland Security. Every U.S. agency even remotely dealing with Islamist terrorism had been informed and had logged the file, but none could respond with helpful intelligence. Who was this man? Where did he come from? Where did he record his broadcasts? He was only tagged as the Preacher and began to climb the lists of HVTs—the high-value targets.

The U.S. has a diaspora of well over a million Muslims, many first generation via their parents from the Middle East and Central Asia, and that was a huge pool of potential converts to the Preacher's ultra-harsh Jihadist sermons and their relentless call for converts to strike just one single blow against the Great Satan before joining Allah in eternal bliss.

Eventually, the Preacher came to be discussed at the Tuesday-morning briefings in the Oval Office and he went onto the kill list.

P eople cope with grief in different ways. For some, only wailing hysteria will prove sincerity. For others, a quiet collapse into weeping helplessness in public is the response. But there are those who take their hurt away to a private place, like an animal his injury.

They grieve alone, unless there is another relative or companion to hold close, and share their tears with the wall. Kit Carson visited his father at his retirement home, but his posting was at Lejeune and he could not stay long.

Alone in his empty house on base, he threw himself into his work and drove his body to the limit with lonely cross-country runs and sessions of gymnasium workout until the physical pain blunted the inner hurt, until even the base medical officer told him to ease up.

He was one of the founder thinkers of the Combat Hunter program, whereby Marines would go on a course to teach them tracking and manhunting techniques in wilderness, rural and urban environments. The theme was: Never become the hunted, always stay the hunter. But while he was at Portsmouth and Lejeune, great events were taking place.

Nine/eleven had triggered a sea change in the American armed forces, and governmental attitudes to any even remotely conceivable possible threat to the U.S. and national alertness inched its way toward paranoia. The result was an explosive enlargement of the world of "intelligence." The original sixteen intel-gathering agencies of the U.S. ballooned to over a thousand.

By 2012, accurate estimates put the number of Americans with top secret clearance at 850,000. Over 1,200 government organizations and 2,000 private companies were working on top secret projects related to counterterrorism and homeland security at over 10,000 locations across the country.

The aim back in 2001 was that never again would the basic intel agencies refuse to share what they had with one another, and thus let nineteen fanatics bent on mass slaughter slip through the cracks. But the outcome a decade later, at a cost that broke the economy, was much the same as the situation of 2001. The sheer size and complexity of the self-defense machine created some fifty thousand top secret reports a year, far too many for anyone to read, let alone understand, analyze, synthesize or collate. So they were just filed.

The most fundamental increase was in Joint Special Ops Command, or J-SOC. This body had existed for years before 9/11, but as a low-profile and principally defensive structure. Two men would convert it into the largest, most aggressive and most lethal private army in the world.

The word "private" is justified because it is the personal instrument of the President and of no other. It can conduct covert war without seeking any sanction from Congress; its multibillion-dollar budget is acquired without ever disturbing the Appropriations Committee, and it can kill you without ruffling the even tenor of the Attorney General's office. It is all top secret.

The first transformer of J-SOC was Defense Secretary Donald Rumsfeld. This ruthless Washington insider was resentful of the power and privileges of the CIA. Under its charter, the Agency needed to be answerable only to the President, not Congress. With its SAD units, it could conduct covert and lethal operations abroad on the Director's say-so. That was power, real power, and Secretary Rumsfeld was determined to have it. But the Pentagon is very much subject to Congress and its limitless capacity for interference.

Rumsfeld needed a weapon outside congressional oversight if he was ever to rival George Tenet, Director of the CIA. A completely transformed J-SOC became that weapon.

With the agreement of President George W. Bush, J-SOC expanded and expanded, in size, budget and powers. It absorbed all the Special Forces of the state. They included Team 6 of the SEALs (who would later kill Osama bin Laden); the Delta Force, or D boys, drawn from the Green Berets; the 75th Ranger Regiment; the Air Force's Special Ops Aviation Regiment (the Night Stalkers' long-range helicopters) and others. It also gobbled up TOSA.

In the summer of 2003, while Iraq was still blazing from end to end and few were looking elsewhere, two things happened that completed the reinvention of J-SOC. A new commander was appointed, in the person of General Stanley McChrystal. If anyone thought J-SOC would continue to play a largely domestic Homeland role, that was the end of that. And in September 2003, Secretary Rumsfeld secured the President's agreement and signed the EXORD.

The Executive Order was an eighty-page document, and within its pages, buried deep, was something like a huge Presidential Finding, the highest decree in America, but without specific terms. The EXORD virtually said do what you want.

About that time, a limping Ranger colonel named Dale Curtis was finishing his one-year, post-injury paid sabbatical and convalescence. He had mastered the prosthetic on his left stump with such skill that the limp was virtually undetectable. But the 75th Ranger Regiment was not for men on prosthetics. His career appeared over.

But like the SEALs, a Ranger does not leave another Ranger in the lurch. Gen. McChrystal was also a Ranger, from the 75th, and he heard of Col. Curtis. He had just taken command of the entire J-SOC and that included TOSA, whose commander was retiring. The post of commanding officer did not have a field-action posting. It could be a desk job. It was a very short meeting, and Col. Curtis jumped at the chance.

There is an old saying in the covert world that if you want to keep something secret, do not try to hide it because some reptile from the press will sniff it out. Give it a harmless name and a thoroughly boring job description. TOSA stands for Technical Operations Support Activity.

Not even "Agency" or "Administration" or "Authority." A support activity could mean changing the lightbulbs or eliminating tiresome Third World politicians. In this case it is more likely to mean the second.

TOSA existed long before 9/11. It hunted down, among others, the Colombian cocaine lord Pablo Escobar. That is what it does. It is the manhunter arm called upon when everyone else is baffled. It has only two hundred and fifty staff and lives in a compound in northern Virginia disguised as a toxic-chemical research facility. No one visits.

To keep it even more secret, it keeps changing its name.

It has been simply the Activity, but also Grantor Shadow, Centra Spike, Torn Victor, Cemetery Wind and Gray Fox. The last title was liked enough to be retained only as the code name of the commander. Upon his appointment, Col. Dale Curtis vanished and became Gray Fox. Later, it became Intelligence Support Activity, but when the word "Intelligence" began to attract attention, it changed again— to TOSA.

Gray Fox had held his post for six years when, in 2009, his chief manhunter retired, took a headful of really top secrets and went off to a log cabin in Montana to hunt steelhead trout. Col. Curtis could hunt only from behind a desk, but a computer and every access code in the U.S. defense machine is quite a head start. After a week, a face came up on the screen that jolted him. Lt. Col. Christopher "Kit" Carson— the man who had carried him out of the Shah-i-Kot.

He checked the career list. Combat soldier, scholar, Arabist, linguist, manhunter. He reached for his desk phone.

Kit Carson did not want to leave the Corps for the second time, but for the second time the argument was fought and won over his head.

A week later, he walked into the office of Gray Fox in the low-rise office block in the center of a woods in northern Virginia. He noted the man who limped as he walked to greet him, the cane propped in the corner, the 75th Ranger tabs.

"Remember me?" said the colonel. Kit Carson thought back to the freezing winds, the boulders beneath the combat boots, the gut-tearing weight on his back, the let-me-die-here-and-now exhaustion.

"Been a long time," he said.

"I know you don't want to leave the Corps," said Gray Fox, "but I need you. By the by, inside this building we use only first names. For the rest, Lt. Col. Carson has ceased to exist. For the entire world outside this complex, you are simply the Tracker."

Over the years the Tracker was alone or instrumental in tracing half a dozen of his country's most wanted enemies. Baitullah Mehsud, Pakistani Taliban, dispatched by a drone strike in a farmhouse, South Waziristan, 2009; Abu al-Yazid, al-Qaeda founder, financier of 9/11, taken out by another drone strike in Pakistan 2010.

It was he, with others, who first identified al-Kuwaiti as bin Laden's personal emissary. Spy drones tracked his last long drive across Pakistan until, amazingly, he turned not toward the mountains but the other way, to identify a compound in Abbottabad.

There was the Yemeni/American Anwar al-Awlaki, who preached online in English. He was found because he invited fellow American Samir Khan, editor of the Jihadist magazine *Inspire*, to join him in northern Yemen. And al-Quso, traced to his home in South Yemen. Another drone launched a Hellfire missile through the bedroom window as he slept.

The buds were coming on the trees this April when Gray Fox came in with a Presidential Finding brought from the Oval Office by courier that morning.

"Another online orator, Tracker. But weird. No name, no face. Totally elusive. He's all yours. Anything you want, just ask for it. The PF covers every requirement." He limped out.

There was a file, but it was slim. The man had gone on air with his first online sermon two years earlier, shortly after the first cyberpreacher had died with five companions by the side of a track in North Yemen, September 30, 2011. While Awlaki, who had been born and raised in New Mexico, had a distinct American accent, the Preacher sounded more British.

Two language laboratories had had a go at trying to trace the voice to a point of origin. There is one at Fort Meade, Maryland, headquarters of the vast National Security Agency. These are the listeners who can pluck any snatch of conversation by cell phone, landline, faxed letter, e-mail or radio out of space anywhere in the world. But they also do translations from a thousand languages and dialects and they do code breaking.

The other belongs to the Army, at Fort Huachuca, Arizona. They had both come up with much the same. The nearest guess was a Pakistani born into a cultured and educated family. There were clipped word endings in the Preacher's tone that smacked of the colonial British. But there was a problem.

Unlike Awlaki, who spoke barefaced, staring into the camera, the newcomer never revealed his face. He wore a traditional Arab *shamagh* but pulled the trailing end up across the face and tucked it in at the other side. Only the blazing eyes could be seen. The fabric, said the file, might distort the voice, making derivation even more of a guess. The computer code-named Echelon, the identifier of accents worldwide, refused to be categoric on a source of that voice.

Tracker issued the usual all-stations, all-services appeal for even a sliver of information. This appeal would go to twenty overseas intelligence services involved in the fight against Jihadism. Starting with the British. Especially the Brits. They once ran Pakistan and still had good contacts there. Their Secret Intelligence Service was big in Islamabad and hand in glove with the even bigger CIA machine. They would all get his message.

His second move was to summon up the entire library of the Preacher's online sermons on the Jihadi website. There would be hours and hours of listening to the sermons the Preacher had been pumping into cyberspace for nearly two years.

The Preacher's message was simple, which could have been why it was so successful in achieving radical conversions to the cause of his own ultra-Jihadism. To be a good Muslim, he told the camera, one had to truly and deeply love Allah, may His name be praised, and His prophet Muhammad, may he rest in peace. Mere words alone were not enough. The True Believer would feel an impulse to turn his love into action.

That action could only be to punish those who made war on Allah and His people, the worldwide Muslim *umma*. And chief among these were the Great Satan, the U.S., and the Little Satan, the United Kingdom. Punishment for what they had done, and were daily doing, was their decreed portion, and bringing that punishment a divine charge.

The Preacher called upon his viewers and listeners to avoid confiding in others, even those who professed to think alike. For even at the mosque there would be traitors prepared to denounce the True Believer for the *kuffar's* (the unbeliever's) gold.

So the True Believer should convert to True Islam in the privacy of his own mind and confide in no one. He should pray alone and listen only to the Preacher who would show the True Way. That way would involve each convert striking one blow against the infidel.

He warned against the devising of complicated plots involving many strange chemicals and many accomplices, for someone would notice the buying or storing of the components of a bomb, or one of the conspirators would betray. The prisons of the infidel were peopled by brothers who had been overheard, watched, spied upon or betrayed by those they thought they could trust.

The message of the Preacher was as simple as it was deadly. Each True Believer should identify one notable *kuffar* in the society in which he found himself and send him to hell, while he himself, blessed by Allah, would die fulfilled in the certain knowledge that he was going to paradise eternal.

It was an extension of Awlaki's "Just do it" philosophy, but better put, more persuasive. His recipe for ultra-simplicity made it easier to decide and act in isolation. And it was clear from the rising number of out-of-nowhere killings in both target countries that even if his message resounded with only a fraction of one percent of young Muslims, that was still an army of thousands.

The Tracker checked for responses from every U.S. agency and their British equivalents, but no one had ever heard reference to any Preacher in the Muslim lands. The title had been given him by the West, for lack of anything else to call him. But clearly he had come from somewhere, lived somewhere, broadcast from somewhere and had a name.

The answers, he came to believe, were in cyberspace. But there were computer experts of near-genius level up at Fort Meade who had been defeated. Whoever was sending the sermons out into cyberspace was keeping them untraceable and untrackable by causing them to appear to emanate from origin after origin, but then to whizz round and round the world, settling on a hundred possible source locations—but all of them false.

T he Tracker refused to bring anyone, however security cleared, to his hideaway in the forest. The secrecy fetish that motivated the entire unit had gotten to him. He also disliked going to other offices within the Washington sprawl, if he could avoid it. He preferred to be seen only by the person he wanted to talk to. He knew he was getting a reputation for being unconventional, but he preferred roadhouses. Faceless and anonymous, both cafeteria and customers. He met the cyberace from Fort Meade at such a roadhouse on the Baltimore road.

Both men sat and stirred their undrinkable coffee. They knew each other from previous investigations. The man the Tracker sat with was reputed to be the best computer detective in the National Security Agency, which is no small reputation.

"So why can't you find him?" asked the Tracker.

The man from the NSA scowled at his coffee and shook his head as the waitress hovered expectantly, carafe poised for a refill. She drifted away. Anyone glancing into the booth would have seen two middle-aged men, one fit and muscled, the other with the pallor of offices without windows and running to fat.

"Because he's freaking clever," he said at last. He hated to be eluded.

"Tell me," said the Tracker. "Layman's language, if you can."

"He probably records his sermons on a digital camcorder or laptop PC. Nothing weird about that. He transmits on a website called *Hejira*. That was the flight of Muhammad from Mecca to Medina."

The Tracker kept a straight face. He did not need explanations about Islam.

"Can you trace *Hejira*?"

"No need. It's just a vehicle. He bought it from an obscure little company in Delhi that is now out of business. When he has a new sermon to transmit worldwide, he sends it on *Hejira*, but he keeps the exact geolocation secret by causing it to emanate from origin after origin, whizzing round and round the world, bouncing it off a hundred other computers whose owners are certainly completely ignorant of the role they are playing. Eventually, the sermon could have come from anywhere."

"How does he prevent tracing back down the line of diversions?"

"By creating a proxy server to create a false Internet protocol. The IP is like your home address with zip code. Then into the proxy server he has introduced a malware or botnet to bounce his sermon all over the world."

"Translate."

The man from the NSA sighed. He spent his entire life talking cyberjargon with colleagues who knew exactly what he was talking about.

"Malware. 'Mal,' as in bad or evil. A virus. 'Bot,' short for robot, something that does your bidding without asking questions or revealing who it is working for."

The Tracker thought it over.

"So the mighty NSA is really defeated?"

The government's computer ace was not flattered, but he nodded.

"We will, of course, keep trying."

"There's a clock ticking. I may have to try some place else."

"Be my guest."

"Let me ask this. Control your natural chagrin. Just supposing you were the Preacher. Who would you absolutely not want on your tail? Who would worry the crap out of you?"

"Someone better than me."

"Is there any such someone?"

The NSA man sighed.

"Probably. Somewhere out there. I would guess from the new generation. Sooner or later, the veterans are overtaken by some beardless kid in every walk of life."

"Do you know any beardless kids? Any specific beardless kid?"

"Look, I've never even met him. But I heard at a recent seminar and trade fair of a youngster right here in Virginia. My informant said he was not at the trade fair because he lives with his parents and never leaves their home. Never, not ever. He's peculiar. In this world he's a bundle of nerves, hardly talks. But he flies like a fighter ace when he enters his own world."

"Which is?"

"Cyberspace."

"You have a name? Even an address?"

"I figured you might ask." He took a slip of paper from a pocket and passed it over. Then he rose. "Don't blame me if he's no use. It was only a rumor, in-trade gossip among us weirdos."

When he had gone, the Tracker settled for the muffins and coffee and left. In the parking lot he glanced at the paper. Roger Kendrick. And an address in Centerville, Virginia, one of myriad small satellite towns that had sprung up in the past two decades and then exploded with commuters since 9/11.

All trackers, all detectives, whatever and wherever the hunt, whoever the quarry, need one break. Just one. Kit Carson was going to be lucky. He was going to get two.

One would come from a strange teenage boy too frightened to leave the attic bedroom of his parents' backstreet house in Centerville, and the other from an old Afghan peasant whose rheumatism was forcing him to lay down his rifle and come in from the mountains.

3

About the only unconventional or audacious thing Lt. Col. Musharraf Ali Shah of the Pakistan regular army had ever done was marry. It was not the fact of marriage but the girl he wed.

In 1979, at the age of twenty-five and single, he had been briefly posted to the Siachen Glacier, a bleak and wild zone in the far north of his country where the border abutted Pakistan's mortal enemy, India. Later, from 1984 to 1999, there would be a low-level but festering border war in the Siachen, but back then it was just cold and bleak, a hardship posting.

The then-lieutenant Ali Shah was a Punjabi, like the majority of Pakistanis, and presumed, as did his parents, that he would make a "good" marriage, possibly to the daughter of a senior officer, which would help his career, or a rich merchant, which would help his bank balance.

He would have been lucky to do either, for he was not an exciting man. He was one of those obeyers of orders to the letter, conventional, orthodox, with the imagination of a *chapati*. But in those jagged mountains, he met and fell in love with a local girl of startling beauty named Soraya. Without the permission or blessing of his family, he married.

Her own family was pleased, thinking a union with a regular army officer would bring elevation in the great cities of the plain. Perhaps a large house in Rawalpindi or even Islamabad. Alas, Musharraf Ali Shah was one of life's plodders, and, over thirty years, he would plod up the rankings to finish as lieutenant colonel, clearly going no higher. A boy was born in 1980, to be named Zulfiqar.

Lieutenant Ali Shah was in the Armored Infantry, getting his commission at twenty-two in 1976. After his first tour on the Siachen, he returned with his heavily pregnant wife and was promoted to captain. He was allocated a very modest house on the officers' patch in Rawalpindi, the military concentration a few miles from the capital of Islamabad.

There were to be no more behavior shocks. Like all officers in the Pakistani army, fresh postings came up every two or three years and were divided into "hard" and "soft." A posting to a city like Rawalpindi, Lahore or Karachi counts as soft and is "with family." Being sent to the garrison of Multan, Kharian, Peshawar in the throat of the Khyber Pass to Afghanistan or the Taliban-infested Swat Valley counted as hard and are for unaccompanied officers only. Through all these postings, the boy Zulfiqar went to school.

Every Pakistani garrison town has schools for the offspring of officers, but they come in three levels. At the bottom come the government schools, then the army public schools and, for those with family funds, the elite private schools. The Ali Shahs had no money outside the very modest salary, and Zulfiqar went to army schools. They have the reputation of being well run, employing many officers' wives as teachers, and they are free.

The boy matriculated at fifteen and passed on to army college, taking engineering on his father's orders. This was the skill that would grant automatic employment and/or a commission in the army. That was in 1996. The parents began to notice a change in their son in his third year.

The now-major Ali Shah, of course, was a Muslim, practicing but not passionately devout. It would have been unthinkable not to attend mosque every Friday or join in the ritual prayers as and when required. But that was all. He habitually dressed in uniform for prestige reasons, but if he had to dress in mufti, it would be the national dress for males: the leg-tight trousers and long, front-buttoned jacket that altogether make up the *shalwar kameez*.

He noticed his son began to grow a straggly beard and wear the fretted skullcap of the devout. He prostrated himself the required five times a day and snapped his disapproval when he saw his father taking a whisky, the tipple of the officer corps, and stormed out of the room. His parents thought the devotions and intense religiosity were a passing phase.

He began to steep himself in written works about Kashmir, the disputed border territory that has poisoned relations between Pakistan and India since 1947. He began to veer toward the violent extremism of Lashkar-e-Taiba, the terrorist group later responsible for the Mumbai massacre.

His father tried to console himself with the thought that his son would graduate in a year and either enter the army or find a good job as a qualified engineer, a talent always sought after in Pakistan. But in the summer of 2000, he flunked his finals, a disaster his father put down to abandoning his studies and poring over the Koran; that and learning Arabic, the only permitted language in which the Koran may be studied.

This event marked the first of a series of blazing quarrels between the son and his father. Maj. Ali Shah pulled such strings as he was able to in order to plead that his son had been unwell and deserved a chance to take the finals again. Then came 9/11.

Like virtually the entire world in possession of a television set, the family watched in horror as the airliners slammed into the Twin Towers. Except their son Zulfiqar. He rejoiced, he noisily jubilated, as the TV station repeated the spectacle over and over again. That was when his parents realized that along with extreme religious devotion, a constant reading of the original Jihadist propagandists Sayyid Qutb and his disciple Azzam, and a loathing of India, their son had developed a hatred of America and the West.

That winter the U.S. invaded Afghanistan, and within six weeks the Northern Alliance, with enormous U.S. Special Forces help and American air power, had toppled the Taliban government. While the Taliban's guest Osama bin Laden fled over the Pakistan border in one direction, the Taliban's one-eyed and bizarre leader Mullah Omar fled into the Pakistani province of Balochistan and settled with his high council, the Shura, in the city of Quetta.

For Pakistan this was a long way from an academic problem. The Pakistani army and indeed all the armed forces are effectively ruled by the Inter-Services Intelligence branch, simply known as the ISI. Everyone in uniform in Pakistan walks in awe of the ISI. And the ISI had created the Taliban in the first place.

More, an unusually large percentage of ISI officers were of the extremist wing of Islam and were not going to abandon their creation, the Taliban, or al-Qaeda guests, to become loyal to the U.S., though they would have to pretend to. Thus began the running sore that has bedeviled U.S.-Pakistan relations ever since. Not only did the senior ranks of the ISI know that bin Laden was in that walled compound in Abbottabad; they built it for him.

In the early spring of 2002, a high-ranking ISI delegation went to Quetta to confer with Mullah Omar and his Quetta Shura. They would normally not have deigned to invite the humble Maj. Ali Shah to accompany them but for one thing. The two senior ISI generals spoke no Pashto; the mullah and his Pashtun followers spoke no Urdu. Maj. Ali Shah spoke no Pashto either, but he had a son who did.

The major's wife was a Pathan from the wild mountains of the north. Her native tongue was Pashto. Her son was fluent in both tongues. He accompanied the delegation, intoxicated by the honor. When he returned to Islamabad, he had the last of the furious rows with his ultra-conventional father who stood ramrod-backed, staring out of the window, as his son stormed out. The parents never saw him again.

The figure that confronted Mr. Kendrick Sr. when he answered his front door was dressed in uniform. Not full dress, but neatly pressed camouflage, with unit flashes, rank tabs and decorations. He could discern that his visitor was a colonel in the Marines. He was impressed.

That was the idea. Working at TOSA, the Tracker hardly ever wore full kit because it drew attention, and in his new environment that was something he avoided at all costs. But Mr. Jimmy Kendrick was a janitor for a local school. He tended the central heating system and swept corridors. He was not accustomed to Marine colonels on the doorstep. He had to be overawed.

"Mr. Kendrick?"

"Yes."

"Colonel Jackson. Is Roger at home?" James Jackson was one of his frequent aliases.

Of course he was at home. He never left home. Jimmy Kendrick's only son was a grievous disappointment to him. Suffering from acute agoraphobia, the boy was terrified of leaving the familiar embrace of his attic hidey-hole and his mother's company.

"Sure. He's upstairs."

"Could I have a word with him? Please?"

He led the uniformed Marine upstairs. It was not a large house; just two rooms down, two up, and an aluminum ladder to a loft space. The father called up into the void.

"Roger, someone to see you. Come on down."

There was a shuffling, and a face appeared in the aperture

atop the ladder. It was a pale face, like that of a night creature accustomed to half-light; young, vulnerable, anxious. About eighteen or nineteen, nervous, with eyes that did not make eye contact. He seemed to be looking at the landing carpet between the two men below.

"Hello, Roger. I'm Jamie Jackson. I need your advice. Can we talk?"

The boy considered the request seriously. There appeared to be no curiosity, just acceptance of the strange visitor and request.

"OK," he said. "Do you want to come up?"

"There's no room up there." The father spoke out of the side of his mouth. Then louder: "Come on down, son." And to the Tracker: "You'd better talk in his bedroom. He doesn't like to come down to the living room except when his mom's here. She works at a grocery store checkout."

Roger Kendrick came down the ladder and into his bedroom. He sat on the edge of the single bed, gazing at the floor. The Tracker took the upright chair. Aside from a small closet and chest of drawers, that was about it. His real life was in the roof space. Tracker glanced at the father, who shrugged.

"Asperger's syndrome," he said helplessly. It was clearly a condition that defeated him. Other men had sons who could date girls and train as car mechanics. The Tracker nodded at him. The meaning was clear.

"Betty will be back momentarily," he said. "She'll make some coffee." Then he left.

The man from Fort Meade had used the word "peculiar," but he had not specified how much and in what way. Before coming, the Tracker had researched both Asperger's syndrome and agoraphobia, the fear of open spaces.

Like Down syndrome and cerebral palsy, both conditions varied in form from mild to severe. After several minutes talking in general terms with Roger Kendrick, there was no need to treat him like a child; no cause for baby talk.

The young man experienced extreme shyness in person-to-person terms, intensified by his fear of the world outside his home. But the Tracker suspected that if he could shift the conversation back to the teenager's comfort zone—cyberspace—he would meet a quite different personality. He was right.

He recalled the case of the Scottish cyberhacker Gary MacKinnon. When the U.S. government wanted to put him on trial, London maintained he was too fragile to travel, let alone take jail. But he had invaded the inner sanctums of NASA and the Pentagon, slicing through some of the most complicated firewalls ever devised like a knife through butter.

"Roger, there's a man out there, somewhere, hiding in cyberspace. He hates our country. He is called the Preacher. He gives sermons online, in English. He asks people to convert to his way of thinking and kill Americans. It's my job to find him and stop him.

"But I cannot. Out there, he's cleverer than me. He thinks he is the cleverest operator in cyberspace."

He noticed the shuffling had stopped. For the first time, the teenager raised his eyes and made contact. He was contemplating a return to the only world a cruel Nature had ever destined him to inhabit. The Tracker opened a pouch and took out a memory stick.

"He transmits, Roger, but he keeps his Internet protocol

address very secret, so nobody knows where he is. If we knew, we could get him to stop."

The teenager toyed with the memory stick in his fingers.

"What I'm here for, Roger, is to ask if you would help us find him."

"I could try," said the teenager.

"Tell me, Roger, what equipment do you have up there?"

The teenager told him. It was not the worst on the market, but it was run-of-the-mill, store-bought stuff.

"If someone came and asked you, what would you really like? What would be your dream setup, Roger?"

He came alive. Enthusiasm flooded his face. He made eye contact again.

"I would really love a dual six-core processor system with thirty-two gigs of RAM, running a Red Hat Enterprise Linux distribution version, six or higher."

The Tracker did not need to take notes. The tiny microphone in his medal display was picking up everything. Just as well; he had not a clue what the lad was talking about. But the eggheads would.

"I'll see what I can do," he said, and rose. "Have a look at the material. It may be you cannot crack it. But thanks for trying."

Within two days, a van with three men and some very expensive cyberequipment arrived at the backstreet house in Centerville. They crawled around in the loft until they had installed it all. Then they left a very vulnerable nineteen-year-old, staring at a screen and believing he had been wafted to heaven. He watched a dozen of the sermons on the Jihadi website and began to tap.

———

The killer crouched low over his scooter and pretended to tinker with the engine as, down the road, the state senator left his house, tossed his golf clubs into the trunk and climbed behind the wheel. It was just after seven on a brilliant early-summer morning. He did not notice the man on the scooter behind him.

The killer did not need to stay close for he had made this run twice before, not dressed as now but in jeans and a hooded jacket, much less noticeable. He followed the senator's car the five miles through Virginia Beach to the golf course. He watched the senator park, take his clubs and disappear into the clubhouse.

The killer cruised past the club entrance, turned left up Linkhorn Drive and disappeared into the woods. Two hundred yards up Linkhorn, he turned left again into Willow Drive. A single car came the other way but took no notice of him despite his garb.

He was dressed from neck to ankles in a snow-white dishdash with a crocheted white skullcap on his shorn head. Passing several rural residences on Willow Drive, he emerged from the trees into the morning sunshine at the point where the tee shot of the fifth hole, known as Cascade, crosses Willow Drive. Here he pulled off the road and dumped his scooter in the tall undergrowth by the side of the fairway of the fourth hole, called Bald Cypress.

There were a few golfers already on other holes, but they were engrossed in their games and took no notice. The young man in white walked calmly down Bald Cypress fairway until he was close to the bridge over the stream, then stepped into the bushes until he was invisible and waited. He knew from earlier observations that anyone playing a round would have to come up the fourth fairway and cross the bridge.

He had been there half an hour, and two pairs had completed Bald Cypress and moved on to the Cascade tee. Watching from deep cover, he let them pass. Then he saw the senator. The man was in a twosome with a partner of similar age. In the clubhouse, the senator had pulled on a green windbreaker, and his opponent wore one of similar color.

As the two elderly men crossed the bridge, the young man emerged from the bushes. Neither golfer paused in his stride, though both glanced at the young man with passing inter- est. It was the clothes he wore, and perhaps his air of calm detachment. He moved toward the Americans until, at ten paces, one of them asked: "Help you, son?"

That was when the man brought his right hand from in- side the dishdash and held it out, as if to offer them some- thing. The something was a handgun. Neither golfer had a chance to protest before he fired. Slightly confused by the similar long-peaked baseball caps and green windbreakers, he fired two shots at each man, at almost point-blank range.

One bullet missed completely and would never be found. Two struck the senator in the chest and throat, killing him instantly. The remaining slug hit the other player mid-chest. The two shot men crumpled, one after the other. The shooter raised his eyes to the duck's egg blue morning sky, murmured, *"Allahu-akhbar,"* put the barrel of the handgun into his mouth and fired.

The players in the foursome were clearing the green of

the fourth hole, Bald Cypress. They would say later they all turned at the sound of the shots in time to see the suicide's head spray blood into the sky, then his body slump to the ground. Two began to run to the scene. A third was already on his cart; he turned it around and gunned the quiet electric engine toward the double murder. The fourth stared for several seconds, mouth agape, then pulled out a cell phone and dialed 911.

The call was taken in the communications center behind the police HQ on Princess Anne Road. The duty telephonist took basic details and alerted the HQ across the compound and the Department of Emergency Medical Services. Both were staffed by experienced local people who needed no directions to the Princess Anne Country Club.

The first to the scene was a police patrol car that had been cruising down 54th Street. From Linkhorn Drive, the officers could see the growing crowd up on the fourth fairway and, without ceremony, drove across the hallowed turf to the crime scene. From police HQ, duty detective Ray Hall arrived ten minutes later to take control. The uniformed men had already secured the scene when the ambulance from the Pinehurst Center on Viking Drive three miles away drove up.

Detective Hall had established that two men were stone dead. The senator he recognized, both from his picture in the papers from time to time and from a police awards ceremony six months back.

The young man with the bushy black beard, identified by the horrified golfers from the foursome as the killer, was also dead, his gun still in his right hand, twenty feet from his victims. The second golfer appeared very badly wounded, with a single gunshot wound, center chest, but still breathing. Hall stepped back to let the paramedics do their job. There were three of them, and a driver.

A glance told them there was only one of the three bodies on the still-dew-flecked grass needing their attention. The other two could wait for transportation to the morgue. Nor was there any cause to waste time attempting to resuscitate, as with a drowning or gassing. This was what paramedics call a load 'n' go.

They were equipped with ALS—advanced life support system—and they were going to need it to stabilize the shot man for the three-mile dash to Virginia Beach General. They loaded the wounded man aboard and raced away, siren wailing.

They covered the miles to First Colonial Road in less than five minutes. Early-morning traffic was light—being a weekend, there were no commuters—the siren cleared the few other vehicles out of the road and the driver kept his foot to the floor all the way.

In the back, two paramedics stabilized the near-dead man as best they could while the third radioed ahead every detail they could discover. At the emergency ambulance entrance, a major trauma team assembled and waited.

Inside the building, a surgical theater was prepared and a surgical team scrubbed up. And cardiovascular surgeon Alex McCrae hurried from a half-eaten breakfast in the cafeteria to the emergency room.

On the fairway of the fourth hole, Det. Hall was left with two bodies, a milling throng of bewildered and horrified Virginia Beach citizens and a hatful of mysteries. As his partner,

Lindy Mills, took names and addresses, he had two things going for him: The first was that all eyewitnesses were adamant there had only been one killer and he had committed suicide immediately after the double shooting. There seemed to be no call to go looking for an accomplice. A single-seat scooter had been discovered in the bushes farther up the fairway.

His second plus was that the witnesses were all sensible mature people, levelheaded and likely to give good and reliable evidence. At that point, the mysteries began, starting with the first: What the hell had just happened and why?

Whatever it was, nothing like it had ever happened in quiet, sedate, law-abiding Virginia Beach before. Who was the killer and who was the man now fighting for his life?

Detective Hall took the second question first. Whoever the wounded man was, he would be likely to have a home somewhere, perhaps a wife and family waiting there, or somewhere a next of kin. Given what he had seen of the chest wound, that next of kin might be urgently needed by nightfall.

No one outside the scene-of-crime tape seemed to know who the senator's partner had been. The wallet and billfold, unless they were in the clubhouse, had gone off with the ambulance, leaving Lindy Mills and the two uniforms to carry on with the routine name taking. Ray Hall asked for and immediately got a lift on a cart back to the clubhouse. There the ashen-faced club professional solved one of his problems. The partner of the dead senator had been a retired general. He was a widower and lived alone in a gated retirement community several miles away. The membership list provided the exact address in seconds.

Hall called Lindy on his cell phone. He asked one of the uniforms to stay with her and the other to bring him the squad car.

As they drove, Det. Hall conferred on the police band with his captain. HQ would take care of the media, even now arriving with a barrage of questions to which no one yet had the answers. HQ would also take care of the miserable business of informing the late senator's wife before she learned it on the radio.

He was told a second, more basic ambulance, the body wagon, was on its way to bring the two cadavers to the hospital morgue, where the medical examiner was preparing himself.

"Priority to the killer please, Captain," said Hall into the mic. "That outfit he was wearing looks like the dress of a Muslim fundamentalist. He acted alone, but there may be more in the background. We need to know who he was—a loner or one of a group."

While he was out at the general's home, he wanted the killer's prints taken and checked against AFIS—the automated fingerprint identification system—and the motor scooter checked with the Virginia state vehicle-licensing bureau. Yes, it was a weekend; people would have to be roused and brought in. He disconnected.

At the gated compound designated by the golf club records, it was clear no one had yet heard of the events on a fairway called Bald Cypress, alias the fourth hole. There were some forty retirement bungalows set among lawns and trees with a small central lake, and the community manager's house.

The manager had finished a late breakfast and was about to mow his lawn. He went white as a sheet, sat down heavily on a garden chair and muttered, "Oh, my God," half a dozen times. Eventually, taking a key from a board in his own hallway, he led Det. Hall to the general's bungalow.

It stood trim and neat amid a quarter acre of mowed lawn, with some flowering shrubs in earthen jars; tasteful without being too labor-intensive. Inside, it was tidy, shipshape, like the abode of a man accustomed to good order and discipline. Hall began the distasteful business of rifling through another person's private affairs. The manager was as helpful as he could be.

The Marine general had come to live at the community some five years earlier, just after losing his wife to cancer. Family? asked Hall. He was going through the desk, looking for letters, insurance policies, some evidence of next of kin. The general seemed to be a man who kept his most private documents with his lawyer or bank. The manager called up the wounded general's closest friend among the neighbors—a retired architect who lived there with his wife and often had the general over for a real home-cooked meal.

He took the call and listened with shocked horror. He wanted to drive straight to Virginia Beach General, but Det. Hall persuaded him there was no chance of visiting. Next of kin? he asked. There is a son, said the architect, a serving Marine officer, a lieutenant colonel, but as to where, he had no idea.

Back at HQ, Hall was reunited with Lindy Mills and his own unmarked car. And there was news. The scooter had been traced. It belonged to a twenty-two-year-old student with a name that was clearly Arabic or a variant of it. He was an American citizen hailing from Dearborn, Michigan, but presently an engineering student at a high-tech college fifteen miles south of Norfolk. The vehicle bureau had sent through a picture.

It had no bushy black beard and the face was intact; not quite what Ray Hall had seen on the grass of the fairway. That face belonged to a head with no back and distorted by the blast pressure of the exploding shell. But close enough.

He put through a call to the U.S. Marine Corps headquarters, next to Arlington Cemetery, across the Potomac from Washington, D.C. He insisted on holding the line until he was speaking with a major from Public Affairs. He explained who he was, speaking from where, and briefly what had happened five hours ago on the Princess Anne golf course.

"No," he said, "I will not wait until after the weekend. I don't care where he is. I need to speak with him now, Major, now. If his father sees the sun rise tomorrow, it will be a miracle."

There was a long pause. Finally, the voice said simply: "Stay by that phone, Detective. I or someone else will be back to you in short order."

It took only five minutes. The voice was different. Another major, this time from Personnel Records. The officer you wish to speak to cannot be reached, he said.

Hall was getting angry. Unless he is in space or at the bottom of the Mariana Trench, he *can* be reached. We both know that. You have my personal cell number. Please give it to him and tell him to call me, and fast. With that, he put the phone down. Now it was up to the Corps.

Taking Lindy with him, he left HQ for the hospital, grabbing an energy bar and a fizzy soda for lunch. So much for healthy eating. At First Colonial, he pulled down the side road, the oddly named Will O Wisp Drive, and around the back to the ambulance entrance. His first stop was the morgue, where the ME was finishing up.

There were two bodies on steel trays, covered by sheets. An assistant was about to consign them to the cooler. The ME stopped him and pulled back one sheet. Det. Hall stared down at the face. It was now scarred and distorted but still the young man in the photo from the vehicle bureau. The bushy black beard jutted upward, the eyes closed.

"Do you know who he is yet?" asked the ME.

"Yep."

"Well, you know more than me. But maybe I can still surprise you."

The ME pulled the sheet down to the ankles.

"Notice anything?"

Ray Hall looked long and hard.

"He has no body hair. Except the beard."

The ME replaced the sheet and nodded to the assistant to remove the steel tray and its cargo to the cooler.

"I've never seen it in person, but I've seen it on camera. Two years ago at a seminar on Islamic fundamentalism. A sign of ritual purification, a preparation for passage into Allah's paradise."

"A suicide bomber?"

"A suicide killer," said the ME. "Destroy an important national of the Great Satan and the gates of immortal bliss open for the servant passing through them as *shahid*, a martyr. We don't see much of it in the States, but it is very common in the Middle East, Pakistan and Afghanistan. There was a lecture on it at the seminar."

"But he was born and raised here," said Det. Hall.

"Well, someone sure converted him," said the ME. "By the by, your crime lab people have already taken the fingerprints away. Other than that, he had nothing on him at all. Except the gun, and I believe that is already with Ballistics."

Detective Hall's next stop was upstairs. He found Dr. Alex McCrae in his office, lunching off a very late tuna melt from the cafeteria.

"What do you want to know, Detective?"

"Everything," said Hall. So the surgeon told him.

When the badly injured general was brought into the emergency room, Dr. McCrae ordered an immediate IVI—an intravenous infusion. Then he checked the vital signs: oxygen saturation, pulse and blood pressure.

His anesthesiologist searched for and found good venous access through the jugular vein, into which he inserted a large-bore cannula and immediately started a saline drip followed by two units of type O rhesus-negative blood as a holding operation. Finally, he sent a sample of the patient's blood for cross-matching in the laboratory.

Dr. McCrae's immediate concern, with his patient stabilized for the moment, was to find out what was going on inside his chest. Clearly there was a bullet lodged there because the entry hole was in view, but there was no exit wound.

He debated whether to use an X-ray or a CT scan, but

chose not to move the patient from the gurney but to settle for an X-ray by sliding the plate beneath the unconscious body and taking the X-ray from above.

This revealed that the general had been lung-shot and the bullet was lodged very close to the hilum, the root of the lung. This gave him a three-choice gamble. An operation using a cardiopulmonary bypass was an option, but it would be likely to cause even further lung damage.

The second choice was to go for immediate invasive surgery with a view to extracting the bullet. But that, too, would be highly risky, as the full extent of the damage was still unclear, and it could also prove fatal.

He chose the third gamble—to allow twenty-four hours without further interference in the hope that, even though resuscitation so far had taken a huge toll on the old man's stamina, he would achieve a partial recovery with further resuscitation and stabilization. This would enable invasive surgery to be undertaken with a better chance of survival.

After that, the general was removed to intensive care, where, by the time the detective conferred with the surgeon, he lay festooned with tubes.

There was one from the central venous line on one side of the neck and the intravenous cannula on the other. Oxygen tubes up the nostrils, known as nasal specs, ensured a constant supply of oxygen. Blood pressure and pulse were displayed on a bedside monitor that, at a glance, revealed the heartbeat.

Finally, there was a chest drain under the left armpit between the fifth and sixth ribs. This was to intercept the constant leakage of air from the punctured lung and guide it down to a large glass jar on the floor, one-third full of water. The expelled air could leave the chest cavity and emerge underwater and bubble to the surface.

But it could not then return to the pleura, for that would collapse the lungs and kill the patient. Meanwhile, he would continue to inhale oxygen via the tubes in each nostril.

Having been told there was not a chance in hell of talking to the general for days to come, Det. Hall left. Back in the parking lot behind the ambulance entrance, he asked Lindy to drive for him. He had calls to make.

His first was to Willoughby College, where the killer, Mohammed Barre, had been studying. He was patched through to the dean of admissions. When he asked for confirmation that Mr. Barre had been a student at Willoughby, she agreed without hesitation. When he told her what had happened on the Princess Anne golf course, there was a stunned silence.

The identification of the morning's killer had not been released to the media. He would be at the college in twenty minutes, he said. He would need the dean to have available all records and access to the student's private quarters. In the interim, she was to inform no one and that included the student's parents in Michigan.

The second call was to Fingerprints. Yes, they had received a perfect set of ten from the morgue and had run them through AFIS. There was no match; the dead student was not in the system.

Had he been a foreigner, there would have been records with Immigration, dating from his visa application. But it was becoming clear Mr. Barre was a U.S. citizen of immigrant parents. But from where? Born Muslim or a convert who had changed his name?

The third call went to Ballistics. The gun was a Glock 17 automatic, Swiss made, with a nearly full magazine, five bullets fired. They were trying to trace the registered owner, whose name was not Barre and who lived near Baltimore, Maryland. Stolen? Purchased? They arrived at the college.

The dead student was of Somali extraction. Those who knew him at Willoughby declared he seemed to have had a change of personality around six months back, from a normal, outgoing, bright student to a silent, withdrawn recluse. The core reason seemed to be religious. There were two other Muslim students on campus, but they had experienced no such metamorphosis.

The dead man had taken to abandoning jeans and windbreakers in favor of long robes. He began to demand time out from studies five times a day for prayers. This was granted without demur. Religious tolerance was supreme. And he grew a bushy black beard.

For the second time that day, Ray Hall found himself going through the private possessions of another person, but there was a fundamental difference. Apart from the engineering textbooks, all the papers were Islamic texts in Arabic. Det. Hall understood not a word but collected them all. The key was the computer. With this, at least, Ray Hall knew what he was doing.

He found sermon after sermon, not in Arabic but in fluent, persuasive English. A masked face, two burning eyes, the calls for submission to Allah, for a completed preparedness to serve Him, fight for Him, die for Him. And, most of all, to kill for Him.

Detective Hall had never heard of the Preacher, but he closed the computer down and impounded it. He signed for everything he had confiscated, leaving the college with permission to inform the parents, to call him when they wished to come south to pick up their son's effects. Meanwhile, he would personally inform the Dearborn police. Taking two trash bags full of books, texts and the laptop, he returned to police HQ.

There were other things on the computer, including a search of Craigslist for a man with a handgun for sale. Clearly the paperwork had not been completed, which would lead to a serious charge for the vendor, but that would come later.

It was eight p.m. when his cell phone rang and a voice introduced himself as the son of the stricken general. He did not say where he was, only that he had received the news and was on his way by helicopter.

Darkness had fallen; there was an open space behind police HQ but no floodlights.

"Where is the nearest Navy base?" asked the voice.

"Oceana," said Hall. "But can you get permission to land there?"

"Yes, I can," said the voice. "One hour from now."

"I'll pick you up," said Hall. While he waited out the first half hour, he consulted police records nationwide for any similar assassinations in the recent past. To his surprise, there had been four. The golf course slaying made the fifth. In two of the previous four cases, the killers had immediately taken their own lives. The other two had been taken alive and even now were awaiting trial for murder one. All had acted alone. All had been converted to ultra-extremism by online sermons.

He picked up the general's son at Oceana at nine and drove him to Virginia Beach General. On his way, he described what had happened since seven-thirty that morning.

His guest questioned him closely on what he had discovered in Mohammed Barre's dorm room. Then he muttered: "The Preacher." Det. Hall thought he was referring to a profession, not a code name.

"I guess so," he said. They reached the hospital main entrance in silence.

The reception desk alerted someone to the arrival of the son of the man in ICU, and Alex McCrae came down from his office. As they went up to the intensive care floor, he explained the seriousness of the wound, which had precluded surgery.

"I can hold out only slim hopes for recovery," he said. "It's touch-and-go."

The son went into the room. He drew up a chair and gazed in the dim light at the rugged old face, locked away in a private place, kept alive by a machine. He sat there throughout the night, holding the sleeping man's hands in his own.

Just before four in the morning, the eyes opened. The heartbeat quickened. What the son could not see was the glass jar on the floor behind the bed. It was rapidly filling with bright red arterial blood. Somewhere, deep inside the chest, there had been a rupture of a major vessel. The general was bleeding out too fast to save.

The son felt a tiny pressure on his own hands from those he held. His father stared at the ceiling and his lips moved.

"Semper Fi, son," he murmured.

"Semper Fi, Dad."

The line on the screen went from mountain peaks to flat-line. The bleep converted to a single wail. A "crash" team appeared at the door. Alex McCrae was with them. He strode past the seated figure of the general's son and glanced at the bottle behind the bed. He held up an arm at the crash team and gently shook his head. The team withdrew.

After a few minutes, the son rose and left the room. He said nothing, just nodded to the surgeon. In the ICU, a nurse drew the sheet up over the face. The son walked the four flights down to the parking lot.

In his car twenty yards away, Det. Hall sensed something and awoke from a light sleep. The general's son walked across the parking lot, stopped and looked up. Dawn was still two hours away. The sky was black, the moon had set. Far above the stars glittered; hard, bright, eternal.

Those same stars, unseen in a pale blue sky, would be looking down on another man, lost to sight in a wilderness of sand. The standing man looked up at the stars and said something. The Virginia detective did not catch it. What the Tracker said was: "You just made this very personal, Preacher."

In a world of code names to hide real identities, the Tracker had given his new helper the pseudonym Ariel. It amused him to choose the sprite from Shakespeare's *Tempest*, who could fly invisibly through space and get up to whatever mischief he wanted.

But if Roger Kendrick struggled on planet Earth, he was nothing like that when he sat before the treasure trove of intoxicating equipment the U.S. taxpayers had provided him. As the man from Fort Meade had said, he became a fighter ace, now at the controls of the best interceptor money could buy.

He spent two days studying the construction the Preacher had built to mask his IP address and thus his location. He also watched the sermons and became convinced of one thing at the outset. The computer genius was not the masked man who preached religious hatred. There was another somewhere, his real opponent, the enemy ace flying against him;

skilled, elusive, capable of spotting any mistake he might make and then shutting him out.

Had Ariel but known it, his cyberenemy was Ibrahim Samir, British, born of Iraqi parentage, schooled at UMIST—the University of Manchester Institute of Science and Technology. Kendrick thought of him as the Troll.

It was he who had invented the proxy server to create the false IP address behind which he could hide his master's real location. But once, at the beginning of the sermon campaign, there had been a real IP, and once he had that, Ariel could place the source anywhere on the face of the Earth.

He also perceived very quickly that there was a fan base. Enthusiastic disciples were able to post messages for the Preacher. He determined to join it.

He realized the Troll would never be deceived unless Ariel's alter ego was detail perfect. Ariel created a young American called Fahad, son of two Jordanian immigrants, born and raised in the Washington area. But first he studied.

He used the background of the long-dead terrorist Abu Musab al-Zarqawi, a Jordanian who had headed al-Qaeda in Iraq until wiped out by Special Forces and a fighter strike. A copious biography was online. He came from the Jordanian village of Zarqa. Ariel created two parents who came from the same village, lived down the same street. If questioned, he could describe it from online information.

He re-created himself, born to his parents two years after they arrived in the USA. He could describe the school he went to, though now supposedly he'd been removed because of panic attacks.

And he studied Islam from online international courses, the mosque he and his parents attended and the name of its resident imam. Then he applied to join the Preacher's fan base. There were questions—not from the Troll personally but from another disciple in California. He answered them. There were days of delay. And then he was accepted. All the while he kept his own virus, his malware, hidden but ready for use.

There were four Taliban fighters in the brick office in the village outside Ghazni, the capital of the Afghan province of the same name. They sat, as they preferred, not on chairs but on the floor.

Their robes and cloaks were wrapped around them, for although it had just turned into the month of May, there was still a chill wind off the mountains, and the brick government building had no heating.

Also seated were three government officials from Kabul and the two *farangi* officers from NATO. The mountain men were not smiling. They never did. The only time they had seen *farangi* (foreign, white) soldiers had been in the sights of a Kalashnikov. But that was a life they had come to the village to abandon.

There is in Afghanistan a little-known program called simply Reintegration. It is a joint venture by the Kabul government and NATO, run on the ground by a British major general named David Hook.

The avant-garde thinking among the best brains has long

been that Taliban body count alone will never win. As fast as Anglo-American commanders congratulate themselves that one hundred, or two or three hundred, Taliban fighters have been taken out, more just seem to appear.

Some come from the Afghan peasantry, as they always have. Some among these volunteer because relatives—and, in that society, an extended family may number three hundred—have been killed by a misdirected missile, a wrong-target fighter strike or careless artillery; others because they are ordered to fight by their tribal elders. But they are young men, little more than boys.

Also young are the students from Pakistan, arriving in droves from the religious *madrassah* schools, where for years they study nothing but the Koran and listen to the extremist imams until they are groomed to fight and die.

But the Taliban army is like no other. Its units are extremely local to the area that bred them. And the reverence to the veteran commanders is total. Take out the veterans, reconvert the clan chiefs, bring in the tribal heads, and an entire county-sized area can simply abandon the fighting.

For years, British and American Special Forces have been disguising as mountain men, slipping through the hills to assassinate the middle- and upper-ranking Talib leaders, reckoning that the small fry are not really the problem.

Parallel with the night hunters is the Reintegration Program that seeks to "turn" veterans, to take the olive branch held out by the Kabul government. That day in the hamlet of Qala-e-Zal, General Hook and his Australian assistant, Captain Chris Hawkins, were representing the Force Reintegration Cell. The four wizened Talib chiefs, crouching along the wall, had been coaxed out of the mountains to return to village life.

As with all fishing, there has to be bait. A "reintegrater" has to attend a course in de-indoctrination. In exchange, there is a free house, a flock of sheep to enable a resumption of farming, an amnesty and the Afghani equivalent of a hundred dollars a week. The purpose of the meeting that bright but crisp May day was to attempt to persuade the veterans that the religious propaganda they had all received for years was, in fact, false.

As Pashto speakers they could not read the Koran and, like all non-Arab terrorists, had been converted because of what they had been told by Jihadi instructors, many pretending to be imams or mullahs while being nothing of the sort. So a Pashtun mullah or *maulvi* was in attendance to explain to the veterans how they had been deceived; how the Koran was, in reality, a book of peace with only a few "kill" passages, which the terrorists deliberately used out of context.

And there was a television set in the corner, an object of fascination to the mountain men. It was not screening live TV but a DVD from a player linked to it. The speaker on the screen was using English, but the mullah had a pause button, enabling him to halt the flow, explain what the preacher had said and then reveal how, according to the Holy Koran, it was all rubbish.

One of the four squatting on the floor was Mahmud Gul, who had been a senior commander as far back as 9/11. He was not yet fifty, but thirteen years in the mountains had aged him; the face beneath the black turban was wrinkled like a walnut, the hands gnarled and aching from incipient arthritis.

He had been indoctrinated as a young man not against the British and Americans, who he knew had helped free his people from the Russians. He knew little of bin Laden and his Arabs, and what he did know he did not like. He had heard of what had happened in downtown Manhattan all those years ago and he did not approve of it. He had joined the Taliban to fight against the Tajiks and Uzbeks of the Northern Alliance.

But the Americans did not understand the law of *pashtunwali*, the sacred rule between host and guest that absolutely forbade Mullah Omar to hand his al-Qaeda guests over to their tender mercies. So they had invaded Mahmud Gul's country. He had fought them for that, and he was still fighting them. Until now.

Mahmud Gul felt old and tired. He had seen many men die. He had put some out of their misery with his own gun when the wounds were so bad that they could live, in pain, for only a few more hours or days.

He had killed British and American boys but could not recall how many. His old bones ached and his hands were turning into claws. The shattered hip of many years ago never gave him peace through the long mountain winters. Half his family was dead, and he had not seen his grandchildren except during hurried night visits, before dawn drove him back to the caves.

He wanted out. Thirteen years was enough. Summer was coming. He wanted to sit in the warmth and play with the children. He wanted his daughters to bring him food, as it

THE KILL LIST

should be in old age. He had decided to take the government offer of amnesty, a house, sheep, an allowance, even if it meant listening to a fool of a mullah and a masked speaker on television.

As the TV was switched off and the mullah droned on, Mahmud Gul uttered something under his breath in Pashto. Chris Hawkins was sitting next to him and he, too, had a command of the language, but not the Ghazni rural dialect. He thought he had heard correctly but could not be sure. When the lecture was over and the mullah had scurried back to his car and his bodyguards, tea was taken. Strong, black, and the *farangi* officers had brought sugar, which was good.

Captain Hawkins slid down beside Mahmud Gul and they sipped in companionable silence. Then the Australian asked: "What did you say when the lecture finished?"

Mahmud Gul repeated the phrase. Spoken slowly and not under his breath, it meant only one thing. He had said: "I know that voice."

Chris Hawkins had two more days to spend in Ghazni and one more reintegration meeting to attend elsewhere. Then back to Kabul. He had a friend at the British embassy who he was pretty certain was there with MI6, the Secret Intelligence Service. He thought he might mention it.

Ariel was right in his assessment of the Troll. The Iraqi from Manchester was possessed of an overweening arrogance. In cyberspace, he was the best and he knew it. Everything in that world to which he put his hand had the stamp of perfection. He insisted on it. It was his hallmark.

He not only recorded the sermons of the Preacher but he alone sent them out into the world, to be watched on who knew how many screens. And he managed the growing fan base. He vetted aspirant members with intense checking before he would accept a comment or deign to reply. But he still did not notice the mild virus that slipped into his program from a dark little attic in Centerville, Virginia. As designed, it began to have its effect a week later.

Ariel's malware simply caused the Troll's website to slow down, periodically and only marginally. But the effect was to cause small pauses in the transmission of the picture as the Preacher spoke. But the Troll noticed at once the tiny aberration from perfection that the pauses made in his work. It was not acceptable. It irritated and finally enraged him.

He tried to correct it, but the flaw remained. He concluded that if website 1 had developed a flaw, he would have to create website 2 and move to it. Which he did. Then he had to transfer the fan base to the new website.

Before he had invented his proxy server to create a false Internet protocol address, he had a real one, the IP that would serve as a sort of mailing address. To move the entire fan base from website 1 to 2, he had to pass back through the true IP. It only took a hundredth of a second, maybe less.

Yet in the move across, the original IP was exposed for that nanosecond. Then it was gone. But Ariel had been waiting for that minuscule window. The IP address gave him a country, but it also had an owner—France Télécom.

If the NASA supercomputers were going to prove no impediment to Gary MacKinnon, the database of France Télécom was not going to hold up Ariel for long. Within a day, he was inside the FT database, unseen and unsuspected. Like a good burglar, he was back out without leaving a trace. He now had a latitude and a longitude—a city.

But he had a message for Col. Jackson. He knew better than send him the news by e-mail. People listen in to that sort of thing.

The Australian captain was right on two counts. The chance remark of the Taliban veteran was indeed worth mentioning, and his friend was indeed part of the large and active SIS unit inside the British embassy. And the tip was acted on without delay. It went by secure encryption to London and thence to TOSA.

For one thing, Britain had also had three deliberate murders encouraged by the faceless and nameless Preacher. For another, an all-points request to friendly agencies had already been disseminated. Given that the Preacher was strongly suspected of being originally from Pakistan, the British SIS stations in Islamabad and neighboring Kabul were particularly alert.

Within twenty-four hours, a J-SOC Grumman Gulfstream 500 with one passenger aboard had lifted off from Andrews field on the outskirts of Washington. It refueled at USAF base Fairford in Gloucestershire, UK, and again at the large U.S. base at Doha, Qatar. Its third stop was at the base still retained by the USA on the enormous sprawl of Bagram, north of Kabul.

The Tracker chose not to go into Kabul. He did not need to and his transport was safer under guard at Bagram than at Kabul International. But his needs had been sent on ahead of him. If there were any financial restraints on the Reintegration Program, they did not apply to J-SOC. The power of the dollar kicked in. Capt. Hawkins was brought by helicopter to Bagram. Refueled, the same chopper brought them and a close-in protection unit drawn from a Rangers company to Qala-e-Zal.

It was midday when they landed outside the impoverished hamlet, and the spring sun was warm. They found Mahmud Gul doing what he had wanted to do for so long: sitting in the sun playing with his grandchildren.

At the sight of the roaring Black Hawk overhead and the soldiers who poured from it when it had landed on the communal threshing floor, the women rushed inside. Doors and shutters slammed. Silent, stony-faced men stood in the only street the hamlet boasted and watched the *farangi* walk into their home.

The Tracker ordered the Rangers to stay with the machine. With just Capt. Hawkins beside him as introducer and translator, he walked down the street, nodding from side to side and uttering the traditional *"Salaam"* greeting. A few grudging *Salaam*s came back. The Australian knew where Mahmud Gul lived. The veteran was sitting outside. Several children scattered in alarm. Just one, a three-year-old girl, more curious than afraid, clung to her grandfather's cloak and stared up with huge saucer eyes. The two white men sat cross-legged in front of the veteran warrior and offered greetings. They were returned.

The Afghan glanced up and down the street. The soldiers were out of sight.

"You are not afraid?" asked Mahmud Gul.

"I believe I have come to visit a man of peace," said the Tracker. Hawkins translated into Pashto. The older man nodded and called something up the street.

"He is telling the village there is no danger," whispered Hawkins.

With pauses only for translation, the Tracker reminded Mahmud Gul of the session with the Reintegration team after Friday prayers the previous week. The Afghan's dark brown eyes remained unblinking on his face. At last he nodded.

"Many years ago, but it was the same voice."

"But on the television he was speaking in English. You do not understand English. How could you know?"

Mahmud Gul shrugged.

"It was the way he spoke," he said, as if no other consideration need apply. With Mozart, they called it perfect pitch—the ability to record and recall sounds exactly as they were. Mahmud Gul might be an illiterate peasant, but if his conviction turned out to be right, he also had that kind of ear.

"Please tell me how it came about."

The old man paused, and his gaze fell to the bundled package the American had carried down the street.

"It is time for gifts," whispered the Australian.

"Forgive me," said the Tracker, jerking loose the binding. He spread out what he had brought. Two buffalo robes, from a Native American memorabilia store, backed with warm fleece.

"Long ago the people of my country used to hunt the buffalo for his meat and his fur. This is the warmest hide known to man. In the winter, wrap one round you. Sleep with one beneath you and one above. You will never be cold again."

Mahmud Gul's walnut face slowly cracked into a smile, the first Capt. Hawkins had ever seen on him. There were only four teeth left, but they did their best to create a broad grin. He ran his fingers through the thick pelt. The jewel box of the Queen of Sheba could not have brought him more pleasure. So he told his story.

"It was in the fight against the Americans just after the invasion against the government of Mullah Omar. There were Tajiks and Uzbeks pouring out of their enclave in the northeast. We could have coped with them, but they had Americans with them, and the *farangi* were directing the airplanes that came from the sky with bombs and rockets. The American soldiers could speak to the airplanes and tell them where we were, so the bombs seldom missed. It was very bad.

"North of Bagram, retreating down the Salang Valley, I was caught in the open. An American warplane fired at me many times. I hid behind rocks, but when he had gone, I saw I had taken a bullet in the hip. My men carried me to Kabul. There I was put in a truck and taken farther south.

"We passed through Kandahar and crossed the border at Spin Boldak into Pakistan. They were our friends and gave us shelter. We came to Quetta. That was the first time a doctor saw me and I had attention to the hip.

"In the spring I had started to walk again. I was young and

strong in those days, and the broken bones healed well. But there was much pain, and I had a stick under my armpit. In the spring I was invited to join the Quetta Shura and sit in the council with the mullah.

"In the spring also a delegation came from Islamabad to Quetta to confer with Mullah Omar. There were two generals, but they spoke no Pashto, only Urdu. But one of the officers had brought his son, just a boy of nineteen. He spoke fluent Pashto, with the accent of the high Siachen area. He translated for the Punjabi generals. They told us that they would have to pretend to work with the Americans, but that they would never abandon us and let our Talib movement be destroyed. And so it has been.

"And I talked with the boy from Islamabad. The one who spoke on the white screen. Behind the mask. That was him. By the way, he had amber eyes."

The Tracker thanked him and left. He walked back down the street to the threshing floor. The men stood or sat in silence and stared. The women peered through the cracks in the shutters. The children hid behind their fathers and uncles. But no one molested him.

The Rangers were in an outward-facing circle. They ushered both officers into the Black Hawk and clambered aboard. The chopper lifted off, sending dust and chaff in all directions, and they flew back to Bagram. There are reasonably comfortable officers' quarters there, with good chow but no alcohol. The Tracker had need of only one thing—ten hours' sleep. While he slept, his message went through to the CIA station in the Kabul embassy.

B efore leaving the States, the Tracker had been advised
that the CIA, despite any interdepartmental rivalry,
was onside to give him the fullest cooperation. He needed
this for two reasons.

One was that the Agency had huge establishments in
Kabul and Islamabad, a capital where any visiting American
was likely to be under the closest secret police surveillance.
The other was that back at Langley the Agency had a superb
facility for the creation of false documents for use abroad.

When he woke, the deputy head of station had flown up
from Kabul to confer, as requested. The Tracker had a list of
requirements, of which the intelligence officer took careful
note. Details would be encrypted and sent to Langley that
day, he was assured. When the papers requested were available, a courier would bring them personally from the U.S.

When the CIA man had returned to Kabul, flying by helicopter from the U.S. compound at Bagram to the grounds
of the embassy, the Tracker took his waiting J-SOC executive
jet and flew to the large American base at Qatar on the Persian Gulf. As far as official records would show, no one called
Carson had even been in the country.

The same applied in Qatar. He could while away the three
days it would cost to prepare the new papers he needed inside the perimeter of an American base. On landing at the
base outside Doha, he dismissed the Grumman to return to
the States. From inside the base he ordered the purchase of
two air tickets.

One was on a cheap local airline for the short hop down

the coast to Dubai and was in the name of Mr. Christopher Carson. The other, from a different travel agency based in a five-star hotel, was for a business-class ticket from Dubai to Washington via London on British Airways. It was in the name of the fictional John Smith. When he received the message he was waiting for, he flew to Dubai International.

On landing, he made his way straight to the transit hall, where the truly vast duty-free shopping mall was thronged with thousands of passengers enjoying the biggest airline hub in the Middle East. Without needing to disturb the transit desk, he walked into the club-class lounge.

The courier from Langley was waiting at the agreed-upon entrance to the men's room and the murmured recognition signals were exchanged. Very old-fashioned, a hundred-year-old procedure, but it still works. They found a quiet corner and two secluded armchairs.

Both men had carry-on baggage only. They were not identical, but that did not matter. The courier had arrived bearing a genuine U.S. passport in the name of John Smith to match the America-bound ticket. He would obtain a boarding pass from the BA desk on the floor below. John Smith, having arrived by Emirates, would depart for home after a remarkably short stopover, but by a different airline and no one the wiser.

They also swapped bags. What the Tracker gave the courier was irrelevant. What he received was a wheelie, containing shirts, suits, toiletries, shoes and any short-stay-traveler's paraphernalia. Scattered among the clothing and airport-purchased thriller novels were various bills, receipts and letters, confirming the owner was Mr. Daniel Priest.

He handed over to the courier every scrap of paperwork he had in the name of Carson. That would also return unseen to the States. What he got in return was a wallet of documents the Agency had spent three days preparing.

There was a passport in the name of Mr. Daniel Priest, a senior staffer with the *Washington Post*. It bore a valid visa from the Pakistani consulate in Washington, securing Mr. Priest entry into Pakistan. The securing of this visa would mean that the Pakistani police were aware of his coming and would be waiting. Journalists are of extreme interest to sensitive regimes.

There was a letter from the publisher of the *Post*, confirming that Mr. Priest was preparing a major series of articles on "Islamabad—the making of a successful modern city." And there was a return ticket via London.

There were credit cards, a driver's license, the usual paperwork and plastic cards to be found in the wallet of a law-abiding American citizen and senior executive, plus a confirmation that a room awaited him at the Serena Hotel, Islamabad, and that the hotel car would be waiting for him.

The Tracker knew better than to emerge from the customs hall at Islamabad International into the seething, surging chaos outside and then allow himself to be hustled into any old taxi.

The courier also handed over the stub of his boarding pass from Washington to Dubai and the unused onward ticket from Dubai to "Slammy," as Islamabad is known in the Special Forces fraternity.

A thorough search of his room, virtually a certainty, would reveal only that Mr. Dan Priest was a legitimate foreign correspondent from Washington with a valid visa and a logical reason for being in Pakistan; further, that he intended to stay a few days and then fly home.

With the exchange of identities and "legends" completed, both men descended separately to different airline desks below to secure boarding passes for their onward flights.

It was nearly midnight, but the Tracker's EK612 flight took off at three twenty-five a.m. He killed the time back in the lounge but was still at the departure gate with an hour to spare, then held back to size up his fellow passengers. He knew that if there were a breeze, he should stay upwind of most of them.

As he suspected, the economy-class passengers were over-whelmingly Pakistani laborers, returning after their statutory two years' virtual forced labor on building sites. It is custom-ary for the construction-trade gang masters to confiscate the laborer's passport on arrival and return it only after the two-year contract is done.

During that time, the laborers live in sub-basic hovels with minimal facilities, working hard in fearsome heat for minuscule wages, some of which they try to send back home. As they crowded to the door for boarding, he caught the first whiff of stale sweat flavored with a diet of constant curry. Mercifully, the economy class and business class were soon separated, and he relaxed into upholstered comfort up front with a complement of Gulf Arab and Pakistani businessmen.

The flight was just over three hours, and the Emirates Boeing 777-300 touched down on time at 0730 local. He watched from the porthole of the taxiing airliner the military C-130 Hercules and the presidential Boeing 737 drift past.

In the passport hall he was separated from the jostling throng of Pakistanis when he joined the queue for foreigners' passports. The new document in the name of Daniel Priest, adorned only by a few European entry and exit stamps and the Pakistani visa, was meticulously examined page by page. The questions were perfunctory and polite, easily answered. He produced proof of his reservation at the Serena. The plainclothesmen stood well back and stared.

He took his wheelie and struggled through the clamoring, pushing, shoving mass of humanity in baggage claim, aware that this was of a Teutonic order compared to the chaos outside. Pakistan does not queue.

Outside the building, the sun was shining. Thousands seemed to have come, bringing entire families, to greet the returnees from the Gulf. Tracker scanned the crowd until he spotted the name Priest on a board held by a young man in the uniform of the Serena. He made contact and was escorted to the limousine, parked in the small VIP parking lot to the right of the terminal.

Since the airport sits within the sprawl of old Rawalpindi, the road, once clear of the airport hub, turns down the Islamabad Highway and into the capital. As the Serena, the only earthquake-proof hotel in Slammy, is on the outskirts of town, the Tracker was taken by surprise as the car swerved into a short dogleg; right, left, past a barrier that would be down for visitor cars but up for the hotel's own limousine, up a short but steep ramp and to the main entrance.

At the reception desk, he was made welcome by name and escorted to his room. There was a letter waiting for him. It bore the U.S. embassy logo. He beamed and tipped the bellhop, pretending to be unaware the counterintelligence police had bugged the room and opened the letter. It was from the press attaché at the embassy, welcoming him to Pakistan and inviting him to dinner that evening at the attaché's home. It was signed Gerry Byrne.

He asked the hotel switchboard operator to put him through to the embassy, asked for and was patched through to Gerry Byrne and exchanged the usual pleasantries. Yes, the flight had been fine, the hotel was fine, the room was fine, and he would be delighted to come for dinner.

Gerry Byrne was also delighted. He lived in town, in zone F-7, Street 43. It was complex, so he would send a car. It would be delightful. Just a small group of friends, some American, some Pakistani.

Both men knew that there was another party to the conversation who was probably more bored than delighted. He would be seated at a console in the basement of a cluster of adobe buildings set among lawns and fountains, looking more like a university or a general hospital than the headquarters of a secret police. But that is what the complex on Khayaban-e-Suhrawardy Street looks like—the home of the ISI.

The Tracker replaced the receiver. So far, so good, he thought. He showered, shaved and changed. It was late morning. He decided on an early lunch and a nap to catch up on the lost sleep of last night. Before lunch he ordered a long, cool beer in his room and signed the declaration to confirm he was not a Muslim. Pakistan is strictly Islamic and dry, but the Serena has a license, only for guests.

The car was there on the dot of seven, an unremarkable (for a reason) four-door sedan of Japanese manufacture.

There would be thousands like it on the streets of Slammy. It would attract no attention. At the wheel was an embassy-employed Pakistani driver.

The driver knew the way—up Ataturk Avenue, across Jinnah Avenue, then left along Nazimuddin Road. The Tracker knew it, too, but only because it had all been in the brief the courier from Langley had given him at the Dubai airport. Just a precaution. He spotted the ISI tail within a block of the Serena and it faithfully followed the sedan past the apartment high-rises and up Marvi Road to Street 43. So, no surprises. The Tracker did not like surprises unless they were his.

The house did not quite have the words "Government Issue" above the front door, but it might have. Pleasant, roomy enough, one of a dozen allocated to embassy staff living outside the compound. He was greeted by Gerry Byrne and his wife, Lynn, who led him through to a terrace in the back, where he was offered a drink.

It might all almost have been a suburban house in the U.S. save for a few details. Each house on Street 43 had seven-foot concrete walls around it, plus steel gates the same height. The gates had opened without any communication, as if someone had been watching from inside. The gateman was in a dark uniform, baseball-capped and with a sidearm. Just normal suburbia.

There was a Pakistani couple already there, a doctor and his wife. Others arrived. One other embassy car, which came inside the compound. Others parked on the street. A couple from an aid agency, able to explain the difficulty of persuading the religious zealots up in Bajaur to permit polio vaccination of local children. Tracker knew there was one man present he had come to see and one not yet arrived. The rest of the guests were cover, like the entire dinner.

The missing man came with his mother and father. The father was forthcoming and jovial. He had concessions in the mining of semiprecious stones in Pakistan, and even in Afghanistan, and was voluble in explaining the difficulties the present situation was causing his business.

The son was about thirty-five, content simply to say he was in the army, though he was in civilian clothes. Tracker had been briefed about him, too.

The other American diplomat was introduced as Stephen Dennis, the cultural attaché. It was a good cover because it would be perfectly natural both for the press attaché to offer a dinner for a star American journalist and for the cultural attaché to be invited along.

Tracker knew he was really the number two in the CIA station. The head of station was a "declared" intelligence officer, meaning that the CIA was perfectly open about who he was and what he did. In any embassy on tricky territory, the fun is working out who the "undeclareds" really are. The host government usually has a number of suspicions, some accurate, but can never be sure. It is the undeclareds who do the espionage, usually using local nationals who can be turned to do a new employer's bidding.

It was a convivial dinner with wine and, later, drams of Johnnie Walker Black Label, which happens to be the tipple of choice of the entire officer corps, Islam or not. As the guests mingled over coffee, Steve Dennis nodded to the

Tracker and drifted to the outside terrace. Tracker followed. The third to join them was the young Pakistani.

Within a few sentences, it became clear he was not only army but also ISI. Because of the westernized education his father had been able to give him, he had been singled out to penetrate British and American society in the city and report back on anything of use that he heard. In fact, the reverse had happened.

Steve Dennis had spotted him in days and done a reverse recruitment. Javad had become the CIA's mole inside the ISI. It was to him that the Tracker's request had been directed. He had quietly entered the archive department on a pretext and searched the records under the year 2002 and Mullah Omar.

"Whoever your source was, Mr. Priest," he murmured on the terrace, "he has a good memory. There was indeed a covert visit in 2002 to Quetta to confer with Mullah Omar. It was headed by then-one-star-general Shawqat, now commander of the entire army."

"And the boy who spoke Pashto?"

"Indeed, though there is no mention of that. Simply that in the delegation was a Major Musharraf Ali Shah of the Armored Infantry. Among the seat allocations on the aircraft, and sharing a room with his father in Quetta, is a listing for a son, Zulfiqar."

He produced a slip of paper and passed it over. It had an address in Islamabad.

"Any further reference to the boy?"

"A few. I checked again under his name and patronymic. It seems he went bad. There are references to him leaving home and going to the Tribal Areas to join Lashkar-e-Taiba. We have had several agents deep inside for many years. A young man of that name was reported to be among them, fanatically Jihadist, seeking action.

"He managed to get acceptance into the 313 Brigade."

Tracker had heard of the 313, named after the warriors, just 313 in number, who stood with the Prophet against hundreds of foes.

"Then he disappeared again. Our sources reported rumors that he had gone to join the Haqqani clan, which would have been facilitated by his Pashto, which is all they speak. But where? Somewhere in the three Tribal Areas—North and South Waziristan or Bajaur. Then nothing, silence. No more Ali Shah."

Others wanted to join them on the terrace. Tracker pocketed the slip of paper and thanked Javad. An hour later, his embassy car took him back to the Serena.

In his room he checked the three or four tiny telltales he had laid; human hairs stuck with saliva across drawers and the lock of his wheelie. They were gone. The room had been searched.

5

The Tracker had a name and an address, along with a street map of Islamabad, brought to him by the departed John Smith in the Dubai transit lounge. He was also certain that when he left the hotel the next morning, he would have a tail. Before going to bed, he went to reception and asked for a taxi to be chartered for the next morning. The clerk asked where he would like to go in it.

"Oh, just a general sightseeing tour of the notable tourist landmarks of the city," he said.

At eight a.m. the next day, the taxi was waiting. He greeted the driver with his usual, amiable harmless-American-tourist beam and they set off.

"I am going to need your help, my friend," he confided, leaning over the front seat. "What do you recommend?"

The car was heading up Constitution Avenue, past the French and Japanese embassies. Tracker, who had memorized the street map, nodded enthusiastically as the Supreme

Court, the National Library, the presidential residence and Parliament were pointed out. He took notes. He also threw several glances out the back window. There was no tail. No need. The ISI man was driving.

It was a long tour with only two breaks. The driver took him past the front entrance of the truly impressive Faisal Mosque, where Tracker asked if photographs were permitted and, on being told they were, took a dozen from the car window.

They swung through the Blue Zone, with its streets of upmarket shops. The first stop came at the tailoring emporium known as British Suiting.

Tracker told the driver a friend had mentioned it as a place to have a very good suit hand-made in only two days. The driver agreed that was so and watched his American client disappear inside.

The staff were attentive and eager to please. Tracker selected a fine wool worsted, dark blue with a faint pinstripe. He was warmly congratulated on his taste and beamed away. Measuring took only fifteen minutes, and he was asked to return the next day for first fittings. He made a cash deposit in dollars, much appreciated, and before leaving asked if he might visit the men's room.

It was, predictably, right at the back, past the stacked rolls of suiting fabric. Next to the lavatory door was another. When the shop assistant who had guided him there left, he gave it a push. It opened onto an alley. He closed the door, used the urinal and returned to the shop. He was ushered out the front. The taxi was waiting.

What he had not seen, but could guess, was that while he

was out back, the driver had put his head through the door to check. He was told his client was "down the back." The fitting rooms were also in that direction. He nodded and returned to his cab.

The only other stop came during a visit to the Kohsar Market, a major landmark. Here Tracker expressed a desire for a midmorning coffee and was pointed to Gloria Jean's coffee shop. After coffee, he bought some British chocolate biscuits at A.M. Grocers, and told his driver they could now head back to the Serena.

Once there, he paid off the driver with a handsome tip, which he was confident would not go into the ISI budget but the driver's pocket. A full report would be filed within the hour and a call would be made to British Suiting. Just to check.

Up in his room he composed and filed a report for the *Washington Post*. It was titled "A Morning Tour of Fascinating Islamabad." It was deeply boring and would never see the light of day.

He had not brought a computer because he did not want any hard drive of his being removed and gutted. He used the telecoms room of the Serena. The dispatch was indeed intercepted and read by the same basement-confined official who had copied and filed the letter from the press attaché.

He lunched in the hotel dining room, then, approaching the front desk, announced he was going to take a stroll. As he left, a rather plump young man, ten years his junior but running to fat, peeled himself off a lobby sofa, stubbed out his cigarette, folded his newspaper and followed.

The Tracker may have been the older man, but he was a

Marine and enjoyed power walking. Within two long avenues, the "tail" was jogging to keep up, puffing and wheezing and drenched in sweat. When finally he lost his quarry, he thought back to the report of the morning. On his second outing of the day, the American was certainly heading in the direction of British Suiting. The policeman headed in the same direction. He was a worried man. He had his unforgiving superiors to think about.

When he put his head around the door of the tailoring shop, his worries evaporated. Yes, the American was indeed inside, but he was "down the back." The tail loitered outside Mobilink, found a friendly doorway, leaned against the wall, unfolded his newspaper and lit up.

In fact, the Tracker had spent no time in the fitting room. After being welcomed, he explained with a display of embarrassment that he had developed an upset stomach and please could he use the loo? Yes, he knew the way.

Farangi sustaining an upset stomach is as predictable as the sun rising. He slipped out the back door, trotted down the alley and into a main boulevard. A passing taxi, seeing his wave, swerved to the curb. This was a genuine cab, driven by a simple Pakistani driver trying to make a living. Foreigners can always be driven the long scenic route without realizing it, and dollars are dollars.

The Tracker knew he was going the long way around, but it was better than making a fuss. Twenty dollars later on a five-dollar fare, he was dropped where he wanted. The junction of two streets in the Pink Zone, the fringes of Rawalpindi and the area of military homes. When the cab had gone, he completed the last two hundred yards on foot.

It was a modest little villa, neat but not generous, with a plaque, in English and Urdu, reading "Col. M. A. Shah." He knew the army started early and broke early. He knocked. There was a shuffling sound. The door opened a few inches. Dark inside, a dark face, careworn but once beautiful. Mrs. Shah? No maid; not a prosperous household.

"Good afternoon, ma'am. I have come to talk with Colonel Ali Shah. Is he in?"

From inside a male voice called, something in Urdu. She turned and replied. The door swung wide open and a middle-aged male appeared. Neatly trimmed hair, a clipped mustache, clean-shaven, very military. The colonel had changed out of uniform into mufti. Even so, he exhaled self-importance. But his surprise at seeing a dark-suited American was genuine.

"Good afternoon, sir. Do I have the honor of addressing Colonel Ali Shah?"

He was just a lieutenant colonel but was not going to object. And the phrasing of the request did no harm.

"Yes, indeed."

"My lucky day, sir. I would have rung, but I had no private phone number for you. I pray I do not come at a bad moment."

"Well, er, no, but what is it . . ."

"The fact is, Colonel, my good friend General Shawqat told me over dinner last night that you were the man to talk to in my quest. Could we . . ."

The Tracker gestured inside, and the bewildered officer backed off and held the door wide open. He would have thrown a quivering salute and stood with his back to the wall if the commander in chief had walked by. Gen. Shawqat, no less, and he and the American dined together.

"Of course, where are my manners? Please come in."

He led the way into a modestly furnished sitting room. His wife hovered. "Chai," barked the colonel, and she scuttled away to prepare the tea, the ritual welcome for honored guests.

The Tracker offered his card: Dan Priest, senior staff writer for the *Washington Post*.

"Sir, I have been tasked by my editor, with the full approval of your government, to create a portrait of Mullah Omar. As you will understand, he is, even after all these years, a very reclusive figure and little known. The general gave me to believe you had met and conversed with him."

"Well, I don't know about . . ."

"Oh, come now, you're too modest. My friend told me you accompanied him to Quetta eleven years ago and played a crucial role in bilateral talks."

Colonel Ali Shah held himself rather straighter as the American lavished on the compliments. So Gen. Shawqat *had* noticed him. He steepled his fingertips and agreed that he had indeed conversed with the one-eyed Taliban leader.

Tea arrived. As she served it, Tracker noticed that Mrs. Ali Shah had the most extraordinary jade green eyes. He had heard of this before. The mountain people from the tribes along the Durand Line, that wild frontier between Afghanistan and Pakistan.

It was said that twenty-three hundred years ago Alexander the Great, Iskandar of Macedon, the young god of the world's morning, had marched through those mountains from his crushing of the Persian empire to his intended conquest of India. But his men were tired, exhausted by his relentless campaigns, and when he marched back from the Indus campaign, they deserted in droves. If they could not return to the hills of Macedon, they would settle in these mountains and valleys, take brides, farm good land and march and fight no more.

The little child who had hidden behind the robe of Mahmud Gul in the village of Qala-e-Zal had bright blue eyes, not brown like the Punjabis. And the missing son?

The tea had not been drunk when the interview ended. He had no idea it would be so abrupt.

"I believe you were accompanied by your son, Colonel, who speaks Pashto?"

The army officer came out of his chair and stood ramrod straight, clearly affronted and deeply so.

"You are mistaken, Mr. Priest, I have no son."

The Tracker rose also, putting down his cup, apologetic.

"But I was given to understand . . . a young lad named Zulfiqar . . ."

The colonel stalked to the window and stood, staring out, hands behind back. He quivered with suppressed anger, though at whom, visitor or son, Tracker could not tell.

"I repeat, sir, I have no son. And I fear I can help you no more."

The silence was freezing. The American was clearly being asked to leave. He glanced across at the colonel's wife.

The jade green eyes were flooded with tears. There was clearly a family trauma going on, and it had been going on for years.

Affecting a few bumbling apologies, the Tracker withdrew toward the door. The wife escorted him. As she held the door open, he whispered: "I am so sorry, lady, so terribly sorry."

It was clear she spoke no English and probably no Arabic. But the word "sorry" is pretty international, and she might have picked up a smattering. She looked up, brimming-eyed, saw the sympathy and nodded. Then he was gone and the door closed.

He walked half a mile before emerging onto Airport Road and hailing a cab heading into town. At the hotel he called the cultural attaché from his room. If the call was monitored, which it would be, it would not matter.

"Hi, this is Dan Priest. I was just wondering whether you had tracked down that material on the traditional music of the Punjab and the tribal agencies?"

"I surely have," said the CIA man.

"Great. I can make a good piece out of it. Can you drop it off for me at the Serena? Take tea in the lounge?"

"And why not, Dan. Seven o'clock suit you?"

"Terrific. See you then."

Over tea that evening, the Tracker explained what he needed for the next day. It was to be Friday, the colonel would be going to the mosque for the prayers on the Muslim holy day. He would not dare miss out. But accompanying wives would not be required. This was not Camp Lejeune.

With the CIA man gone, he used the concierge to reserve himself passage on the Etihad evening departure for Qatar, connecting via British Airways for London.

The car was there the next morning when he settled up and emerged with his single bag. It was the usual nondescript car but with CD plates so it could not be entered or its inhabitants harassed.

At the wheel was a middle-aged white American with gray hair—a veteran embassy servant who had been driving this city long enough to know it intimately. With him was a young and junior State Department staffer who, at a language course back home, had chosen and mastered Pashto as his specialty. The Tracker climbed in the back and gave the address. They came down the ramp from the Serena, and their ISI tail slid in behind them.

At the end of the street containing Col. Ali Shah's house they parked and waited until every male in the road had left for the mosque and Friday prayers. Only then did the Tracker order that he be dropped at the door.

It was again Mrs. Shah who answered. She at once appeared flustered and explained that her husband was not there. He would return in an hour, maybe more. She spoke in Pashto. The embassy man replied that the colonel had bade them wait for him. Uncertain that she had had no such instructions, she nevertheless let them in and took them to the sitting room. She hovered, embarrassed, but did not sit. Nor did she leave. The Tracker gestured to the armchair opposite his own.

"Please, Mrs. Shah, do not be alarmed to see me again. I came to apologize for yesterday. I did not mean to upset your husband. I brought a little gift to express my regrets."

He placed the bottle of Black Label on the coffee table. It, too, had been in the car, as requested. She gave a nervous smile, as the translator interpreted, and sat down.

"I had no idea there had been a rift between father and

son," said the Tracker. "Such a tragedy. I had been told your lad—Zulfiqar, is it not?—was so talented, speaking English as well as Urdu and Pashto—which, of course, he must have learned from you."

She nodded, and again tears welled in her eyes.

"Tell me, do you not somewhere have a picture of Zulfiqar, even when he was your little boy?"

A large drop emerged from each eye and ran down the cheek. No mother of a son quite forgets the once beautiful little boy she held on her lap. She nodded slowly.

"May I see it . . . please?"

She rose and left the room. Somewhere she had a secret hiding place and there she defied her husband by keeping a photo of her long-lost boy. When she came back, she was holding a single photo in a leather frame.

It was a graduation-day picture. There were two teenage boys in the frame, grinning happily at the camera. It was from the days before the conversion to Jihad, the carefree school-end days, a rolled baccalaureate scroll and harmless friendship. There was no need to ask which boy was which. The one on the left had luminous amber eyes. He handed back the photo.

"Joe," said the Tracker quietly, "use your mobile to ask our driver to come knock on the door."

"But he'll be waiting outside."

"Do as I ask, please."

The junior staffer made the call. Mrs. Shah did not understand a word. A few seconds later, there was a sharp rap on the front door. Mrs. Shah looked alarmed. Not her husband; too early, and he would simply enter. No other visitors were expected. She rose, looked helplessly around, pulled open a drawer in the credenza by the wall and pushed the photo into it. The door knocker rapped again. She left the room.

The Tracker was across it in two strides. He removed the photo and snapped it twice with his iPhone. By the time Mrs. Shah returned with their puzzled driver, her older visitor was back in his chair, the younger one standing bewildered by him. The Tracker rose with a warm smile.

"Ah, time to go, I see. I have a plane to catch. I am so sorry to have missed your husband. Please give him my best regards and my apologies for upsetting him."

This was all translated, and they saw themselves out. When they were gone, Mrs. Shah retrieved her precious photo and returned it to her secret place.

In the car to the airport, the Tracker expanded the picture and stared at it. He was not a cruel man and did not want to deceive the once-beautiful woman with the jade green eyes. But how, he mused, do you tell a mother still crying for her lost baby boy that you are going to hunt him down and kill him for the monster he has become?

Twenty hours later, he touched down at Washington Dulles.

The Tracker crouched in the tiny space available to him in the attic of the small house in Centerville and stared at the screen. Beside him, Ariel sat in front of his keyboard, as a pianist before his concert grand. He was in total control; through the equipment TOSA had donated him, the whole world was his.

His fingers flickered over the keys, and images came and went as he explained what he had done.

"Troll's Internet traffic is coming out of here," he said.

The images were from Google Earth, but he had somehow enhanced them. From space, the watcher plunged downward like aerial daredevil Felix Baumgartner diving to Earth. The Arabian Peninsula and the Horn of Africa filled the screen, then seemed to rush past his ears as the camera roared down and down. Eventually, it halted its insane dive, and he was staring at a roof; square, pale gray. There seemed to be a courtyard and a gate. Two vans were parked in the yard.

"He's not in Yemen, as you might have thought, he's in Somalia. This is Kismayo, on the coast at the southern end of the country," said Ariel.

Tracker stared, fascinated. They had all been wrong—CIA, TOSA, Counter-Terrorism Center—to think their quarry had emigrated from Pakistan to Yemen. He had probably been there but had moved on to seek sanctuary not with the AQAP, the al-Qaeda in the Arabian Peninsula, but with the fanatics controlling AQHA. Al-Qaeda in the Horn of Africa, formerly called al-Shabaab, which controlled the southern half of Somalia, among the wildest countries in the world.

There was much to research. So far as he knew, Somalia, outside the guarded enclave surrounding the token capital Mogadishu, was virtually out of bounds since the slaughter of eighteen Rangers in the incident known as Black Hawk Down, which was die-stamped onto the American military memory—and not in a pleasant way.

If Somalia had any fame at all, it was for the pirates who

for ten years had been hijacking ships off the coast and ransoming vessels, cargoes and crews for millions of dollars. But the pirates were in the north, in Puntland, a great and desolate wilderness peopled by clans and tribes that the Victorian explorer Sir Richard Burton had once termed "the most savage people in the world."

Kismayo was in the deep south, two hundred miles north of the Kenyan border; in colonial days a thriving Italian trade center, now a teeming slum ruled by Jihadi fanatics more extreme than any others in Islam.

"Do you know what that building is?" he asked Ariel.

"No. A warehouse, a large shed, I don't know. But that is where the Troll operates the fan base. That is where his computer is located."

"Does he know you know?"

The young man smiled quietly.

"Oh, no. He never spotted me. He is still running the fan base. He would have shut down if he knew I was watching him."

The Tracker backed out of the loft and eased himself down the ladder to the landing below. He would have it all transferred to TOSA. He would have a UAV, a drone, circling silently and invisibly over that shed within days, watching, listening for any cyberspace whisper, sensing body-heat movements, photographing comings and goings. It would transmit everything it saw in real time to screens at Air Force Base Creech, Nevada, or Tampa, Florida, and thence to TOSA. Meanwhile, there was much to do with what he had brought back from Islamabad.

———

The Tracker stared for hours at the photograph he had swiped from the picture treasured by Mrs. Ali Shah. He had had the laboratory enhance the quality until it was pin sharp. He looked at the two smiling faces and wondered where they were now. The one on the right was irrelevant. It was the boy with amber eyes whom he studied, as in World War Two General Montgomery had studied the face of Rommel, the German Desert Fox, trying to imagine what he would do next.

The boy in the photograph was seventeen. That was before he converted to ultra-Jihadism, before 9/11, before Quetta, before he walked out on his family and went to live with the killers of Lashkar-e-Taiba and the 313 Brigade and the Haqqani clan.

The experiences, the hatred, the inevitable killings witnessed, the harsh life in the mountains of the Tribal Agencies— all that would have aged the face of the laughing boy.

The Tracker sent a clear picture of the Preacher now, masked though he was, and the left-hand side of the picture from Islamabad to a very specialist unit. At the Criminal Justice Information Services, an FBI facility in Clarksburg, West Virginia, there is a laboratory that is expert in aging faces.

He asked them to give him a face—the face of now. Then he went to see Gray Fox.

The director of TOSA examined the evidence with approval. At last they had a name. They would soon have a face. They had a country, maybe even a city.

"Do you think he lives there, in that warehouse in Kismayo?" he asked.

"I doubt it. He has a paranoia about being elusive. I would bet he resides elsewhere, records his sermons in a single room with a camcorder, backed by a bedsheet-sized backdrop inscribed with the usual Koranic verses as we see on the screen, then lets his assistant, the one we now call the Troll, take it away and transmit it from Kismayo. He's not in any trap yet, not by a long shot."

"So what next?"

"I need a UAV over that warehouse on virtually permanent station. I'd ask for a low-flying mission to take side-on pictures of that building to see if there is a company name on it, except for one thing. I believe it would be a waste of time. But I have to identify who owns it."

Gray Fox stared at the image from space. It was clear enough, but military technology would be able to count the rivets in the roof from 50,000 feet.

"I'll get on to the drone boys. They have launch facilities in Kenya to the south, Ethiopia to the west, Djibouti to the north, and the CIA has a very covert unit inside the Mogadishu enclave. You'll get your pictures. Now that you have his face, which he seems so keen to keep covered, and his name, are you going to blow his cover away?"

"Not yet. I have another idea."

"Your call, Tracker. Go for it."

"One last thing. I could ask, but the weight of J-SOC behind it would be helpful. Does the CIA or anyone else have a secret agent buried inside South Somalia?"

———

A week later, four things happened. Tracker had spent the time steeping himself in the tragic story of Somalia. Once, it had been three regions. French Somaliland in the far north was now Djibouti, still with a strong French influence, a resident Foreign Legion garrison and a huge American base whose rent was crucial to the economy. Also in the north, former British Somaliland was now just Somaliland, also quiet, peaceful, even democratic, but bizarrely unrecognized as a nation/state.

The bulk was former Italian Somaliland, confiscated after World War Two, administered for a while by the British and then given independence. After a few years of the usual dictatorship, the once thriving and elegant colony where wealthy Italians used to vacation had lapsed into civil war. Clan fought clan, tribe fought tribe, warlord after warlord sought supremacy. Finally, with Mogadishu and Kismayo just seas of rubble, the outside world had given up.

A belated notoriety had returned when the beggared fishermen of the north turned to piracy and the south to Islamic fanaticism. Al-Shabaab had arisen not as an offshoot but an ally of al-Qaeda and conquered all of the south. Mogadishu hovered as a fragile token capital of a corrupt regime living on aid but in an encircled enclave whose border was guarded by a mixed army of Kenyans, Ethiopians, Ugandans and Burundians.

Inside the wall of guns, foreign money poured into aid projects, and various spooks scuttled about pretending to be something else.

As the Tracker read, head in hands, or studied images on the plasma screen in his office, an RQ-4 Global Hawk took up station over Kismayo. It was not weaponized, for that was not the mission. It was known as a HALE version, for high altitude, long endurance.

It came out of the nearby Kenyan facility, where a few American soldiers and technicians sweltered in the tropical heat, resupplied by air and dwelling in air-conditioned housing units like a film crew on location. They had four Global Hawks and two were now airborne.

One had been aloft before the new request arrived. The job was watching the Kenya/Somali border and the offshore waters for raids and incursions over the border. The new order was to circle over a once commercial zone in Kismayo and watch a building. As the Hawks would have to spell each other, that meant all four were now operational.

The Global Hawk has an extraordinary "loiter time" of thirty-five hours. Being close to its base, it could circle above its target for thirty hours. At 60,000 feet, almost twice the height of an airliner, it could scan up to 40,000 square miles a day. Or it could narrow that beam to four square miles and zoom in for pin-sharp clarity.

The Hawk over Kismayo was equipped with synthetic-aperture radar, electro-optical and infrared for night and day, clear or cloud, operation. It could also "listen" to the tiniest transmission on the lowest possible power and "sniff" changing heat centers as humans moved about below. All intelligence gathered went straight to Nevada in a nanosecond.

The second thing that happened was the return of the pictures from Clarksburg. The technicians there had noticed that on the masked images off the TV, the fabric of the mask seemed to be slightly bulked out from the face beneath. They theorized there could be a full black beard under there. So they sent two alternates, with and without beard.

They had the creases across the forehead and those around the eyes to work on, so the updated face was markedly older. And hard. There was a cruelty about the mouth and jaw. The boy's softness and merriment was gone.

Hardly had Tracker finished studying the new photos than a message came from Ariel.

"There seems to be a second computer in that building," he said. "But it is not emitting the sermons. Whoever is on it, and I think it is the Troll, has acknowledged receipt with thanks. No indication of what. But someone else is communicating by e-mail with that building."

And Gray Fox came back. A total negative. No one has any "asset" living among the al-Shabaab.

"The message seems to be: If you want to go into that hellhole, you're on your own."

6

He should have thought of it while he was in Islamabad and mentally kicked himself for the oversight. Javad, the CIA's mole inside the ISI, had told him the young Zulfiqar Ali Shah had vanished off all radar screens by 2004 after disappearing into Lashkar-e-Taiba, the anti-Kashmir terror group.

Since then—nothing. But nothing under that name. It was only when staring at the face in his office that another line occurred to him. He asked the CIA to recontact Javad with a simple query: Did any of their agents inside the various terror groups along the deadly frontier hear mention of a terrorist with amber eyes?

Meanwhile, he had another call to make with the same request he had vainly put to Langley.

He took an official car again but this time went in a civilian suit with shirt and tie. Since 9/11, the British embassy on Massachusetts Avenue has also been heavily protected. The grandiose building stands next to the Naval Observatory, home of the Vice President and also heavily guarded.

Access to the embassy avoids the columned portico at the front and is achieved down a small street to one side. His car stopped at the hut beside the barrier pole, and he offered his pass through the car's open window. There was a consultation by handheld phone. Whatever the reply, it was enough for the pole to be lifted and the car to roll into the small parking lot. Less important creatures park outside and enter on foot. Space is scarce.

The door was much less grand than the front entrance, for security reasons now hardly used and only then by the ambassador and American visitors of exalted rank. Once inside, Tracker turned to the glass-windowed booth and again offered his identity card. It mentioned a certain Col. James Jackson.

Another phone conference, then the invitation to take a seat. Within two minutes, the elevator door opened and a young man emerged, evidently a junior in the pecking order.

"Colonel Jackson?" There was no one else in the lobby. He, too, examined the ID card. "Please come with me, sir."

It was, as Tracker knew it would be, the fifth floor, the defense attachés' floor, the level the American cleaning staff never entered. Cleaning had to be done by the lowest, albeit British, forms of life.

On the fifth floor, the young man led Tracker down a corridor past several door plaques announcing the inhabitants, and finally to a door with no marking but with a card-swipe mechanism instead of a handle. He knocked and on the command from inside swiped the card, swung the door open and gestured Tracker to enter. He did not follow but quietly closed the door.

It was an elegant room, with bulletproof windows giving onto the avenue. It was an office but definitely not the "bubble," which was where conferences only of cosmic clearance level took place. That room was in the center of the building, surrounded on all sides, including floor and ceiling, by a vacuum and without windows. The technique of beaming a ray onto window glass and reading the conversation inside from the vibrations had been used against the American embassy in Moscow during the Cold War and required the reconstruction of the entire building.

The man coming around the corner of his desk, hand outstretched, was also in a suit with a striped tie that Tracker, after his years in London, presumed to be the hallmark of a rather good school. He was not quite expert enough to recognize the colors of Harrow.

"Colonel Jackson? Welcome. Our first meet, I think. Konrad Armitage. I took the liberty of ordering coffee. How do you take it?"

He could have asked one of the glamorous young secretaries employed on that floor to enter from the side door and serve it but chose to do so himself. Recently arrived from London, Konrad Armitage was the head of station for the British Secret Intelligence Service, or SIS.

He knew perfectly well who his visitor was from his predecessor and welcomed the meeting. The awareness of common cause, common interest and common enemy was mutual.

"So, what can I do for you?"

"An odd request but brief. I could have sent it the usual way, but I figured we probably ought to meet one day anyway so I just cut to the chase."

"Quite right. And the request?"

"Does your service have a contact or, better still, an asset buried down among the al-Shabaab in Somalia?"

"Wow. That's an odd one, all right. Not my specialty. We have a desk, of course. I'll have to ask. May I inquire: Is it the Preacher?"

Armitage was no clairvoyant. He knew who the Tracker was and what he did. Britain had just had its fourth murder committed by a young fanatic inspired by the online sermons of the Preacher, as opposed to America's six, and both services knew how their governments wanted to put an end to this man.

"Could be," said the Tracker.

"Well, excellent, then. As you know, we have a presence, as do your friends at Langley, inside Mogadishu, but if they have anyone out in the wild places, I'd be surprised if they haven't proposed a joint operation. But I'll have the request in the London office by morning."

The reply took only two days, but it was the same as that from the CIA. And Armitage was right: If either country was running a source inside South Somalia, it would have been too valuable not to share—both the costs and the "product."

The reply from Javad inside the ISI was much more helpful. One of those to whom he pretended to report back about his spying on the Americans was a contact in the notorious S Wing, which "covered," in every sense, myriad groups dedicated to Jihadism and violence that inhabited the border strip from Kashmir to Quetta.

It would have been far too risky for Javad to have asked outright; it would have blown his cover and revealed his true employers. But part of his ISI job was to have authorized access to the Americans and to frequent their company. He pretended he had eavesdropped on a conversation between diplomats at a cocktail party. Out of curiosity, the S Wing officer consulted the archive database, and Javad, standing behind him, noted the file he accessed.

When he had shut down, the S Wing officer ordered that the Yankees be told there was no such trace. Later, by night, Javad reaccessed the database and punched up the file.

There was such a mention but years old. It came from an ISI spy in Ilyas Kashmiri's 313 Brigade of fanatics and killers. It mentioned a new arrival from Lashkar-e-Taiba, a fanatic for whom the raids against Kashmir had proved too tame. The young recruit spoke Arabic and Pashto, which was what had facilitated his acceptance into 313. The Brigade was composed mainly of Arabs and cooperated closely with the Pashto-speaking Haqqani clan. The report added that this was his usefulness, but he had yet to prove himself as a fighter. He had amber eyes, and styled himself Abu Azzam.

So that was why he had disappeared nine years ago. He had changed his terror group and changed his name.

The U.S.'s Counter-Terrorism Center has a vast database on Jihadist terror groups, and punching in Abu Azzam produced a cornucopia.

Back during the Soviet occupation of Afghanistan, there

were seven great warlords who comprised the Mujahideen, applauded and supported by the West as "patriots," "partisans" and "freedom fighters." To them, and them alone, went the huge quantities of money and weapons channeled into the Afghan mountains to defeat the Russians. But the moment the last Soviet tank rolled back into Russia, two of them reverted to the vicious killers they had always been. One was Gulbuddin Hekmatyar and the other was Jalaluddin Haqqani.

Though a warlord and master of his native province of Paktia, Haqqani switched sides when the Taliban swept the warlords aside and came to power and he became commander of the Taliban forces.

After their defeat by the Americans and Northern Alliance, he moved again, crossing the border and setting himself up in Waziristan, inside the Pakistan border. Succeeded by his three sons, he created the Haqqani network; basically, the Pakistani Taliban.

This became a hub for terror strikes against American and NATO forces over the border and against the Pakistani government of Pervez Musharraf, which became an ally of the U.S. He attracted to his network the remaining al-Qaeda forces not dead or in jail and any other Jihadist fanatic. One of these was Ilyas Kashmiri, who brought with him his 313 Brigade, part of the Shadow Army.

What the Tracker could surmise was that the fanatical and eager-to-rise Zulfiqar Ali Shah, now calling himself Abu Azzam, was among them.

What he could not know was that Abu Azzam, while avoiding going into mortal danger in raids into Afghanistan, developed a taste for killing and became the 313 Brigade's most enthusiastic executioner.

One by one, the leading figures of Haqqani, Taliban, al-Qaeda and the Brigade were identified by the Americans, located with local information and targeted for drone strikes. In those mountain fastnesses, they were immune to army attack, as Pakistan discovered with huge losses, but could not hide for long from the UAVs, endlessly patrolling over their heads, soundless, invisible, watching everything, photographing everything and listening to everything.

The HVTs, the high-value targets, were blown to pieces, replaced by others, who were, in turn, blown away, until leadership became virtually a sentence of death.

But the old links with S Wing of Pakistan's ISI never died. The ISI had created the Taliban in the first place and never lost sight of a single prediction: The Yankees have the clocks, but the Afghans have the time. One day, they calculated, the Americans will pack up and go. The Taliban might well retake Afghanistan, and Pakistan does not want two enemies, India and Afghanistan, on her borders. One will be enough, and that will be India.

There was one more chapter in the mass of data that the Tracker had unleashed. The 313 Brigade, with its leaders, including Kashmiri, blasted into infinity, ebbed away but was replaced by the even more fanatic and sadistic Khorosan, and Abu Azzam was at the heart of it.

Khorosan was no more than two hundred and fifty ultras, mostly Arabs and Uzbeks, targeted at the local natives who were selling information to U.S.-paid agents, particularly the whereabouts of the top targets. Khorosan had no talent for gathering its own intelligence, but a limitless capacity to terrify by public torture.

Whenever a drone-launched missile wiped out a house containing a terror leader, the Khorosan would arrive to snatch a sample of local citizens and inflict so-called courts, preceded by extreme interrogation involving electric shocks, electric drills or red-hot irons. The court would be presided over by an imam or mullah, often self-styled. Confessions were almost guaranteed and sentences other than death exceptional.

The habitual method of death was throat cutting. The merciful procedure involves the knife penetrating from the side, razor edge forward. A quick slice outward will open the jugular vein, carotid artery, trachea and esophagus, bringing instant death.

But a goat is not killed that way because maximum blood loss is needed to tenderize the meat. Then the throat is opened by a hacking, seesawing motion from the front. To make a human prisoner suffer and to demonstrate contempt, the goat method is used.

Having passed sentence, the presiding priest would then sit and watch it carried out. One of them was Abu Azzam.

There was one more item in the file. About 2009, a roaming preacher began to sermonize in the mosques along the peaks of North and South Waziristan. The CTC file gave him no name, saying only that he spoke Urdu, Arabic and Pashto and was a most powerful orator who could bring his audiences to extremes of religious exultation. Then, about 2010, he vanished. He had never been heard of in Pakistan since.

The two men sitting in the corner of the bar of the Washington Mandarin Oriental attracted no attention. There was no reason why they should. Both were early to mid-forties, both in dark suits with white shirt and neutral tie. Both looked lean and hard, slightly military, with that indefinable air that says "Been in combat."

One was the Tracker. The other had introduced himself as Simon Jordan. He did not like to meet with complete strangers inside the embassy if it could just as well be done outside. Hence the meeting in the discreet bar.

Back in his home country, his first name was really Shimon, and his surname had nothing to do with any river. He was the head of station of the Mossad in the Israeli embassy.

The Tracker's request was the same as he had placed with Konrad Armitage and the result was much the same. Simon Jordan also knew perfectly well who the Tracker was, what TOSA really did and, as an Israeli, thoroughly approved of both. But he did not have any answer at his fingertips.

"Of course, there is someone back home at the Office who will cover that part of the world, but I will have to put the question to him. You are, I suppose, in a hurry?"

"I'm an American. Are we ever anything else?"

Jordan laughed with genuine appreciation. He liked self-deprecation. Very Israeli.

"I'll ask at once and request no delay." He held up the card in the name of Jackson that the Tracker had given him. "I suppose this is a secure number?"

"Very."

"Then I'll use it. And on one of our secure lines."

He knew perfectly well that the Americans would listen to anything coming out of the Israeli embassy, but allies try to maintain the courtesies.

They parted. The Israeli had a car waiting, with a driver at the wheel. It would take him to the door. He did not like to be ostentatious, but he was "declared," which meant he might be recognized. Driving himself or taking a cab was not a wise way of avoiding a kidnap. Having a former Golani Brigade commando at the wheel and an Uzi in the back was better. On the other hand, he did not, like an "undeclared," have to go through a lot of rigmarole involving double-backs and side entrances.

The Tracker, among his other habits that raised official eyebrows, did not like a chauffeur-driven car if he could avoid it. Nor did he like to spend hours in the gridlocks between downtown D.C. and his office in the forest. He used a motorcycle, with helmet and visor in a pannier under the seat. But it was not a rolling armchair; it was a Honda Fireblade, a transport with which there is not much point in arguing.

Having read the file from Javad, the Tracker was convinced, though he could not know it rightly, that Abu Azzam had fled the too-dangerous mountains of the Afghan/Pak border for what seemed the safer climes of the Yemen.

In 2008, al-Qaeda in the Arabian Peninsula, AQAP, was in its infancy, but among its leaders was an American-raised Yemeni called Anwar al-Awlaki, fluent in English with an

American accent. He was establishing himself as a brilliantly effective online sermonizer, reaching out to the teeming diaspora youth of Britain and the U.S. He also became the mentor of the newly arrived, also English-speaking Pakistani.

Awlaki had been born of Yemeni parents in New Mexico, where his father was studying agriculture. Raised virtually as an American boy, Awlaki was first brought to Yemen, age seven, in 1978. He completed secondary education there, then returned to the U.S. for college in Colorado and San Diego. In 1993, age twenty-two, he went to Afghanistan, and it seems it was there that he converted to ultra-violent Jihadism.

Like most Jihadi terrorists, he had no Koranic scholarship at all, confining himself to extremist propaganda. But back in the States, he managed to become resident imam at the Rabat Mosque in San Diego, and at another in Falls Church, Virginia. On the threshold of arrest for passport fraud, he quit for Britain.

Here he traveled widely on speaking tours. Then came 9/11, and the West woke up at last. The net tightened, and in 2004 he left Britian and returned to Yemen. He was briefly arrested and imprisoned on kidnap and terrorism charges but was released after pressure from his influential tribe. By 2008, he had discovered his true slot—as a firebrand sermonizer, using the Internet as his pulpit.

And he had an effect. Several killings took place at the hands of ultras converted by listening to his lectures calling for murder and destruction. And he formed a partnership with a brilliant Saudi bombmaker named Ibrahim al-Asiri. It was Awlaki who persuaded the young Nigerian Abdulmutal-

lab to agree to die by suicide bomb in an airliner over De-
troit, and Asiri who built the undetectable bomb into his
undershorts. Only a malfunction saved the plane—but not
the Nigerian's genitalia.

As Awlaki's sermons became more and more effective
on YouTube—he was regularly downloaded 150,000 times—
Asiri became more and more skilled with his bombs. Eventually, both went on the kill list in April 2010. By then, he had
been joined by his secretive and self-effacing disciple from
Pakistan.

Two attempts were made to track him and destroy him:
one involved the Yemeni army, who let him slip away when
his village was surrounded; the other was when a U.S. missile
from a drone destroyed the house he was supposed to be in.
But he had left.

Justice finally caught up with him on a lonely track in
North Yemen on 30 September 2011. He had been staying at
the village of Khashef and was identified by a junior acolyte,
who took dollars to make the "squeal." Within hours, a Predator, launched out of a secret pad in the Saudi desert across
the border, was circling over him.

In Nevada, eyes watched the three parked Toyota Land
Cruisers—the al-Qaeda vehicle of choice—in the village
square, but permission to launch was denied because of the
women and children nearby. At dawn on the thirtieth, he
was seen to climb into the lead vehicle. The cameras were so
good that when he looked up, his face filled the entire plasma
screen at Creech Air Force Base.

Two Land Cruisers set off, but the third seemed in trouble. Its hood was up, and someone seemed to be working on the engine. Unbeknownst to the watchers, there were three more waiting to board that vehicle, and the U.S. would have liked them all.

One was Asiri the bombmaker himself. Another was Fahd al-Quso, deputy head under Awlaki at AQAP. He had been one of those behind the killing of seventeen U.S. sailors on the destroyer *Cole* in Aden harbor in 2000. He would later die in another drone strike in May 2012.

The third was an unknown to the Americans. He never looked up, his head was shrouded and masked against the dust, and no one saw that he had amber eyes.

The two leading SUVs set off down a dusty track into Jawf Province, but they kept apart so the watchers in Nevada did not know which to strike. Then they stopped for breakfast and parked side by side. There were eight figures grouped around the vehicles. Two drivers and four bodyguards, and the other two were American citizens: Awlaki himself and Samir Khan, editor of the English-language online Jihadi magazine *Inspire*.

The NCO at Creech told senior authority what he had in the target frame. From Washington, a voice murmured: "Take the shot." It was a J-SOC major, a soccer mom, about to take her kids to evening practice.

The trigger was pressed in Nevada. Over North Yemen, 60,000 feet high in a beautiful sunrise, two Hellfire missiles detached themselves from the Predator, sniffed the nose-cone signal like hunting dogs and tilted down to the desert. Twelve seconds later, both Land Cruisers and eight men vaporized.

Within six months, J-SOC had ample evidence that Asiri, still only thirty, had continued making bombs, and they were getting more and more sophisticated. He began to experiment with the implantation of explosives inside the human body, where no scanner could spot them.

He sent his kid brother to assassinate the Saudi head of counterterrorism, Prince Muhammad bin Nayef. The youth claimed he had renounced terrorism, wished to come home, possessed much information and sought an interview. The prince agreed to see him.

As he entered the room, the young Asiri simply blew up. The prince was lucky; he was blown backward through the door he had come in by, taking only some cuts and bruises.

The young Asiri had a small but powerful bomb up his anus. The detonator was a mobile-telephone-based device across the border. It was his own brother who designed and triggered it.

And the dead Awlaki had a successor. A man known only as the Preacher began to launch sermons into cyberspace. Just as powerful, just as hate filled, just as dangerous. Yemen's ineffectual president fell to the Arab Spring. A new man took over, younger, more vigorous, prepared to cooperate with the U.S. in exchange for substantial developmental aid.

The drone coverage of Yemen increased. U.S.-paid agents proliferated. The army was launched against AQAP leaders. Quso was wiped out. But still it was presumed the Preacher, whoever he was, remained in Yemen. Now, thanks to a boy in a loft in Centerville, the Tracker knew better.

As Tracker closed the file on the life of Awlaki, a report came through from those Gray Fox had simply called the drone boys. For this operation, J-SOC was not using the CIA drone facility out of Nevada but its own dedicated unit out of Pope Air Force Base near Fayetteville, North Carolina.

The report was succinct and to the point. Trucks had been seen visiting the target warehouse/shed in Kismayo. Some came, went undercover and left. They arrived loaded but left empty. Two were open-topped over the cargo area. What they seemed to be carrying was a cargo of fruit and vegetables. Endit.

Tracker turned and stared at the portrait of the Preacher on his wall. What the hell do you want with fruit and vegetables? he mused.

He stretched, rose and walked out into the summer warmth. Ignoring the smiles of those in the parking lot, he hauled his Fireblade off its stand, pulled on his helmet with the visor down and cruised out through the gate. When he hit the highway, he turned south for D.C., then off the main road for Centerville.

"I want you to check something for me," he told Ariel, as he crouched in the semidarkness of the attic. "Someone is buying fruit and vegetables in Kismayo. Can you find out where it is coming from and where it is going to?"

There were others at computer consoles he could have approached, but in a vast arms-industrial-espionage complex teeming with rivals and loose mouths Ariel had two unpurchasable advantages: He reported to only one man and he never talked to anybody. Ariel's fingers flickered away. The map of lower Somalia swam into view.

"It's not all desert," he said. "There is a richly forested and planted area along both banks of the Lower Juba Valley. Look, you can see the farms."

Tracker studied the patchwork quilt of orchards and plantations, a splash of green against the dull ocher desert. The country's only fertile zone, the food bowl of the south. If those cargoes were harvested in the plantations he was staring at and trucked to Kismayo, where thence? Local markets or export?

"Go to Kismayo port zone."

Like everything else, the port was pretty shattered. Once it had thrived, but the quay was broken in a dozen places, the old derricks tilted and damaged beyond use. It could be that a freighter came in occasionally. Not to discharge. What could al-Shabaab's bankrupt ministate import and pay for? But to pick something up? Fruit and vegetables? Maybe. But destination where? And for what?

"Search the commercial world, Ariel. See if any company trades with Kismayo. Anyone buying fruit and vegetables raised in the Lower Juba Valley. If so, who are they? Maybe they own the warehouse."

He left him to it and returned to TOSA.

In the extreme northern suburbs of Tel Aviv, off the road to Herzliya, in a quiet street just down from a food market, is a large, nondescript office block that its inhabitants simply call the Office. It is the headquarters of Mossad. Two days after Tracker's meeting with Simon Jordan at the Mandarin Oriental, three men in short-sleeved, open-necked shirts met in the director's office. That room had seen quite a few momentous conferences.

It was where, in the autumn of 1972 after the summer slaughter of Israeli athletes at the Munich Olympics, Zvi Zamir had ordered his *kidonim* (bayonets) to go out, find and kill the Black September fanatics responsible. Such was the decision by Prime Minister Golda Meir to launch Operation Wrath of God. Over forty years later, it was still shabby.

The men were of different ranks and ages but only used first names. The oldest had been there twenty years and needed only the fingers of one hand to recall the times he had heard surnames. The grizzled director was Uri, the chief of operations was David and the youngest, running the Horn of Africa desk, Benny.

"The Americans are asking for our help," said Uri.

"Surprise me," muttered David.

"It seems they have tracked down the Preacher."

He had no need to explain. Jihadi terrorism has several targets for its violence, and Israel is far up the list, along with the U.S. Everyone present knew of the top fifty in the world, even though Hamas to their south, Hezbollah to their north and Iran's al-Quds thugs to their east jostled for first in the queue. The Preacher's sermons might target America and Britain, but they knew who he was.

"It appears he is in Somalia, sheltering with al-Shabaab. Their request is very simple: Do we have an asset implanted in South Somalia?"

Both senior men looked at Benny. He was a former member of the elite Sayeret Matkal commando, fluent in Arabic to the point where he could pass unnoticed across the border, and thus one of the *mistaravim*. He studied the pencil in his hands.

"Well, Benny, do we?" David asked gently. They all knew what was coming, and agent runners hate to lend one of their assets for a foreign agency's concerns.

"Yes, we do. Just one. He is embedded in the port of Kismayo."

"How do you communicate with him?" asked the director.

"With extreme difficulty," said Benny. "And slowly. It takes time. We can't just send in a message. He can't send a card. Even e-traffic could be monitored. There are trainee bombers in there now. Western-educated. Technology-savvy. Why?"

"If the Yankees want to use him, we would have to speed up communications. A miniaturized two-way transceiver," said David. "And it ought to cost them."

"Oh, it would cost them, all right," said the director. "But you could leave that to me. I'll tell them 'maybe,' and we'll discuss price."

He did not mean money; he meant help in a score of other ways—the Iranian atomic bomb program, the release of very high-tech classified equipment. He would have quite a shopping list.

"Does he have a name?" asked David.

"Opal," said Benny. "Agent Opal. He's a tally clerk on the fishing dock."

G ray Fox did not waste time.
"You've been talking to the Israelis," he said.
"True. Have they come back?"

"With a vengeance. They have a man. Deep inside. In Kismayo, as it happens. They are prepared to help, but there are outrageous demands. You know the Israelis. They don't give away sand in the Negev."

"But they want to discuss price?"

"Yes," said Gray Fox, "but not at our level. It's above our pay grade. Their top man at the embassy went straight to the commander of J-SOC."

"Did he turn them down?"

"Amazingly, no. Demands acceded. You can go ahead. Your contact man is their head of station. Do you know him?"

"Yes. Fleetingly."

"Well, you can go ahead. Tell them what you want and they'll try to deliver."

T here was a message from Ariel when he got back to his office.

"There seems to be one purchaser of Somali fruit, vegetables and spices. A company called Masala Pickles. It makes hot chutneys and pickles, the sort the British eat with their curries. The produce is bottled or frozen or canned in a plant in Kismayo, then shipped to the main factory."

The Tracker rang him. To a listener the exchange would have been meaningless, so he did not encrypt.

"Got your message, Ariel. Well done. Just a detail: Where is the main factory?"

"Oh, sorry, Colonel. It's in Karachi."

Karachi. Pakistan. Of course.

7

A twin-engined, propeller-driven Beech King Air took off before dawn from Sde Dov, the military airfield north of Tel Aviv, turned southeast and began to climb. It passed over Be'er Sheva, flew through the no-fly zone over the atomic plant at Dimona and left Israeli airspace south of Eilat.

Its livery was snow white, with the words "United Nations" down the fuselage. The tailfin bore the large letters *WFP* for World Food Programme. Had anyone checked its registration number, the latter would have revealed it was owned by a shell company lodged in Grand Cayman and on long-term charter to the WFP. All of which was nonsense.

It belonged to the Metsada (Special Ops) division of Mossad and lived in the Sde Dov hangar that once housed the black Spitfire of Ezer Weizman, founder of the Israeli air force.

South of the Gulf of Aqaba, the King Air followed a

course between the landmasses of Saudi Arabia to the east and Egypt/Sudan to the west. It remained in international airspace the length of the Red Sea until it crossed the coast of Somaliland and on over Somalia. Neither state had interceptor facility.

The white plane recrossed the Somali coast with the Indian Ocean north of Mogadishu and altered course southwest to fly parallel to the coast at 5,000 feet and just offshore. Any observer would have presumed it came from a nearby charity/aid base, since it had no external fuel tanks and therefore limited range. That same observer would not have seen that much of the interior was occupied by two huge fuel tanks.

Just south of Mogadishu, the cameraman readied his equipment and began to film after Marka. Excellent images of the entire beach were obtained from Marka to a point fifty miles north of Kismayo, a total stretch involving two hundred miles of sandy shore.

Then the cameraman shut down, and the King Air peeled away. It retraced its flight, switched from internal fuel tanks to main supply and returned home. After twelve hours airborne, it just squeezed in to Eilat airport, refueled and went on to Sde Dov. A motorcyclist took the camera pack to the Mossad's photographic analysis unit for study.

What Benny wanted, and got, was a clearly unmissable rendezvous spot along the coast road where he could meet Agent Opal with fresh instructions and the necessary equipment. The spot he wanted would have to be unmistakable for someone motoring up the highway and a fast inflatable coming off the sea.

When he had his spot, he prepared his message for Opal.

W arden Doherty tried to run a decent penitentiary, and, of course, it had a chapel. But he did not want his daughter married there. As the father of the bride, he was prepared to make her day truly memorable, so the ceremony was planned at St. Francis Xavier Catholic Church, with a reception at the Clarendon Hotel downtown.

There had been mentions of the wedding, time and place, in the social diary column of the *Phoenix Republic*, so it was no surprise that a crowd of both the curious and the well-wishers had gathered outside the doors of the church when the happy couple emerged.

No one paid much attention to the swarthy young man among the crowd, the one with the long white robes and far-away gaze. Not until he burst through the press of onlookers, ran up to the father of the bride with something in his right hand, as if he were offering a gift. It was not a gift; it was a Colt .45 handgun. He fired four times at Warden Doherty, who was thrown backward by the force of the impact and went down in a heap.

There were, as always when a true horror has not yet impacted, two seconds of uncomprehending silence. Then the reactions. Screams, shouts and, in this case, more shots, as two on-duty Phoenix police officers drew and fired. The assailant also went down. Others threw themselves flat amid the ensuing chaos; the hysterical Mrs. Doherty, the weeping bride ushered away, the wailing police cars and ambulances, the panicking crowd running in all directions.

Then the system took over. Crime scene taped off, firearm recovered and dropped in an evidence bag, identification of the assassin. Newscasts out of Arizona that evening told all the U.S. that there had been another one. And the recovered laptop of the fanatic, found in his room above the garage, where he worked, disgorged its long list of online sermons by the Preacher.

The U.S. Army film unit is called TRADOC (Training and Doctrine Command), and it lives at Fort Eustis, Virginia. Normally, it makes training films and documentaries, explaining and extolling every aspect of the Army's work and function. So the commanding officer had no hesitation in acquiescing to a request to meet with a certain Col. Jamie Jackson, serving with J-SOC headquarters at MacDill Air Force Base, outside Tampa, Florida.

Even within the military, the Tracker saw no reason to reveal he was really Col. Kit Carson, came from TOSA and was assigned only a few miles away in the same state. It is simply called need to know.

"I want to make a short movie," he said. "But this would have a classification of top secret, and the finished product would be seen by an extremely limited group of people."

The CO was intrigued, slightly impressed but not fazed. He was proud of his unit's talent for filmmaking. He could not recall such a strange request before, but that could make the offered assignment more interesting. He had filming facilities and sound studios right on the base.

"It will be a very small, short movie with one scene. There will be no location filming. It will involve one set, probably

off base. It will involve no cameras save a single camcorder—
sound and picture. It will be seen, if at all, only on the Internet. The unit will therefore be extremely small, probably no
more than six, all sworn to secrecy. What I need is a young
filmmaker steeped in movies," said the visitor.

The Tracker got what he wanted: Captain Damian
Mason. The CO did not get what he wanted, which was an
answer to his numerous questions. What he did get was a
call from a three-star general, telling him that, in this man's
army, orders are obeyed. Damian Mason was young, eager
and a movie buff since he was knee-high in White Plains,
New York. When he had served his time with TRADOC, he
wanted to go west to Hollywood and make real movies, with
stories and stars.

"Will this be a training film, sir?" he asked.

"I hope it will be instructive, in its way," said the Marine
colonel. "Tell me, is there one single directory with the photographs of every available actor in the country?"

"I think you mean the Academy players directory. Every
casting director in the country has one."

"Is there one on base?"

"I doubt it, sir. We don't use professional actors."

"We do now. Or one, at least. Can you get me a copy?"

"Sure, Colonel."

It took two days to arrive by FedEx, and it was a very thick
book, page after page of the faces of aspiring actors and
actresses, juveniles right through to veterans.

Another science that police forces and intelligence agencies employ across the world is face comparison. It helps detectives trace down runaway criminals who try to change their appearance.

Computerization has codified what used to be little more than a policeman's hunch into a science. In the USA, the software is called Echelon, and it is lodged with the FBI's Engineering Research Facility at Quantico, Maryland.

Basically, hundreds of facial measurements are taken and stored. Ears alone are like fingerprints—never the same. But with long hair, they are not always visible. The distance between eye pupils, measured to the micron, can eliminate a match in a fraction of a second. Or help confirm. Echelon has refused to be deceived by felons who have had extensive plastic surgery.

Terrorists caught by the cameras of drones have been identified in seconds as the real top target and not some bag carrier. It saves an expensive missile. The Tracker flew back east and set Echelon a task: Scan every male face in the players directory and find me a doppelgänger to this man. He offered them the face of the Preacher without the full beard. That could go back on later.

Echelon scanned nearly a thousand male faces and came up with one who, more than any other, looked like the Pakistani called Abu Azzam. Ethnically, he was Hispanic. His name was Tony Suárez. His résumé stated he had had bit parts and walk-on parts, appearances in crowds and even a few words to speak in a commercial for barbecue equipment.

The Tracker went back to his office at TOSA. There was a report from Ariel. His father had found a store selling foreign foodstuffs and brought him a jar of Masala pickles and another of mango chutney. The computer revealed that almost all the fruit and spice ingredients were grown in the plantations of the Lower Juba Valley.

There was more. Commercial data banks revealed Masala was highly successful in Pakistan and the Middle East, and also Great Britain, with its taste for spicy foods and Indian curries. It was wholly owned by its founder, Mr. Mustafa Dardari, who had a mansion in Karachi and a town house in London. Finally, there was a photo of the tycoon, blown up from a boardroom "smiley" picture.

Tracker stared at the face. Smooth, clean-shaven, beaming—something vaguely familiar. He took from his desk drawer the original print of the photo he had brought back from Islamabad on his iPhone. It was folded over to eliminate the half he did not want. He wanted it now. The other grinning schoolboy, fifteen years ago.

As a single son, the Tracker knew that when two such form a schooltime friendship of best buddies, the bond sometimes never dies. He recalled the warning from Ariel—someone sending e-traffic to the warehouse in Kismayo. The Troll responding to acknowledge receipt with thanks. The Preacher had a friend in the West.

Captain Mason studied the presumed face of the Preacher, former Zulfiqar Ali Shah, former Abu Azzam, as he would now look. And by its side the picture of the unsuspecting Tony Suárez, out-of-work bit-part actor dwelling in a squat in Malibu.

"Sure, it can be done," he said at length. "With makeup, hair, wardrobe, contact lenses, script with rehearsal, autocue." He tapped the photo of the Preacher.

"Does this guy ever speak?"

"Occasionally."

"Can't answer for the voice."

"Leave the voice to me," said the Tracker.

Captain Mason, in civilian clothes and calling himself Mr. Mason, flew to Hollywood with a block of dollars and came back with Mr. Suárez. He was lodged in a very comfortable suite in a chain hotel twenty miles from Fort Eustis. To ensure he did not wander, he was assigned a minder in the person of a stunning blond corporal, who was assured all she need do to serve her country was prevent the Californian guest from wandering out of the hotel or into her bedroom for forty-eight hours.

Whether Mr. Suárez believed his services were really desired because of preproduction for an art-house movie being made for a Middle East client with a lot of money to spend was irrelevant. Whether the movie had a plot did not concern him. He was simply content to be in a luxurious suite with a champagne bar, enough dollars to purchase several years of barbecue equipment and the companionship of a blonde who could stop traffic. Capt. Mason had reserved a large conference room in the same hotel and told him the "screen test" would take place the next day.

The team from TRADOC arrived in two unmarked

cars and a small van. They took over the conference room and covered all the windows with black paper and masking tape. That done, they constructed the world's simplest film set.

Basically, it was a bedsheet pinned to the wall. It, too, was black, and there were Koranic inscriptions on it in cursive Arab script. The sheet had been prepared in the workshop of one of the sound sets at Fort Eustis. It was a replica of the backdrop to all the broadcasts of the Preacher. In front of it was placed a simple wooden chair with arms.

At the other end of the hall, chairs, tables and lights created two working spaces for "Wardrobe" and "Makeup." No one doing any of this had the faintest idea why.

The camera technician set up his camcorder, facing the chair. One of his colleagues sat in the chair to assist with range, focus and clarity. The sound engineer checked levels. The autocue operator set up his screen just under the camera lens so that the speaker's eyeline would appear to be straight into the camera.

Mr. Suárez was led in and taken to Wardrobe, where a matronly senior sergeant, in civvies like everyone else, was waiting with the robe and headdress he would wear. These, too, had been selected by the Tracker from TRADOC's enormous resources, with alterations performed by the wardrobe mistress, studying photographs of the Preacher.

"I don't have to speak any Ayrab, do I?" protested Tony Suárez. "No one mentioned Ayrab."

"Absolutely not," he was assured by Mr. Mason, who now appeared to be directing. "Well, a couple of words, but it doesn't matter about the pronunciation. Here, check them out, just to get the lip synch about right." He gave Suárez a card with several Arabic words on it.

"Shit, man, these are complicated."

An older man, who had been waiting quietly against the wall, stepped forward.

"Try and imitate me," he said, and pronounced the foreign words like an Arab. Suárez tried. It was not the same, but the lips moved in the right direction. The dubbing would complete the job. Tony Suárez moved to the makeup chair. It took an hour.

The experienced makeup artist deepened the skin tone to make it slightly more swarthy. The black beard and mustache were applied. The *shamagh* headdress covered the hair of the scalp. Finally, the contact lenses gave the actor those arresting amber eyes. When he rose and turned, the Tracker was sure he was facing the Preacher.

Tony Suárez was led to the chair and sat down. Camcorder and sound levels, focus and autocue, received minor adjustments. The actor had spent an hour in the makeup chair, studying the text he would be reading off the autocue. He had most of it memorized, and though the Arabic did not sound like an Arab speaker, he had ceased to stumble over it.

"And cue," said Capt. Mason. One day, he dreamed, he would be saying that to Brad Pitt and George Clooney. The film extra began to speak.

The Tracker murmured in Mason's ear.

"More solemn, Tony," said Mason. "It's a confession. You're

the Grand Vizier telling the Sultan he got it all wrong, and he's sorry. OK, roll again. And cue."

After eight takes, Suárez had peaked and was fading. The Tracker called a halt.

"OK, people, it's a wrap," said Mason. He loved that phrase. The crew dismantled everything they had built. Tony Suárez was restored to his jeans and sweatshirt, clean-shaven and smelling faintly of cleansing cream. Wardrobe and Makeup were repacked and went back to the truck. The bedsheet came down, was rolled up and removed. The windows were cleared of black paper and tape.

While this was going on, the Tracker had the camcorder technician give him the five best takes of the brief speech. He chose the one he wanted and had the others erased.

The voice of the actor was still pure Californian. But the Tracker knew of a British TV mimic who had his audiences in stitches with his uncanny imitations of celebrities' voices. He would fly across for the day and be well paid. Technicians would get the lip synch exact.

They handed the rented conference hall back to the hotel. Tony Suárez regretfully checked out of his suite and was driven back to Washington National and his night plane to Los Angeles. The Fort Eustis team was much closer to home and were there by sundown.

They had had a fun day, but they had never heard of the Preacher and had not the faintest idea what they had done. But the Tracker knew. He knew that when he launched what was in the cassette in his hand, there was going to be absolute chaos among the forces of Jihadism.

The man who descended with a smattering of Somalis from the Turkish airliner at Mogadishu airport had a passport that declared him to be a Dane, and other papers in five languages, including Somali, that identified him as working for the Save the Children fund.

His real name was not Jensen, and he worked for the Collections Division (general espionage) of Mossad. He had flown the previous day from Ben Gurion Airport to Larnaca in Cyprus, switched name and nationality, then flown on to Istanbul.

There was a long and tiresome wait in the business-class transit lounge for the flight south to Somalia, with a staging stop at Djibouti. But Turkish Airlines was still the only national flag carrier to serve Mogadishu.

It was eight a.m. and already hot out on the tarmac as the fifty passengers straggled into the arrivals building, the Somalis from economy class shouldering the three from business out of the way. The Dane was in no hurry; he waited his turn in front of the passport officer.

He had no visa, of course; visas are purchased on arrival, as he knew, having been there before. The passport officer studied the previous entry and exit stamps and studied his list. There was no ban on anyone called Jensen.

The Dane slipped a fifty-dollar bill under the glass screen.

"For the visa," he murmured in English. The officer slid the note toward him, then noticed another fifty-dollar bill in the pages of the passport.

"A little something for your children," murmured the Dane.

The passport officer nodded. He did not smile but stamped in the visa, glanced at the yellow fever chit, folded the passport, nodded and handed it back. For his children, of course. An honorable gift. Nice to meet a European who knew the rules.

There were two dilapidated taxis outside. The Dane hefted his single grip into the first, climbed in and said, "Peace Hotel, please." The driver headed for the gated entrance to the airport compound, guarded by Ugandan soldiers.

The airport is in the center of the African Union military base, an inner zone of the Mogadishu enclave, surrounded by barbed wire, sandbags, blast walls and patrolled by Casper armored personnel carriers of the Union. Within the fortress is another fortress: Bancroft camp is where the "whiteys" live, the several hundred staff of contractors, aid agencies, visiting media and a few ex-mercenaries working as bodyguards for the fat cats.

The Americans lived inside their own compound at the far end of the runway, home to their embassy, some hangars of undisclosed contents and a training school for young Somalis being schooled to, one day, slip back into dangerous Somalia as American agents. Those who knew Somalia from long and disenchanting experience felt this to be a very fond hope indeed.

Also in the inner sanctuary, passing the windows of the moving car, were the other minisettlements for the United Nations, African Union senior officers, European Union and even the dowdy British embassy, which insisted with passion and mendacity that it was not another "spook central."

The Dane Jensen did not dare stay inside Bancroft. He might meet another Dane or a real worker with Save the Children. He was headed for the one hotel outside the blast walls where a white man might stay with reasonable security.

The taxi passed through the last manned gate—more red-and-white-striped poles, more Ugandans—and out on the one-mile strip to central Mogadishu. Though it was not his first trip, the Dane was still amazed at the sea of rubble to which twenty years of civil war had reduced the once elegant African city.

The cab turned up an alley; a paid street urchin hauled aside a tangle of barbed wire, and a nine-foot-high steel gate creaked open. There had been no communication; someone was watching through a hole.

With the cab paid off, the Dane checked in and was shown to his room; small, just functional, with frosted windows (against occupant recognition) and curtains drawn (against the heat). He stripped off, stood for a while under the tepid dribble from the shower, did his best to soap and dry, and changed clothing.

In flip-flops, rough canvas jeans and a long, no-button cotton shirt, he was wearing much what a local Somali might wear. There was a satchel slung over one shoulder and wrap-around dark glasses. The hands were tanned from the Israeli sun. The pale face and blond hair were clearly European.

He knew a place that rented scooters. A second taxi, summoned by the Peace Hotel, took him there. In the cab he removed the *shamagh* from his satchel. He wrapped the basic

Arab headdress around the blond locks and drew the trailing tail across the face, tucking the hem into the fold on the other side. There was nothing suspicious in this; those who wear a *shamagh* often protect the nose and mouth against the constant dust and sand gusts.

He rented a rickety white Piaggio moped; the renter knew him from previous visits. Always requiring a substantial dollar deposit, the vehicle always returned intact, no need for silly formalities like a license.

Joining the stream of donkey carts, falling-to-pieces trucks, pickups and other scooters, avoiding the occasional camel or pedestrian, looking exactly like a Somali going about his business, the Dane puttered down Maka al-Mukarama, the highway slicing through the center of Mogadishu.

He passed the gleaming white Isbahaysiga Mosque, impressive for its lack of damage, and glanced across the road to something less attractive. The Darawsha refugee camp had not been moved or improved since his last visit. It was still a sea of hovel/squalor, housing ten thousand hungry and frightened refugees. They had no sanitation, food, employment or hope, and their children played in the urine pools. They were truly, he thought, those Frantz Fanon had called the wretched of the Earth, and Darawsha was one of eighteen poverty cities inside the enclave. The Western aid agencies tried, but it was an impossible job.

The Dane glanced at his cheap watch. He was on time. The meetings were always at twelve noon. The man he had come to see would glance at the usual spot. If he was not there—ninety-nine percent of the time—the other man would get on with his life. If he was there, the signals would be exchanged.

The moped took him to the ruined Italian Quarter. A white man going there without a large armed escort would be a fool. The danger was not murder but kidnapping. A European or American could be worth up to two million dollars. But with Somali sandals, African shirt and *shamagh* around his head and face, the Israeli agent felt safe if he kept it short.

The fish come ashore every morning at a small horseshoe bay opposite the al-Uruba Hotel, where the surge of the Indian Ocean throws the fishing skiffs out of the swell and onto the beach. Then the skinny dark men who have fished all night carry their jacks, kings and shark up to the market shed, hoping for buyers.

The market is two hundred yards from the bay, a ninety-foot, unlit shed stinking of fish, some fresh, some not. The Dane's agent was the market manager. At noon, as he was paid to do every day, Mr. Kaamal Duale stepped out of his office and surveyed the crowd gazing at the market.

Most had come to buy, but not yet. Those with money would get the fresh fish; in one-hundred-degree heat, without any form of refrigeration, it would start to smell quite quickly. Then bargains were to be had.

If Mr. Duale was surprised to see his handler in the crowd, he did not give a sign of it. He simply stared. He nodded. The man astride the Piaggio nodded back and raised his right hand across his chest. Fingers spread, closed, spread again. There were two more slight nods, and the scooterist wheeled away. The rendezvous was set: usual place, ten tomorrow morning.

The next day the Dane descended for breakfast at eight. He was in luck, there were eggs. He took two, fried, with bread and tea. He did not want to eat much; he was trying not to use the lavatory.

His scooter was parked by the compound wall. At half past nine he kicked it into life, waited for the steel gate to open and let him out and headed back toward the gate of the African Union camp. As he approached the concrete blocks and the guardhouse, he reached up to snatch off his *shamagh*. The blond hair at once gave him away.

A Ugandan soldier emerged from the shelter, rifle unslung. But just short of the barrier pole, the blond rider swerved away, raised a hand and called, *"Jambo."*

The Ugandan, hearing his native Swahili, lowered his gun. Another crazy *mzungu*. He just wanted to go back home, but the pay was good, and he would soon have enough for cattle and a wife. The *mzungu* swerved into the parking lot of the Village Café beside the entrance gate, stopped and went in.

The fish market manager was at a table, taking coffee. The Dane went to the bar and ordered the same, thinking of the rich, aromatic coffee he could get at the cafeteria back at the office in Tel Aviv.

They did the exchange in the men's room of the Village Café, as always. The Dane produced dollars, the world's common currency even in the hostile lands. The Somali watched with appreciation as they were counted out.

There would be a portion for the fisherman who would carry the message south to Kismayo in the morning, but he would be paid in virtually valueless Somali shillings. Duale would keep all the dollars, saving for the day when he had enough to emigrate.

And there was the consignment, a short aluminum tube like the sort used to protect fine cigars. But this was custom-made, stronger and heavier. He secreted it inside his waist-band.

Back in his office, he had a small, rugged generator, se-cretly donated by the Israelis. It ran on the most dubious kerosene, but it made electricity. This could power his air conditioner and his fridge/freezer. He was the only man in the fish market who always had fresh fish.

Among these was a yard-long kingfish, purchased that morning and now frozen rock-solid. In the evening his fisher-man would take it, with the tube rammed deep into its en-trails, and sail south, fishing all the way, landing two days later at the fish dock at Kismayo.

There he would sell the kingfish, no longer quite fresh, to a tally clerk at the market and say it was from his friend. He did not know why nor did he care. He was just another poor Somali trying to raise four sons to take over his skiff when they were able.

The two men in the Village Café emerged, finished their coffee separately and left, also separately. Mr. Duale took his tube home and rammed it into the deep stomach of the frozen kingfish. The blond man wrapped his *shamagh* around his head and face and motored back to the rental ga-rage. He returned the Piaggio, recovered most of his deposit, and the renter gave him a lift to the hotel. There were no cabs about, and he did not want to lose a good, if irregular, client.

The Dane had to wait until the departing Turkish Airlines flight at eight the next morning. He killed the time reading a novel in English in his room. Then a bowl of camel stew and bed.

In the dusk the fisherman put the kingfish, wrapped in wet sacking, in the fish locker of his skiff. But he slashed the tail to mark it out from any others he might catch. Then he put to sea, turned south and spread his lines.

At nine the next day, after the usual boarding chaos, the Turkish airliner lifted off. The Dane watched the buildings and fortifications of Bancroft camp fall away. Far to the south, a fishing skiff, lateen sail bending to the wind, plodded past Marka. The airliner turned north, refueled at Djibouti and in midafternoon landed at Istanbul.

The Dane from the Save the Children fund stayed airside, raced through the transit procedures and caught the last flight to Larnaca. He changed name, passport and ticket in his hotel room and took the first flight the next day back to Tel Aviv.

"Any problems?" asked the major known as Benny. It was he who had sent "the Dane" down to Mogadishu with fresh instructions for Opal.

"No. Routine," said the Dane, who had now become Moshe again.

There was an encrypted e-mail from the Office to Simon Jordan, head of station in Washington. As a result, he met with the American known as the Tracker. He preferred hotel bars, but not the same one twice in a row. The second meeting was at the Four Seasons, Georgetown.

It was high summer. They met in the garden bar under the awnings. There were other middle-aged men taking cocktails with their jackets off. But they all looked rather plumper than the two who sat right at the back.

"I am told your friend in the south is now fully briefed," said Simon Jordan. "So I must ask you: What exactly is it you want him to do?"

He listened intently while the Tracker explained what he had in mind. He stirred his club soda thoughtfully. He had not the slightest doubt as to the fate the former U.S. Marine next to him had in mind for the Preacher, and it would not be vacationing in Cuba.

"If our man is able to assist you in this way," he said at length, "and there is any question of terminating him along with the quarry in a missile strike, there would be a serious refusal from us to cooperate with you for a long while to come."

"I never had that in mind," said the Tracker.

"I just want us to be clear on that, Tracker. Are we clear?"

"As the ice in your glass. No missile strike unless Opal is miles away."

"Excellent. Then I will see the instructions are given."

Y ou want to go where?" asked Gray Fox.

"Only London. They are as keen to see the Preacher silenced as we are. His apparent outside man is in residence there. I want to be nearer to the center of events. I think we may be moving toward closure with this man Preacher. I have mentioned this to Konrad Armitage. He says I would be welcome, and his people will do everything they can. It's only a phone call away."

"Stay in touch, Tracker. I have to report up to the admiral on this."

O n the fishing dock at Kismayo, a dark-skinned young man with a clipboard scanned the faces of the fisher- men arriving from the sea. Kismayo, lost to government forces in 2012, had been regained by al-Shabaab after bloody fight- ing the following year, and the vigilance of the fanatics was ferocious. Their religious police were everywhere to ensure absolute piety from the population. The paranoia regarding spies from the north was pandemic. Even the fishermen, nor- mally boisterous unloading their catch, were subdued by fear.

The dark young man spotted a face he knew, one he had not seen for weeks. With his clipboard and pen poised to note the size of the catch being landed, he approached the man.

"Allahu-akhbar," he intoned. "What have you got?"

"Jacks and just three kingfish, *inshallah,*" said the fisher- man. He gestured to one of the kings, which had lost the sil- very glitter of the fresh-caught and had a slash across its tail. "From your friend," he murmured.

Opal signaled that all were permitted for sale. As the fish were removed to the stone slabs, he slipped the marked one into a burlap bag. Even in Kismayo it was permitted for a tally clerk to take a fish for supper.

When he was alone in his cabin by the shore, just out of town, he extracted the aluminum tube and unscrewed the top. There were two rolls, one of dollars and one of instruc- tions. The latter would be memorized and burnt. The dollars buried under the earthen floor.

The dollars were one thousand, in ten hundred-dollar bills, the instructions simple.

"You will use the dollars to acquire a reliable scooter, trail bike or moped and canisters of fuel to attach to the pillion. There is motoring to be done.

"Second, acquire a good radio with a range able to pick up Kol Israel. On Sunday, Monday, Wednesday and Thursday, there is a late-night talk show on Channel Eight. It comes on at 23.30. It is called *Yanshufim* (*The Night Owls*).

"It is always preceded by the weather report. Somewhere up the coast highway toward Marka, there is a new rendezvous spot marked out for a face-to-face meeting. You will find it on the attached map. It is unmistakable.

"When you hear the coded instruction, wait until the following day. Set off at dusk. Motor to the RV spot, arriving at dawn. Your contact will be there with fresh funds, equipment and instructions.

"The words in the weather report you are waiting for are: 'Tomorrow there will be slight rain over Ashkelon.' Good luck, Opal."

The fishing boat was old and battered, but that was the idea. She was rusted and needed a lick of paint or more, but that also was deliberate. In a sea full of inshore fishing boats, she was not supposed to attract attention.

She slipped her mooring in the dead of night from the cove where Rafi Nelson used to have his beach bar outside Eilat. By dawn, she was south of the Gulf of Aqaba, chugging her way into the Red Sea and past the scuba-diving resorts of the Egyptian Sinai coast. The sun was high when Taba Heights and Dahab went by; there were a couple of early dive boats out over the reefs, but no one took any notice of the grubby Israeli fisherman.

There was a captain at the wheel, his first mate making coffee in the galley. There were only two real seamen on-board. There were also two real fishermen, who would handle the long lines and the nets when she took up her drifting role. But the other eight were Sayeret Matkal commandos.

The fish hold had been scoured and cleansed of the old stink to create accommodation for them: eight bunks along the walls and a common mess area on deck. The hatch covers were closed so that the air-conditioning in the cramped space, as the burning sun rose in the sky, could do its job.

As she cruised down the Red Sea between Saudi Arabia and Sudan, she changed her identity. She became the *Omar al-Dhofari*, out of the Omani port of Salalah. Her crew looked the part; all could pass for Gulf Arabs by appearance and mastery of the language.

In the narrows between Djibouti and Yemen, she skirted the Yemeni island of Perim and turned into the Gulf of Aden. From here on she was in pirate territory but virtually immune from danger. Somali pirates look for a prey with a commercial value and an owner prepared to pay the price of recovery. An Omani fishing boat did not fit that pattern.

The men onboard saw a frigate from the international naval flotilla that had made life extremely hard for the pirates, but she was not even challenged. The sun caught the glint of the lenses of the powerful binoculars that studied her, but that was all. Being Omani, she was of no interest to the pirate catchers either.

On the third day out, she rounded Cape Guardafui, the easternmost mainland point of Africa, and turned south, with only Somalia to starboard, heading on down to her operational station off the coast between Mogadishu and Kismayo. When she reached her station, she hove to. The nets were cast to continue the pretense, and a brief and harmless message was sent by e-mail to the imaginary girlfriend, Miriam, at the Office, to say she was ready and waiting.

The division chief Benny headed south also, but much faster. He flew El Al to Rome and changed planes there for Nairobi. Mossad has long had a particularly strong presence in Kenya, and Benny was met by the local head of station, in plainclothes and in a plain car. It had been a week since the Somali fisherman with the smelly kingfish had handed over his cargo to Opal, and Benny had to hope a motorcycle of some type had been acquired by then.

It was a Thursday, and that evening, close to midnight, the talk show *The Night Owls* was broadcast as usual. It was preceded by the weather report. This one mentioned that, despite a heat wave in most parts, there would be light rain over Ashkelon.

Full cooperation with the Tracker from the British was a foregone conclusion. The United Kingdom had sustained four murders by young fanatics seeking glory or paradise or both, inspired by the Preacher, and the authorities wanted him closed down as eagerly as the Americans did.

Tracker was lodged in one of the U.S. embassy's safe houses, a small but well-appointed cottage down a cobbled mews in Mayfair. There was a brief meeting with the J-SOC chief of the defense staff at the embassy and with the CIA chief of station. Then he was taken to meet the Secret Intelligence Service at their HQ at Vauxhall Cross. Tracker had been in the green-and-sandstone pile by the Thames twice before, but the man he met was new to him.

Adrian Herbert was much the same age, mid-forties, so he had been at college when Boris Yeltsin terminated Soviet communism and the Soviet Union in 1991. He had been a fast-track entrant, after a degree in history at Lincoln College, Oxford, and a year at SOAS, the School of Oriental and African Studies in London. His specialty was Central Asia, and he spoke Urdu and Pashto, with some Arabic.

The boss of the SIS, often but wrongly called MI6, is always and only known as the Chief; he popped his head around the door to say hello and then left Adrian Herbert alone with his guests. Also present, as a courtesy, was a staffer from the Security Service, or MI5, at Thames House, five hundred yards down the river on its northern bank.

There was the almost ritual offering of coffee and biscuits, then Herbert glanced at his three American guests and murmured: "How do you think we can help?"

The two from the U.S. embassy left it to the Tracker. No one present was in ignorance of what the man from TOSA was charged with. Tracker saw no need to explain what he had done so far, how far he had got or what he intended to do next. Even between friends and allies, there is always need to know.

"The Preacher is not in Yemen, he's in Somalia," he said. "Exactly where he is lodged, I do not yet know. But we do know that his computer, and thus the source of his broadcasts, is in a warehouse-cum-bottling-plant in the port of Kismayo. I am pretty certain he is not there in person."

"I believe Konrad Armitage told you we have no one in Kismayo," said Herbert.

"It seems no one has," the Tracker lied. "But that is not my quest here. We have established that someone is communicating with that warehouse and has received acknowledgment and thanks for his messages. The warehouse is owned by Masala Pickles, based in Karachi. You may have heard of it."

Herbert nodded. He enjoyed Indian and Pakistani food and sometimes took his "assets" to curry restaurants on their visits to London. Masala mango chutney was well known.

"By an extraordinary coincidence, which we none of us believe in, Masala is wholly owned by Mr. Mustafa Dardari, who was a boyhood friend of the Preacher in Islamabad. I would like to have this man investigated."

Herbert glanced at the man from MI5, who nodded.

"Should be possible," the man murmured. "Does he live here?"

Tracker knew that although MI5 had representatives in the main foreign stations, their principal obligations were in the country. The SIS, although principally charged with foreign espionage and counterespionage against perceived enemies of Her Majesty abroad, also had the facility to mount an operation at home.

He also knew that, as with CIA and FBI in America, there had been periods when the rivalry between the internal and external secret services had led to animosity, but the common threat of Jihadist extremism, and its offspring terrorism, had for ten years led to a far greater degree of cooperation.

"He migrates," said the Tracker. "He has a mansion in Karachi and a town house in London. Pelham Crescent. My information is that he is thirty-three, single, personable and a presence on the social map."

"I may have met him," said Herbert. "Private dinner, two years ago, hosted by a Pakistani diplomat. Very smooth, I seem to recall. And you want him watched?"

"I want him burgled," said the Tracker. "I would like his pad bugged, sound and picture. But, most of all, I want his computer."

Herbert glanced at Donald Firth, the man from 5.

"Joint op?" he suggested. Firth nodded.

"We have the facilities, of course. I'll need the go from higher authority. Shouldn't be a problem. Is he in town at the moment?"

"Don't know," said the Tracker.

"Well, not a problem to find out. And I presume the whole bun fight must be invisible and remain so?"

Yes, thought the Tracker, a very invisible bun fight indeed. It was agreed both services would get clearance for a very black operation with no sanction from any magistrate—in other words, totally illegal. But both British spooks were confident that with the Preacher's trail of blood and death across the country, there would be no objection, right up to ministerial level if need be. The only political caveat would be the usual: Do what you feel you must, but I want to know nothing about it. Leading from the front, as ever.

As he was driven back to his mews cottage in the embassy car, the Tracker mused that there were now two possible routes to the exact location of the Preacher: One was Dardari's personal desktop computer, if it could be tapped into. The other he was keeping up his sleeve for the moment.

It was just after dawn the next day, that the MV *Malmö* eased her way out of Gothenburg port and headed for the open sea. She was a 22,000-ton general-cargo freighter, what in the merchant shipping world is called handy-sized. The yellow-and-blue flag of Sweden fluttered from her stern.

She was a part of the considerable merchant fleet of Harry Andersson, among the last one-of-a-kind tycoons left in Sweden. Andersson had founded his shipping line many years ago with a single aged tramp steamer and had built the line to forty ships and made himself the biggest merchant marine tycoon in the country.

Despite the taxes, he had never relocated abroad; despite the fees, he had never adopted flags of convenience for his vessels. He had never "floated" except on the sea, never the stock exchange. He was sole owner of Andersson Line and, rare in Sweden, a billionaire in his own right. He had had two marriages and seven children, but only his youngest son, young enough to be his grandchild, was eager to become a mariner like his father.

The *Malmö* had a long trip ahead of her. She had a cargo of Volvo cars, destination Perth, Australia. On her bridge was Captain Stig Eklund; the first and second officers were Ukrainian and the chief engineer Polish. There were ten Filipino crew, including a cook, cabin steward and eight deckhands.

The only supernumerary was the cadet Ove Carlsson, studying for his merchant officer's ticket and on his first long-distance voyage. He was just nineteen. Only two men on that ship knew who he really was: Capt. Eklund and the lad himself. The old tycoon was determined that if his youngest son was to go to sea on one of his ships, there would be neither bullying caused by resentment nor sycophancy from those seeking favor.

So the young midshipman traveled under the identity of his mother's maiden name. A friend in government had authorized a genuine passport in the false name, and the passport had secured papers from the Swedish merchant marine authorities in the same name.

The four officers and the cadet were on the bridge that summer morning when the steward brought them coffee as the *Malmö* pushed her blunt nose into the rising swell of the Skagerrak.

Agent Opal had indeed managed to acquire a rugged trail bike from a Somali who was desperate to get out of the country with his wife and child and needed the dollars to start afresh in Kenya. What he was doing was utterly illegal under al-Shabaab law and liable to bring him a flogging or worse if he were caught. But he also had a scruffy pickup truck and believed he could make the border if he drove by night and lay up all day in the dense vegetation between Kismayo and the Kenyan frontier.

Opal had also strapped to the rear pillion a large wicker basket in which anyone might carry their meager shopping but which in his case would hide a large extra canister of petrol.

The map he had acquired from the belly of the kingfish

showed him his handler's chosen meeting point was on the coast almost a hundred miles north. On the pitted, rutted track the coast highway had become, he could manage it between dusk and dawn.

His other purchase was an old but serviceable transistor radio on which he could listen to various foreign stations—also forbidden by al-Shabaab. But living alone in his cabin out of town, pressing the tranny to his ear with the sound low, he could pick up Kol Israel and not be heard by anyone a few yards away. That was how he heard about showers over Ashkelon.

The inhabitants of that merry borough might look up the next day and be perplexed by a blue sky with not a cloud in sight, but that was their problem.

Benny was already with the fishing boat. He had arrived by helicopter, a machine owned and flown by another Israeli on what purported to be a private charter for a wealthy tourist from Nairobi to the Oceans Sports Hotel at Watamu on the coast north of Malindi.

In fact, the helicopter had flown past the coast, turned north past Lamu Island, east of Somalia's Ras Kamboni Island, until the GPS system located the fishing boat below.

The helicopter held position twenty feet up as Benny fast-roped down to the pitching deck and the hands waiting to grab him.

That evening, Opal set off under cover of darkness. It was Friday, the streets were almost empty, the population at their prayers and the road traffic thin. Twice when the agent saw headlights coming up behind him, he pulled off the road and hid until the truck went by. He did the same when he saw the glow of lights on the horizon ahead. And he rode only by the light of the moon.

He was early. When he knew he must be a few miles short of the meeting point, he pulled off again and waited for dawn. At first light, he went on, but slowly, and there it was: a dry wadi, coming from the desert to his left, but large enough to merit a bridge to pass under. It would flood in the coming monsoon and become a raging torrent, passing under the concrete span of the bridge and through the cluster of giant casuarina trees between the highway and the shore.

He left the road and coaxed his trail bike the hundred yards to the water's edge. Then he listened. After fifteen minutes, he heard it: the faint snarl of an outboard engine. He flicked his lights twice: up, down, up, down. The buzz turned toward him, and the shape of the rigid inflatable came out of the dark sea. He looked back at the road behind him. No one.

Benny stepped ashore. Passwords were exchanged. Then he gave his agent a hug. There was news from home, eagerly awaited. A briefing, and equipment.

The latter was extremely welcome. He would have to bury it, of course, under the earthen floor of his cabin, and then cover the patch with plywood sheeting. A small but state-of-the-art transceiver. It would take messages from Israel and hold them for thirty minutes, while they were transcribed or memorized. Then it would self-erase.

And it would send messages from Opal to the Office, which, spoken "in clear," would be compressed into a single "squirt" so short that any listener would need ultra-technology to catch the tenth-of-a-second burst and record it. In Tel Aviv, the burst would be extended back into normal speech.

And there was the briefing. The warehouse, the need to know who lived in it, if they ever left it and, if so, where did they go? A description of any vehicle used by any inhabitant or regular visitor to the warehouse. And if any visitor lived away from the warehouse, a complete description of that residence and its exact location.

Opal did not need to know, and Benny could only presume, but there would be an American drone up there somewhere; a Predator, or Global Hawk, or perhaps the new Sentinel, turning slowly, hour after hour, looking down, seeing everything. But in the tangle of Kismayo's streets, the watchers could still lose one vehicle among hundreds unless that vehicle was precisely described to the last detail.

With another hug, they parted. The inflatable, manned by four armed commandos, slipped away to the sea. Opal refueled his motorcycle and headed south to his cabin to bury his transceiver and the battery, energized by the sun via a photovoltaic cell.

Benny was lifted back off the sea by a rope ladder dangled from the helicopter. When he was gone, the commandos settled for another day of hard exercises, swimming and fishing to stave off the boredom. They might not be needed again, but in case they were, they had to stay.

Benny was dropped at Nairobi airport and took flight for Europe and thence Israel. Opal scoured the streets around the warehouse and found a room to rent. From a crack in its warped shutters, he could survey the single, double-gated entrance.

He would have to continue with his job as a tally clerk or arouse suspicion. And he had to eat and sleep. Between these, he would stake out the warehouse as best he could. He hoped something would happen.

Far away in London, the Tracker was doing his best to make something happen.

The installers of the security system at the house in Pelham Crescent were sufficiently confident of their skill and renown that they announced who they were. Pinned to the outside wall underneath the eaves was a tasteful plaque announcing "This property is protected by Daedalus Security Systems." It was discreetly photographed from the leafy park at the center of the crescent of houses.

Daedalus, mused the Tracker when he saw the picture, was the Greek engineer who designed a not very secure pair of wings for his son, who fell into the sea and died when the wax melted. But he also constructed a maze of fiendish ingenuity for King Minos of Crete. No doubt the modern Daedalus was trying to evoke the skill of the builder of a puzzle system that no one could break.

He turned out to be Steve Bamping, who had founded and still ran his own company, which was very upmarket and serviced a wealthy client list with antiburglar protection. With the permission of the director of G Branch of MI5, Firth and the Tracker went to see him. His first reaction to what they wished was of flat refusal.

Firth did the talking until the Tracker produced a sheaf of

photos and laid them on Mr. Bamping's desk in two rows. There were eleven of them. The head of Daedalus Security stared at them uncomprehending. Each was of a dead man, on a morgue slab, eyes closed.

"Who are these?" he asked.

"Dead men," said the Tracker. "Seven Americans and four British. All harmless citizens doing their best for their countries. All murdered in cold blood by Jihadist assassins inspired and impelled by a preacher on the Internet."

"Mr. Dardari? Surely not."

"No. The Preacher launches his hate campaign out of the Middle East. We have pretty much proof his London-based helper is your client. That is what has brought me across the Atlantic."

Steve Bamping continued to stare at the eleven dead faces.

"Good God," he muttered. "So what do you want?"

Firth told him.

"Is this authorized?"

"At the cabinet level," said Firth. "And, no, I do not have the Home Secretary's signature on a piece of paper to say so. But if you wish to talk with the director general of MI5, I can give you his direct-line number."

Bamping shook his head. He had already seen Firth's personal identification as an officer of 5's anti-terrorist division.

"Not one word of this gets out," he said.

"Not from either of us," said Firth. "Under any circumstances whatsoever."

The system installed at Pelham Crescent was from the Gold Menu. Every door and every window was fitted with invisible-ray-based alarms linked to the central computer. But the owner himself would enter only by the front door when the system was activated.

The front door appeared normal, with a Bramah lock operable with a key. When the door opened with the alarm system on, a bleeper would begin to sound. It would not alert anyone for thirty seconds. Then it would shut off but trigger a silent alarm at the Daedalus emergency center. They would alert the police and send their own van.

But to confuse any prospective burglar who might wish to chance his luck, the bleeper would sound from a cupboard in one direction, while the computer was in a completely different direction. The householder would have thirty seconds to go to the right cupboard, reveal the computer and punch a six-digit code into the illuminated panel. That gave millions of computations. Only someone knowing the right one could stop the bleeper in less than thirty seconds and prevent activation.

If he made a mistake and the thirty seconds elapsed, there was a phone, and a four-figure call would put him through to the center. He would then have to recite his personal, memorized pin number to cancel the alarm. One wrong number would tell the center he was under duress, and despite the courtesy of the response, the "Armed intruder on premises" procedure would be followed.

There were two further precautions. Invisible rays across reception rooms and stairwells would trigger silent alarms if broken, but their turn-off switch was very small and tucked away behind the computer. Even with a pistol pointed at his head, the threatened householder did not need to deactivate the ray beams.

Finally, a hidden camera behind a pin-sized hole covered the entire hall and was never switched off. From any point in the world, Mr. Dardari could dial a phone number that would stream his own hallway onto his iPhone.

But, as Mr. Bamping later explained to his client with extreme apologies, even high-technology systems occasionally malfunction. When a false alarm was registered while Mr. Dardari was in London but not at home, he had to be summoned and was not pleased. The Daedalus team was apologetic, the Metropolitan Police very courteous. He was mollified, and agreed a technician should put the minor fault right.

He let them in, saw them start in the computer cupboard, became bored and went into the sitting room to mix himself a cocktail.

When the two technicians, both from MI5's computer specialist office, reported to him, he put down his drink and agreed with lofty amusement to a test run. He went out, then let himself in. The bleeper sounded. He went to the cupboard and silenced it. To make sure, he stood in the hall and dialed his own spy camera. On his screen he saw himself and the two technicians in the middle of his hall. He thanked them and they left. Two days later, he also left, but for a week in Karachi.

The trouble with computer-based systems is that the computer controls everything. If the computer "goes rogue," it is not only useless, it collaborates with the enemy.

When they came, the MI5 team did not use the hoary device of the gas company truck or the telephone van. Neighbors might know the man next door had gone for a while. They came at two in the morning in dead silence, dark clothes and rubber shoes. Even the streetlights failed for a few minutes. They were through the door in seconds, and not a light went on up and down the crescent.

The leading man quickly deactivated the alarm, reached behind the box and killed the infrared rays. A few more taps on the computer panel and it told the camera to freeze on a shot of the hall entirely empty and the camera obeyed. Mr. Dardari could phone in from the Punjab and he would see an empty hall. In fact, he was still airborne.

There were four this time and they worked fast. Tiny microphones and cameras were installed in the three most important rooms: sitting, dining and study. When they were done, it was still pitch-black outside. A voice in the earpiece of the team leader confirmed that the street was empty, and they left unseen.

The only remaining problem was the Pakistani businessman's personal computer. It had gone with him. But he was back in six days, and two days after that he went out for a black-tie dinner. The third visit was the shortest of all. The computer was on his desk.

The hard drive was removed and inserted into a drive duplicator known by the technicians as the box. Mr. Dardari's hard disk went into one side of the box and a blank into the other. It took forty-four minutes for the entire database to be sucked out and "imaged" into the duplicate, then put back without leaving any trace. So much for the past.

A USB stick, or universal serial bus, or memory stick, was inserted and the computer turned on. Then the malware was fed in, instructing the computer to, in future, monitor every keystroke pressed, and the same for every e-mail coming in. This data would then be passed to the Security Service's own listening computer, which would log every time the Pakistani used his computer. And he would not notice a thing.

The Tracker was happily prepared to concede that the MI5 people were good. He knew that the stolen material would also go to a doughnut-shaped building outside the Gloucestershire town of Cheltenham, home of the Government Communications HQ, the British equivalent of Fort Meade. There cryptographers would study the back file to see if it was in clear or in code. If the latter, the code would have to be broken. Between them, the two bodies of aces should be able to lay the Pakistani's life bare.

But there was something else he wanted, and his hosts had no objection. It was that both the harvest of past transmissions and all future keystrokes be passed to a young man hunched over his machine in a half-dark attic in Centerville. He had special instructions that needed to go to only Ariel.

The first information was very quick. There was not the slightest doubt Mustafa Dardari was in constant contact with the computer at the canning warehouse in Kismayo, Somalia. He was exchanging information and warnings with the Troll and he was the personal cyberrepresentative of the Preacher.

Meanwhile, the code breakers were seeking to discover exactly what he had said and what the Troll had said to him.

A gent Opal kept watch on the warehouse for a week before his sleep-deprived vigil was rewarded. It was evening when the gate swung open. What emerged was not an empty delivery truck but a pickup truck, old and battered, with a cab and an open back. This is the standard vehicle for both halves of Somalia, north and south. When the back is fitted with half a dozen clan fighters clustered around a machine gun, it is called a technical. The one that passed down the street into which Opal was peering at through his crack was empty, and with just a driver at the wheel.

The man was the Troll, but Opal could not know that. He just had his handler's orders: If anything leaves, except produce trucks, follow it. He left his rented room, unchained his trail bike and followed.

It was a long, brutal drive, through the night and into the dawn. The first part he knew already. The coast road led northeast, along the shoreline, past the dry wadi and the clump of casuarinas where he had met Benny and on toward Mogadishu. It was midmorning, and even his spare tank was almost empty when the pickup turned into the shoreside town of Marka.

Like Kismayo, Marka had been a rock-solid al-Shabaab stronghold until 2012, when federal forces, with huge backup from African Union Mission in Somalia (AMISOM) troops, had retaken it from the Jihadists. But 2013 had seen a reversal. The fanatics had come storming back and in bloody fighting clawed back both towns and the land between.

Dizzy with fatigue, Opal followed the pickup until it stopped. There was a gate guarding some kind of a courtyard. The driver of the pickup hooted. A small trap opened in the timber gate and half a face looked out. Then the gate began to swing open.

Opal dismounted, crouching behind his machine, pretending to attend to the front tire, peering through the spokes. The driver seemed to be known, for there were greetings, and he rolled inside. The gate began to close. Before it sealed off Opal's view, he saw a compound, with a central yard and three low-built off-white houses with shuttered windows.

It looked like one of a thousand compounds that make up Marka, a sprawling complex of low white cubes between the ocher hills and the sandy shore, with the glittering blue ocean beyond. Only the minarets of the mosques reached higher than the houses.

Opal went a few littered alleys farther on, found a pool of shade against the rising heat, pulled his *shamagh* over his head and slept. When he woke, he patrolled the town until he found a man with a barrel of petroleum and a hand pump. This time, there were no dollars; too dangerous. He could have been denounced to the *mutawa*, the religious police, with their hate-filled eyes and canes. He paid in a sheaf of shillings.

He motored again through the cool of the night. He arrived in time for his shift at the fish market. Only in the afternoon could he compose a short verbal message, dig up his canvas-wrapped transceiver, hook it to the newly charged battery and hit the send button. The message was received at the Office north of Tel Aviv and, by agreement, passed on to TOSA in Virginia.

Within a day, a Global Hawk out of the American launch site in Yemen had found the compound. It took a while, but the message from Mossad mentioned a fruit market, with stalls and produce spread across the ground, just a hundred yards from the compound. And the minaret two blocks away. And the multi-exit roundabout built by the Italians, six hundred yards in a straight line due north, where the Mogadishu highway skirted the town. There could only be one like that.

Tracker had had a link from the J-SOC drone-operating center outside Tampa patched through to the U.S. embassy. He sat there and stared at the three houses enclosing the compound. Which one? None of them? Even if the Preacher were there, he was safe from drone strike. A Hellfire or a Brimstone would flatten up to a dozen of the close-packed houses. Women, children. His war was not with them, and he had no proof.

He wanted that proof, he needed that proof, and when the cryptographers were finished, he figured the Karachi-based chutney maker would provide it.

In his Kismayo cabin, Opal was sleeping when the MV *Malmö* joined the queue of merchant ships waiting to enter the Suez Canal. For them, motionless under the Egyptian sun, the heat was stupefying. Two of the Filipinos had lines out, hoping for a catch of fresh fish for supper. Others sat under awnings rigged in the lee of the steel sea containers, themselves like radiators, that contained the cars. But the Europeans stayed inside where the air-conditioning run off the auxiliary engine made life bearable. The Ukrainians played cards, the Pole was in his engine room. Capt. Eklund tapped out an e-mail to his wife, and the cadet Ove Carlsson studied his navigation lessons.

Far to the south, a Jihadist fanatic, filled with hatred for the West and all its doings, scanned the printouts of messages brought to him from Kismayo.

And in a mud-brick fort in the hills behind the bay of Garacad, a sadistic clan chief known as al-Afrit, the Devil, planned to send a dozen of his young men back to sea, despite the risks, to hunt for prey.

9

There was indeed a code in the messages from Dardari in London and the Troll in Kismayo and it was broken. The two men communicated apparently in clear because both GCHQ in England and Fort Meade in Maryland are suspicious of transmissions that are clearly in code.

So vast is the commercial and industrial traffic flying through cyberspace that not everything can be subjected to rigorous scrutiny. So both centers of interception tend to prioritize the evidently suspicious. Somalia being a highly suspect place, only the harmless-looking would be studied but not subjected to the top-of-the-list decryption tests. So far the London/Kismayo traffic had got away with it. That ended.

The traffic purported to be between the head of a large foodstuffs manufacturer based in London and his manager in a location producing raw materials. The traffic out of London appeared to be queries concerning local availability of fruits, vegetables and spices, all locally grown, and their prices. The traffic out of Kismayo seemed to be the manager's replies.

The code's key was in the lists of prices. Cheltenham and Ariel got it about the same time. There were discrepancies. Sometimes the prices were too high, sometimes too low. They did not match the real prices on the world markets for those products at that time of year. Some of the figures were genuine, others unrealistic. In the latter category, the figures were letters, the letters made words and the words made messages.

The months of exchanges between a fashionable town house in London's West End and a warehouse in Kismayo proved that Mustafa Dardari was the Preacher's outside man. He was both financier and informer. He advised and warned.

He subscribed to technical publications dealing intensively with the West's counterterrorism thinking. He studied the work of think tanks on the subject, taking technical papers from the Royal United Services Institute and the International Institute for Strategic Studies in London and their U.S. equivalents.

His e-mails to his friend revealed he frequented, at a social level, the tables of those who might have a senior civil servant, military or security figure as their guest. In short, he was a spy. He was also, behind the urbane, westernized façade a Salafist and Jihadist extremist like his boyhood friend in Somalia.

Ariel spotted something else. There were single-letter typing errors in the texts, but they were not random. Very few nonprofessionals can type long passages without occasionally hitting the wrong key and creating a one-letter typo. In journalism and publishing, the correction of these is what copy editors are for. But so long as the meaning is clear, many amateurs do not bother.

The Troll bothered, but Dardari did not. Because his typos were deliberate. They occurred only once or twice per send, but their appearance was rhythmic, not always in the same place but always in sequence with the ones in the previous message. Ariel deduced they were "tells"—small signs which, if they were not there, would warn the reader the sender was under duress or the computer was being operated by an enemy.

What the traffic did not confirm was two things the Tracker needed. The messages referred to "my brother," but that could be a greeting between fellow Muslims. They referred to "our friend," but never Zulfiqar Ali Shah or Abu Azzam by name. And they never confirmed that our friend was resident not in Kismayo but in a compound in the heart of Marka.

The only way he would achieve these two proofs and the authority to go for a terminal strike would be positive identification by a reliable source or the Preacher being goaded to make a terrible mistake and go online from his home. The Global Hawk high above the Marka compound would hear it instantly and snatch it out of space.

To achieve the first, it would need someone in a distinctive and preassigned headdress or baseball cap to stand in the courtyard, look up at the sky and nod. Tampa would see that staring face, as Creech had seen Anwar al-Awlaki look fatally at the sky, his exposed face filling a whole TV screen in an underground bunker in Nevada.

As to the second, the Tracker still had an ace of his own to play.

The MV *Malmö* eased out of the canal at Port Suez and into the Red Sea. Capt. Eklund offered his thanks and farewells as the Egyptian pilot slipped over the side to his waiting launch. Within hours, he would be on another freighter heading north.

The *Malmö*, back under her own command, nosed south toward Bab al-Mandab and the eastward turn into the Gulf of Aden. Capt. Eklund was content. She had made good time so far.

Opal returned from his work at the fish dock, checked that he was completely alone and unobserved and retrieved his radio from beneath the floor. He knew these daily checks to see if there had been an incoming message were the danger points in his life as a spy inside the al-Shabaab fortress.

He took the set, linked it to the charged battery, put on his earphones, took out pen and notepad and prepared to transcribe. The message, once slowed down to reading speed, took only a few minutes, and his pen raced over the paper making Hebrew characters.

It was short and to the point. Warm congratulations on tracing the pickup from the warehouse to Marka. The next time that happens, do not follow immediately. Return to the set and alert us that it is heading north. Then hide the set and follow. Endit.

The Taiwanese trawler was well east of the Somali coast and had not been stopped. There was no reason why she should be. A low-flying patrol plane, spotting for one of the international naval forces now trying to protect international shipping from Somali pirates, had dipped to have a look but had flown on.

The vessel was clearly what she was—a deep-sea, long-distance fisherman out of Taipei. Her trawl was not down, but there was nothing odd about that if she was looking for fresh and better waters. She had been captured by al-Afrit weeks before, and that had been noted—but under her real name. That name had been changed. Her Chinese crew, under threat, had been forced to paint a new name on her bows and stern.

Two of the same crew, all that were needed, were now on the bridge. The ten Somali pirates were crouching out of sight. The patrol plane crew, scanning with binoculars, had seen the two Asian men at the wheel and suspected nothing. The two men had been warned that any attempt to gesture for help would result in death.

The trick was not new, but it remained extremely hard for the international force to detect. Somali skiffs, pretending to be innocent fishermen if seen and intercepted, did not take long to expose. They might protest they needed their AK-47 Kalashnikovs for self-protection, but that could hardly apply to rocket-propelled grenades. The clincher was always the light aluminum ladder. You do not need it to fish, but you do to scale the side of a merchantman.

Somali piracy had taken some devastating knocks. Most big and valuable ships had taken on a team of professional ex-soldiers, who carried rifles and knew how to use them. About eighty percent were so protected. The drones now flying out of Djibouti could scan up to 40,000 square miles of sea in a day. The warships of the four international flotillas were helped by helicopters as wide-ranging scouts. And, finally, the pirates, captured in greater numbers, were simply being tried, found guilty and detained in the Seychelles with international support. The heyday was over.

But one ruse still worked: the mother ship. The *Shan-Lee 08*, as she was now named, was one such. She could stay at sea far longer than an open skiff, and her range was immense. The attack skiffs with their fast outboard motors, were stored belowdecks. She looked innocent, but the attack skiffs could be on deck and in the water in a few minutes.

Out of the Red Sea and into the Gulf of Aden, Capt. Eklund was meticulous in following the internationally recommended transit established to give maximum protection to merchant shipping passing the dangerous Gulf of Aden.

The corridor runs parallel to the Adeni and Omani coast, from the 45th to the 53rd longitude east. These eight longitude zones bring the merchantman past the north coast of Puntland, the start of the pirate havens, and far out beyond the Horn. For ships wishing to round the southern tip of India, this brings them many miles too far north before they can turn south for the long haul across the Indian Ocean. But it is heavily patrolled by naval vessels and keeps them safe.

Captain Eklund followed the prescribed passage to the 53rd longitude, then, convinced he was safe, he turned southeast for India. The drones could indeed patrol 40,000 square miles of sea in a day, but the Indian Ocean is many millions of square miles, and in this vastness a ship can disappear. The naval vessels of NATO and the European EU NAVFOR could be thickly gathered in the corridor, but they were scattered far and wide out on the ocean. Only the French have a force dedicated to the Indian Ocean. They call it *L'indien*.

The *Malmö*'s master was convinced that he was now too far east for anything from the Somali coast to threaten him. The days, and even the nights, were sweltering hot.

Almost all ships traveling in these waters have used engineers at home to construct an inner fortress protected by steel doors locked from the inside and equipped with food, water, bunks and toiletries, enough for several days. Also included are systems to disconnect the engines from outside interference and run both them and the steering mechanism from inside. Finally, there is a fixed-message distress call that will broadcast from the mast top.

Protected inside the citadel, the crew, if they can seal themselves inside in time, can await rescue, pretty sure that it is on its way. The pirates, though they have the run of the ship, cannot control it or threaten the crew, though they will try to break in. The crew can only hope for the arrival of a frigate or destroyer.

But as the *Malmö* ran south past the Laccadive Islands, the crew slept in the greater comfort of their cabins. They did not see or hear the skiffs racing through the wake or hear the clatter of ladders against the stern as the Somali pirates boarded by moonlight. The helmsman raised the alarm, but too late. Dark, agile figures with guns were racing into the superstructure and up to the bridge. Within five minutes, the *Malmö* was captured.

Opal watched the gates of the warehouse compound open as the sun went down and the pickup emerged. It was the same one as before. It turned in the same direction as before. He straddled his trail bike and followed it to the northern outskirts of Kismayo until he was sure it was on the coast highway toward Marka. Then he went back to his cabin and lifted his transceiver from its hole beneath the floor. He had already composed his message and compressed it into a fraction-of-a-second burst transmission. When he had removed the battery from its photovoltaic recharger and connected it, he just hit send.

The message was taken by the permanent listening watch inside the Office. It was decrypted by the officer of the watch, who passed it to Benny, still at his desk in the same time zone as Kismayo. He composed a short instruction, which was encoded and beamed to a boat masquerading as a Salalah-based fisherman twenty miles off the Somali shore.

The rigid inflatable left the side of the fisherman a few minutes later and sped toward the shore. It contained seven commandos and a captain in command. Only when the sand dunes of the coast came into sight in the moonlight did the engine level decrease to a slow growl, in case of listening ears even on this desolate stretch of sand.

As the nose ground into the sand, the captain and six men leapt ashore and ran for the road. The spot, they already knew; it was where a dry wadi ran under a concrete bridge and a clump of casuarinas grew. One of the men jogged three hundred yards up the road toward Kismayo, found a spot in the sedge by the roadside, lay down and fixed his powerful night vision goggles on the road south. He had been told exactly what vehicle to look for and even its plate number. Behind him, the ambush party also lay in the cover roadside and waited.

The captain lay with the communicator in his hand, where he could not miss the pulsing red light when it came. Four vehicles went past, but not the one they wanted.

Then it came. In the green half-light of the night vision goggles, the commando down the road could not mistake it. Its dirty off-white original color was irrelevant in the all-green glow of the NVGs. But the battered grille was there, along with the twisted roll bar that had clearly not done its job. And the front number plate was the one he was looking for. He pressed the send button on his pulser.

Behind him the captain saw the red glow in his hand and hissed, "Kadima," to his men. They came out of the ground, from both sides of the road, holding the broad red-and-white tape between them. In the darkness, it looked like a horizontal pole. The captain stood in front of it, shining a shaded torch at the ground, his other hand raised.

They were not dressed in camouflage but in long white robes and Somali headdresses. They all carried Kalashnikovs. No Somali would dare drive through a roadblock manned by the religious *mutawa*. The engine of the oncoming pickup truck coughed as the driver changed down a gear, then another.

The pirates had left two of their number to keep the Taiwanese skipper and his first-mate prisoner. The other eight had boarded the *Malmö*. One spoke a smattering of English. He came from the Garacad pirates' nest, and this was his third capture. He knew the routine. Capt. Eklund did not, despite his briefing from a Swedish naval officer back in Gothenburg.

He knew he had had time to press the send button of the perpetual Mayday signal from his cabin. He knew it would be transmitting from his mast top, alerting a listening world that he was captured.

The pirate leader, who was twenty-four and called Jimali, knew it, too, and did not care. Let the infidel navies come; it was too late now. They would never attack and trigger a bloodbath. He knew of the *kuffar* obsession with human life and despised it. A good Somali feared neither pain nor death.

The five Europeans and ten Filipinos were gathered on deck. Capt. Eklund was told that if any more were hiding, one of the officers would be thrown into the sea.

"There are no more," said the captain. "What do you want?"

Jimali gestured to his men.

"Food. No pig," he said. Capt. Eklund told the Filipino cook to go to his galley and prepare food. One of the pirates went with him.

"You. Come." Jimali beckoned the captain, and they went to the bridge. "You steer Garacad, you live."

The captain consulted his maps, presumed the Somali coast and found the village a hundred miles south of Eyl, another pirate concentration. He worked out an approximate heading and turned the helm.

A French frigate from *L'indien* was the first to find them, just after dawn. It took up station several cables to port and reduced speed to stay in formation. The French captain did not intend to use his marines to board the *Malmö*, and Jimali knew it. He stared across the water from the bridge wing, almost challenging the infidels to have a go.

Far away from the seemingly harmless maritime spectacle of a French frigate escorting a Swedish freighter with a Taiwanese trawler far behind, a whirlwind of electronic communication was taking place.

The *Malmö*'s automatic identification system had been picked up instantly. It was monitored by the British Maritime Trade Operations out of Dubai and the American MARLO, the maritime liaison out of Bahrain. A score of NATO and EU warships were alerted to her problem, but, as Jimali knew, none would attack.

The Andersson Line maintained a night-and-day operations room in Stockholm, which was immediately advised. The shipping HQ called the *Malmö*. Jimali indicated that Capt. Eklund could take the call but put it on the bridge speaker and converse only in English. Even before he spoke, Stockholm knew he was in the presence of armed Somalis and every word should be guarded.

Captain Eklund confirmed that the *Malmö* had been taken in the night. His men were all safe and were being well treated. There were no injuries. They were steaming under orders for the coast of Somalia.

The shipowner, Harry Andersson, was roused over breakfast in his palatial home in a walled park in Östermalm, Stockholm. He finished dressing while his car was brought to the door, then drove straight to his operations room. The fleet controller of the night shift had stayed on. He explained everything that the emergency services and Capt. Eklund had been able to tell him.

Mr. Andersson had become a very successful, and thus rich, man because he had two very useful talents, among others. One was to assimilate a situation with extreme speed and, having done so, create a plan of action based on realities, not fantasies, and then go for it.

He stood, plunged in thought, in the middle of his operations room. No one dared disturb him. His ship had been taken by pirates, his first ever. Armed assault at sea would trigger a massacre and was simply not going to be attempted.

The *Malmö* would therefore make the Somali coast and be anchored there. His first duty was to his fifteen employees, then to recover ship and cargo if possible. And then there was the question of his son.

"Bring my car to the door," he said. "Call Björn, wherever he is, and tell him to get the plane ready for immediate take-off. Flight plan for Northolt, London. Book me a suite at the Connaught. Hannah, you have your passport with you? Then come with me."

Minutes later, in the back of his Bentley, his PA Hannah beside him, speeding to Bromma airport, he used his mobile phone to plan the immediate future.

It was a matter for the insurers now. He insured through a specialist syndicate of underwriters at Lloyd's. They would have the whip hand because the money at risk was theirs. That was what he paid them an annual fortune for.

Before he was airborne, he had learned his underwriters' negotiator of choice—and they definitely had been down this road before—was a firm called Chauncey Reynolds, which had a track record of negotiated recoveries. He knew he would be in London long before his ship would reach the Somali shore. Before his Learjet reached the Swedish coast, he had an appointment with the lawyers at six p.m. Well, they would damn well have to work late.

While he was on the glide path of Northolt touchdown, Chauncey Reynolds was preparing. They were trying the Surrey home of their negotiator of choice, the half-retired ace of his strange profession. His wife fetched him from among the beehives in the garden.

He had learned his skills as a hostage-recovery negotiator for the Metropolitan Police. He was a deceptively slow-spoken Welshman named Gareth Evans.

The Troll was very dead when Opal arrived. Opal had been seen by the spotter down the road and recognized because the captain had seen him before, at the earlier beach meeting with Benny. Again the pulse went red in the captain's hand and the roadblock came into being.

Opal suddenly saw the group of robed figures in his dim headlight, the swinging torch, the pointing assault rifles. Like all secret agents far behind enemy lines and facing a bad death in the event of unmasking, he had a small panic attack.

Were his papers in order? Would his story of job seeking in Marka stand up? What could the *mutawa* possibly want on that road in the middle of the night?

The man with the torch approached and stared at his face. The moon came out from behind a bank of clouds, harbinger of the coming monsoon. Two black faces, inches apart in the night, one dark by nature, the other smeared with commando's night-fighting cream.

"*Shalom*, Opal. Come, off the road. There is a truck coming."

The men vanished into the trees and couch grass, taking the trail bike with them. The truck passed. Then the captain showed Opal the crash site.

The Troll's pickup had seemingly had a complete blowout of the front offside wheel. The nail was still protruding from the tread, where human hands had hammered it. Out of control, the pickup must have slewed to one side. By ill chance, this was in the center of the concrete bridge.

It had toppled at speed over the edge, slamming into the far steep bank of the wadi. The impact had hurled the driver into the windshield and the steering wheel into his chest with enough force to shatter both head and thorax. Someone had seemingly eased him out of the cab and laid him beside the vehicle. In death he stared unseeing up at the wispy tips of the casuarina trees between him and the moon.

"Now, let us talk," said the captain. He briefed Opal exactly as Benny had told him on the secure line between the trawler and Tel Aviv. Word for word. Then he gave him a sheaf of papers and a red baseball cap.

"These are what the dying man gave you before he passed away. You did your best, but there was no hope. He was too far gone. Any questions?"

Opal shook his head. The story was feasible. He tucked the papers inside his windbreaker. The captain of the Sayeret Matkal held out a hand.

"We must go back to the sea. Good luck, my friend. *Mazel tov.*"

It took a few moments to brush the last footprints from the dust, all save those of Opal. Then they were gone, back across the dark ocean to the waiting fishing boat. Opal hauled his trail bike back to the road and continued to the north.

Those who gathered in the office of Chauncey Reynolds were all experienced at what, over a decade of piracy, had become a mutually agreed ritual. The pirates were all clan chiefs of Puntland, operating out of an eight-hundred-mile coast from Boosaaso in the north to Mareeg, just up the coast from Mogadishu.

They were in piracy for money and that was all. Their excuse was that, years ago, fishing fleets from South Korea and Taiwan had arrived and gutted their traditional fishing grounds, from which they had made a livelihood. Whatever the rights and wrongs, they had turned to piracy and since then made huge earnings, far more than those generated by a few tuna.

They had started by boarding and capturing merchant vessels steaming past their coast just offshore. With time and expertise, they had ranged farther and farther east and south. In the beginning, their captures were small, their negotiations clumsy, and suitcases of dollar bills were dropped by light aircraft, flying up from Kenya, at a preagreed drop zone at sea.

But no one trusts anybody on that coast. There is no honor among these thieves. Ships captured by one group were stolen by another clan while at anchor. Rival packs fought over floating suitcases of cash. Eventually, a kind of agreed-upon procedure prevailed.

The crew of a captured vessel was rarely, if ever, brought ashore. Lest an anchor drag in the pounding rollers, captured ships were anchored up to two miles offshore. The officers and crew lived onboard in barely reasonable conditions, but with a dozen guards, while negotiations between their principals—shipowner and clan chief—dragged on.

On the Western side, certain companies of insurers, lawyers and negotiators became expert with experience. On the Somali side, educated negotiators—not simply Somalis but from the right clan—took over the talking. This was now done with modern technology—computers and iPhones. Even the money was rarely dropped like bombs from on high; the Somalis had numbered bank accounts, in which the money would immediately appear.

With the passage of time, negotiators from the two sides came to know each other, each simply concerned about getting the job done. But the Somalis held the aces.

For the insurers, a cargo delayed was a cargo lost. For the shipowners, a vessel not earning was an operating loss. Add to that the distress of the crew and their desperate families, and a speedy conclusion was their pressing aim. The Somali pirates knew this, and they had all the time in the world. That was the basis of the blackmail: time. Some vessels had been moored off that coast for years.

Gareth Evans had negotiated ten releases of ships and cargoes of varying values. He had studied Puntland and its maze-like tribal structures as if for a doctorate. When he heard the *Malmö* was steaming for Garacad, he knew which tribe controlled that stretch of coast and how many clans comprised the tribe. Several of them used the same negotiator, a smooth, urbane Somali graduate of a Midwestern American university named Mr. Ali Abdi.

All this was explained to Harry Andersson as a summer dusk settled over London and, half a world away, the *Malmö* steamed west to Garacad. Takeaway dinners were nibbled at the polished table of the conference room, and Mrs. Bulstrode, the tea lady who had agreed to stay on, served relay after relay of coffee.

A room was set aside as operations control for Gareth

Evans. If a new Somali negotiator was going to be appointed, Capt. Eklund would be told by Stockholm which London number to call to get the ball rolling.

Gareth Evans studied the details of the *Malmö* and her cargo of gleaming new cars and privately calculated that they ought to be able to settle for about five million dollars. He also knew that the first demand would be miles too high. More, he knew that to agree with alacrity would be disastrous. It would immediately double. To demand speed would also be self-defeating; that, too, would raise the price. As for the imprisoned crew, that was their bad luck. They would just have to wait in patience.

Tales from repatriated seamen related that as the weeks dragged by, the onboard Somalis, mostly ill-educated tribesmen from the hills, turned the once-spruce vessel into a stinking pesthole. Lavatories were ignored, urinations took place as and when Nature called. And where, inside or out. The heat did the rest. Oil to power the generators, and thus the air-conditioning, would run out. Unfrozen food would rot, putting the crew onto the Somali goat diet, slaughtered on deck. The only diversions were fishing, board games, cards and reading, but they held boredom at bay for only just so long.

The meeting broke at ten p.m. If set on maximum power, which she probably would be, the *Malmö* should enter the bay of Garacad around noon London time. Shortly thereafter, they should learn who had taken her and who the nominated negotiator was. Then Gareth Evans would introduce himself, if need be, and the intricate gavotte would begin.

Opal arrived in Marka as the town slumbered in the blazing post-noon heat. He found the compound and hammered on the door. This compound was not sleeping. He could hear voices and running steps, as if someone was expected but was late.

The latch door in the heavy timber gate flicked open and a face peered out. It was an Arab face but not Somali. The eyes scanned the street but saw no pickup truck. Then they settled on Opal.

"Yes," snapped a voice, angry that a mere nobody should seek admittance.

"I have papers for the Sheikh," said Opal in Arabic.

"What papers?" The voice was plainly hostile but with curiosity.

"I don't know," said Opal. "That was what the man on the road told me to say."

There was a buzz of conversation behind the timber. The first face was pulled aside and another took its place. Neither Somali nor Arab, but Arabic-speaking. Pakistani?

"Where are you from and what papers?"

Opal fumbled under his windbreaker and produced a sealed package.

"I come from Marka. I met a man on the road. He had crashed his pickup truck. He asked me to bring these and told me how to find this place. That is all I know."

He tried to stuff the package through the aperture.

"No, wait," shouted a voice, and the gate began to open.

Four men stood there, fiercely bearded. He was grabbed and hauled inside. A teenage boy ran out, seized his trail bike, wheeling it inside. The gate closed. Two held him. The man who might be a Pakistani towered over him. He studied the package and sucked in a deep breath.

"Where did you get these, dog? What have you done with our friend?"

Opal played the terrified nobody, which was not hard.

"The man driving the truck, sir. I fear he is dead . . ."

That was as far as he got. A right-handed slap with full force laid him on the ground. There was confused shouting in a language he did not understand, though he spoke English, Somali and Arabic apart from his native Hebrew. Half a dozen hands picked him up and hustled him away. There was a shed of sorts built into the compound wall. He was thrown inside and heard a bolt slam. It was dark, and the place stank. He knew he had to keep up the act. He sank onto a pile of old sacks and buried his head in his hands, the universal posture of bewildered defeat.

It was half an hour before they returned. The two or three of bodyguard stature were there, but also a new one. He was indeed Somali, and with a cultured voice. Some education perhaps. He beckoned. Opal stumbled, blinking, into the harsh sunlight.

"Come," said the Somali, "the Sheikh wishes to see you."

He was marched under close escort into the main building, facing the gate. In the lobby he was given a skilled and thorough frisking. His tattered wallet was taken and handed to the Somali. He extracted the usual papers and scanned them, comparing the grainy photograph to the face. Then he nodded, pocketing the wallet, turned and walked on. Opal was hustled in his wake.

They entered a well-appointed sitting room, where a large fan turned from the ceiling. There was a desk with papers and writing materials. A man sat in a swivel chair, facing away from the door. The Somali approached and murmured in the man's ear. Opal could have sworn he had switched to Arabic. He offered the seated man the wallet and identification papers.

Opal could see the package he had brought was open and several sheets lay on the desk. The seated man turned, lifted his eyes from the wallet and stared at him. He had a full black beard and amber eyes.

Hardly had the *Malmö* dropped her anchor in twenty fathoms of water in the bay of Garacad than three aluminum skiffs were seen heading toward her from the village.

Jimali and his seven co-pirates were eager to be back on land. They had been at sea for twenty days, most of them cooped up in the Taiwanese trawler. Their supplies of fresh food were long gone, and they had been existing on European and Filipino cuisine, which they did not like, for two weeks. They wanted to get back to their native goat stew diet and the feel of sand under their feet.

The dark heads crouching in the oncoming skiffs from the shore a mile away were those of the relief crew, who would guard the ship at anchor for as long as it took.

Only one of those approaching the *Malmö* was not a ragged tribesman. Primly at the back of the third skiff sat a neatly dressed Somali in a well-cut fawn safari jacket and trousers. He held an attaché case on his knees. This was al-Afrit's chosen negotiator, Mr. Abdi.

"Now it begins," said Capt. Eklund. He spoke in English, the language common to the Swede, Ukrainians, the Pole and Filipinos onboard. "We must be patient. Leave the talking to me."

"No speak," snapped Jimali. He disliked his captives speaking even in English because his grasp of it was not very strong.

A ladder was lowered over the side and the mainly teenage relief guards came up it, hardly seeming to touch the rungs. Mr. Abdi, who did not like being at sea, even a mile out, took his time and clung firmly to the guy ropes as he climbed. His attaché case was passed up to him when his feet hit the deck.

Captain Eklund did not know who he was but recognized from his dress and manner that this was at least an educated man. He stepped forward.

"I am Captain Eklund, master of the *Malmö*," he said.

Mr. Abdi held out his hand. "I am Ali Abdi, the appointed negotiator for the Somali end of things," he said. His English was fluent, with a slight American intonation. "You have never been . . . how shall I put it? . . . a guest of the Somali people before?"

"No," said the captain. "And I would prefer not to be now."

"Of course. Most distressing, from your point of view. But you have been briefed, no? There are certain formalities that must be gone through, then meaningful negotiations can begin. The sooner an accord is reached, the sooner you will be on your way."

Captain Eklund knew that, far away, his employer would be in conclave with insurers and lawyers, and they, too, would appoint a single negotiator. Both, he hoped, would be skilled and experienced and would accomplish a quick ransom payment and release. He clearly did not know the rules. Speed was now the concern of the Europeans only.

Abdi's first concern was to be escorted to the bridge to make contact on the ship's satellite phone with the control center in Stockholm and then the negotiation office, presumably in London, the home of Lloyd's, which would be the epicenter of the whole bargaining process. As he surveyed the deck from the vantage of the bridge, he murmured: "It might be wise to rig canvas awnings in the spaces left by the deck cargo. Then your crew can take the sea air without being roasted by the sun."

Stig Eklund had heard of the Stockholm syndrome, the procedure whereby kidnappers and captives formed a friendship bond based on shared proximity. He had no intention of relaxing his inner loathing for the people who had seized his ship. On the other hand, the neatly dressed, educated and well-spoken Somali, in the person of Ali Abdi, was at least someone he could communicate with on a civilized basis.

"Thank you," he said. His first and second officers were standing behind him. They had heard and understood. He nodded to them and they left the bridge to hang the awnings.

"And now, if you please, I must speak to your people in Stockholm," said Abdi.

The sat phone had Stockholm on the line in seconds. Abdi's face lit up when he heard the ship's owner was even then in London with Chauncey Reynolds. He had twice negotiated, albeit for other clan chiefs, for the release of vessels through Chauncey Reynolds and each time they had been successful, with only a few weeks of delay. Given the number, he asked Capt. Eklund to raise the London lawyers. Julian Reynolds came on the line.

"Ah, Mr. Reynolds, we speak again. This is Mr. Ali Abdi on the bridge of the *Malmö*, with Captain Eklund beside me."

In London, Julian Reynolds looked pleased. He covered the mouthpiece and said, "It's Abdi again." There was a sigh of relief, and that included Gareth Evans. Everyone at the London end had heard of the foul reputation of al-Afrit, the cruel old tyrant who ruled Garacad. The appointment of the urbane Abdi caused a flicker of light in the gloom.

"Good morning, Mr. Abdi. *Salaam aleikhem.*"

"*Aleikhem as-salaam,*" responded Abdi over the airwaves. He suspected the Swedes and British would happily wring his neck if they had a free choice, but the Muslim greeting was a nice attempt at civility. He appreciated civility.

"I am going to pass you to someone I think you already know," said Reynolds. He passed the receiver to Gareth Evans and switched to conference call. The voice from the Somali shore was clear as a bell. It was just as clear to the ears at Fort Meade and Cheltenham, who were recording everything.

"Hello, Mr. Abdi. This is Mr. Gareth. We meet again, if only in space. I have been asked to handle the London end of things."

In London, five men—the shipowner, two lawyers, an insurer and Gareth Evans—heard Abdi's chortle over the speaker system.

"Mr. Gareth, my friend. I am so glad it is you. I am sure we can lead this matter to a good conclusion."

Abdi's habit of putting the "Mr." in front of the given name was his way of landing between frostily formal and too intimate. He always referred to Gareth Evans as Mr. Gareth.

"I have a room set aside for me in the law office here in London," said Evans. "Shall I move in there so that we can start?"

It was too fast for Abdi. The formalities had to be observed. One was to impress on the Europeans that the hurry was all on their side. He knew Stockholm would already have calculated just how much the *Malmö* was now costing them on a daily basis; ditto the insurers, of which there would be three.

One firm would cover the hull and machinery, a different firm the cargo, and a third would be the war risk underwriters holding cover on the crew. They would all have different calculations of loss, ongoing or pending. Let them stew with their figures a while longer, he thought. What he said was: "Ah, Mr. Gareth, my friend, you are ahead of me. I need a little more time to study the *Malmö* and her cargo before I can propose a reasonable figure that you can confidently put to your principals for settlement."

He had already been online from his private room, set aside for him in the sand-blasted fortress in the hills behind Garacad, which was the headquarters of al-Afrit. He knew there were factors such as age and condition of the freighter, perishability of the cargo and loss of future likely earnings to be computed.

But he had done all that and had decided on a starting figure of twenty-five million dollars. He knew he would probably settle on four million, maybe five if the Swede was in a hurry.

"Mr. Gareth, let me propose we begin tomorrow morning. Say, nine o'clock London time? That will be midday here. I shall by then be back in my office onshore."

"Very well, my friend. I shall be here to take your call."

It would be a satellite call by computer. There would be no question of using Skype. Facial expressions can give too much away.

"There is one last thing before we break for the day. Do I have your assurance that the crew, including the Filipinos, will be detained safely onboard and not molested in any way?"

No other Somali heard this, for those on the *Malmö* were out of earshot of the bridge and could not speak English anyway. But Abdi caught the meaning.

By and large, the Somali warlords and clan chiefs treated their captives humanely, but there were one or two notable exceptions. Al-Afrit was one, and the worst, a vicious old brute with a reputation.

At a personal level, Abdi would work for al-Afrit, and his fee would be twenty percent. His labors as hostage negotiator for pirates were making him a wealthy man much younger than usual. But he did not have to like his principal and he did not. He despised him. But he did not have a corps of bodyguards around him.

"I am confident that all the crew will remain onboard and be well treated," he intoned, then ended the call. He just prayed he was right.

The amber eyes gazed at the young prisoner for a dozen seconds. Silence reigned in the room. Opal could sense the educated Somali, who had let him into the courtyard, and two Pakistani bodyguards behind him. When the voice came, it was surprisingly gentle and in Arabic.

"What is your name?"

Opal gave it.

"Is that a Somali name?"

Behind him, the Somali shook his head. The Pakistanis did not understand.

"No, Sheikh, I am from Ethiopia."

"That is a mainly *nasrani* country. Are you a Christian?"

"Thanks be to Allah the Merciful, the Compassionate. No, no, Sheikh, I am not. I am from the Ogaden, just over the border. We are all Muslims and much persecuted for it."

The face with the amber eyes nodded approvingly.

"And why did you come to Somalia?"

"There were rumors in my village that recruiters from the Ethiopian army were coming to press-gang our people into the army to fight in the invasion of Somalia. I escaped and came here to join my fellow brothers in Allah."

"You came from Kismayo to Marka last night? Why?"

"I am looking for work, Sheikh. I have a job as tally clerk at the fish dock, but I hoped for something better in Marka."

"And how did you come by these papers?"

Opal told his rehearsed story. He had been motoring through the night to avoid the blinding heat and sandstorms of the day. He noted his petrol was low and stopped to fill up from his spare jerrycan. This was, by chance, on a concrete bridge over a dry wadi.

He heard a faint cry. He thought it might be the wind in the high trees that stand near there, but then he heard it again. It seemed to come from below the bridge.

He climbed down the bank into the wadi and found a pickup truck, badly crashed. It seemed to have come off the bridge and dived into the wadi bank. There was a man at the wheel, but terribly injured.

"I tried to help him, Sheikh, but there was nothing I could do. My motor bicycle would never carry two, and I could not bring him up the bank. I pulled him out of the cab in case it caught fire. But he was dying, *inshallah*."

The dying man had begged him, as a brother, to take his satchel and deliver it to Marka. He described the compound: near the street market, down from the Italian roundabout, a timber double door with a latched door for the lookout.

"I held him while he died, Sheikh, but I could not save him."

The robed figure considered this for some while, then turned to look through the papers that had come from the satchel.

"Did you open the satchel?"

"No, Sheikh, it was not of my business."

The amber eyes looked thoughtful.

"There was money in the satchel. Perhaps we have an honest man. What do you think, Jamma?"

The Somali smirked. The Preacher let out a torrent of Urdu at the Pakistanis. They moved forward and seized Opal.

"My men will return to that spot. They will examine the

wreck, which must surely still be there. And the body of my servant. If you have lied, you will surely wish you had never come here. Meanwhile, you will stay and wait for their return."

He was imprisoned again, but not in the decrepit shed in the yard from which an agile man might escape in the night. He was taken to a cellar with a sand floor and locked in. He was there for two days and a night. It was pitch-dark. He was given a plastic bottle of water, which he sipped sparingly in the blackness. When he was let out and brought upstairs, his eyes puckered and blinked furiously in the sunlight from the shutters. He was taken to the Preacher again.

The robed figure held something in his right hand, which he turned over and over in his fingers. His amber eyes moved to his prisoner and settled on the frightened Opal.

"It seems you were right, my young friend," he said in Arabic. "My servant had indeed crashed his truck into the bank of the wadi and died there. The cause"—he held up the object in his fingers—"this nail. My people found it in the tire. You spoke the truth."

He rose and crossed the room to stand in front of the young Ethiopian, looking down at him speculatively.

"How is it you speak Arabic?"

"I studied in my spare time, sir. I wanted the better to read and understand our Holy Koran."

"Any other language?"

"A little English, sir."

"And how did you come by that?"

"There was a school near my village. It was run by a missionary from England."

The Preacher went dangerously quiet.

"A *nasrani*. An infidel. A *kuffar*. And from him you also learned to love the West?"

"No, sir. Just the opposite. It taught me to hate them for the centuries of misery they have inflicted on our people and to study only the words and the life of our prophet Muhammad, may he rest in peace."

The Preacher considered this and smiled at last.

"So we have a young man"—he was clearly speaking to his Somali secretary—"who is honest enough not to take money, compassionate enough to fulfill the wish of a dying man and wishes to serve only the Prophet. And who speaks Somali, Arabic and some English. What do you think, Jamma?"

The secretary fell into the trap. Seeking to please, he agreed their discovery was fortunate indeed. But the Preacher had a problem. He had lost his computer expert, and the man who brought him his downloaded messages from London, while never revealing that he himself was in Marka, not Kismayo. Only Jamma could replace him in Kismayo; the rest were not computer literate.

That left him short a secretary but facing a young man who was literate, spoke three languages apart from his Ogaden dialect and sought work.

The Preacher had survived for ten years on the basis of a caution bordering on paranoia. He had seen most of his contemporaries from Lashkar-e-Taiba, the 313 Brigade, the Khorosan executioners, the Haqqani clan and al-Qaeda in the Arabian Peninsula, the Yemen group, traced, tracked down, targeted, wiped out. More than half of these had been betrayed.

He had shunned cameras as the plague, changed residence constantly, altered his name, hid his face, masked his eyes. And stayed alive.

He would tolerate in his personal entourage only those he was convinced he could trust. His four Pakistani bodyguards would die for him but had no brains. Jamma was clever, but he needed him now to oversee the two computers in Kismayo.

The new arrival pleased him. There was proof of his honesty, his truthfulness. If he took him into his employ, he could be monitored night and day. He would communicate with no one. And he needed a personal secretary. The idea that the young man facing him was a Jew and a spy was inconceivable. He decided to take the risk.

"Would you like to become my secretary?" he asked gently. There was a gasp of dismay from Jamma.

"It would be a privilege beyond words, sir. I would serve you faithfully, *inshallah*."

The orders were given. Jamma was to take one of the pickups in the compound and drive to Kismayo to take over the managership of the Masala warehouse and the Preacher's sermon-broadcasting computer.

Opal would take over Jamma's room and learn his duties. An hour later, he pulled on the bright red baseball cap with the New York logo on it that he had been given by the wrecked truck. It had belonged to the Israeli skipper of the fishing boat who had had to give it up when fresh orders came through from Tel Aviv.

Out in the courtyard, he wheeled his trail bike over to the decrepit shed in the wall to store it out of the sun. Halfway across, he stopped and looked up. Then he slowly nodded and walked on.

In a buried control room outside Tampa, the figure far below the circling Global Hawk was seen and noted. An alert call was made and the image patched through to a room in the U.S. embassy in London.

The Tracker looked at the slim figure in dishdash and red cap, staring at the sky in faraway Marka.

"Well done, kid," he murmured. Agent Opal was inside the fortress and had just confirmed all Tracker needed to know.

The last killer neither stacked shelves nor served on a garage forecourt. He was a Syrian by birth, well educated and with a diploma in dental studies, and he worked as assistant to a successful orthodontist on the outskirts of Fairfax, Virginia. His name was Tariq Hussein.

He was neither refugee nor student when he arrived from Aleppo ten years earlier but a legal immigrant who had passed all the tests for legitimate entry. It was never established whether he bore with him, that far back, the raging hatred for the West in general and America in particular that his writings revealed when his neat suburban bungalow was raided by the Virginia state police and the FBI or whether he developed it during his residence.

His passport revealed three journeys back to the Middle East during that decade, and it was speculated he may have become "infected" with his rage and loathing during those visits. His diary and his laptop disclosed some of the answers but not all.

His employers, neighbors and social circle were all intensively questioned, but it seemed he had fooled them all. Behind his polite, smiling exterior, he was a dedicated Salafist, subscribing to the meanest and harshest brand of Jihadism. In his writings, his contempt and loathing of American society emerged from every line.

Like other Salafists, he saw no need to wear traditional Muslim robes nor grow a beard nor pause for the five daily prayers. He was clean-shaven daily, with neat, short black hair. Living alone in his detached suburban bungalow, he nevertheless socialized with work colleagues and others. With the American love of friendly-sounding diminutives for first names, he was Terry Hussein.

Among these friends at the local bar, he could explain his teetotalism as a desire to "keep in shape," and this was accepted. His refusal to touch pork or sit at a table where it was being consumed was not even noticed.

Because he was single, a number of girls made eyes at him, but his rebuffs were always polite and gentle. There were one or two gay men who frequented the neighborhood bar, and he was asked once or twice whether he was one of them. He remained polite as he denied it, simply saying he was waiting for Miss Right.

His diary made plain he believed gay men should be stoned to death as slowly as possible, and the thought of lying beside some fat, white pig-eating infidel cow filled him with revulsion.

It was not the teaching of the Preacher that created his rage and hatred, but it channeled it. His laptop showed he had followed the Preacher avidly for two years but never betrayed himself by joining the fan base, though he longed to contribute. Finally, he decided to follow the Preacher's urging: to perfect his adoration of Allah and His prophet by the act of supreme sacrifice, and go to join them in paradise eternal.

But also to take with him as many Americans as he could and die a *shahid*, a martyr, at the hands of their infidel police. For this, he would need a gun.

He already had a Virginia driver's license, the principal photo ID, but it was in the name of Hussein. Given the media coverage that several assassinations that spring and summer had already generated, he thought the name might be a problem.

Staring at his face in the mirror, he realized that with black hair, dark eyes and a swarthy skin, he looked as if he might have come from the Middle East. The surname would prove it.

But one of his coworkers in the laboratory was similar in appearance and he was of Hispanic origin. Tariq Hussein determined to secure a driver's license in a more Spanish-sounding name and began to scour the Internet.

He was surprised by the simplicity. He did not even have to present himself in person nor write a letter. He simply applied online in the name of Miguel "Mickey" Hernandez, up from New Mexico. There was a fee, of course: seventy-nine dollars to Global Intelligence ID Card Solutions, plus fifty-five-dollar express delivery charge. The Virginia license to replace his "lost" one came in the mail.

But his principal research online had been for the right gun. He spent hours poring over the thousands of pages concerning guns and gun magazines. He knew more or less what he wanted and what he needed it to do. He just sought advice on which gun to buy.

He dawdled over the Bushmaster, used at Sandy Hook, but discarded it due to its lightweight 5.6mm bullets. He wanted something heavier and more penetrating. He finally settled on the Heckler & Koch G3, a variant of the A4 military assault rifle, using standard NATO ordnance of 7.62mm, which, he was assured, would tear through tinplate without shredding.

The online research engine informed him he would be unlikely to secure the fully automatic version under U.S. law, but the semiautomatic version would suit his purpose. It would fire a round for every time the trigger was squeezed—fast enough for what he had in mind.

If he was surprised at the ease of obtaining a driver's license, he was bewildered by the simplicity of buying a rifle. He went to a gun show at the Prince William County Fairgrounds at Manassas, hardly an hour away and still in Virginia.

He wandered in some perplexity through the sales halls, offering an array of lethal weaponry sufficient to start several wars. Finally, he found the HK G3. On production of his driver's license, the beefy salesman was delighted to sell him the "hunting rifle" for cash dollars. He just walked out with it and loaded it into the trunk of his car. No one raised an eyebrow.

The ammunition for the twenty-round magazine was just as easy, but from a gun shop in Falls Church. He bought a hundred rounds, an extra magazine and a magazine clamp, to clip the two mags together and give him forty rounds without the need to reload. When he had all he needed, he drove quietly back to his small house and prepared to die.

It was on the third afternoon that al-Afrit came to visit his new prize. From the bridge of the *Malmö*, Capt. Eklund saw the larger fishing dhow when it was already halfway between the shore and the ship. His binoculars picked out the suit of Mr. Abdi, beside a white-robed figure, under an awning amidships.

Jimali and his fellow pirates had been replaced by another dozen youths, who were indulging in a Somali practice the Swedish mariner had never seen before. When they boarded, the new guard crew brought with them large bundles of green leaves, not sprigs but bushes of them. This was their *khat*, which they were chewing steadily. Stig Eklund noticed that by sundown they were high on it. Then they varied between somnolent and easily angered.

When the Somali standing beside him followed his eye-line and spotted the dhow, he sobered up fast, ran down the companionway to the deck and shouted to his companions, lounging under the awning.

The old clan chief climbed the aluminum ladder to the deck, straightened and looked around him. Capt. Eklund had his cap on and saluted. Better safe than sorry, he thought. Mr. Abdi, who had been brought along as interpreter, made the introductions.

Al-Afrit had a lined and almost coal black face beneath his headdress, but his legendary cruelty showed in his mouth. In London, Gareth Evans had been tempted to warn Capt. Eklund but could not know who might be standing beside him. Mr. Abdi had also said nothing. So the captain was unsure exactly whose prisoner he was.

With Abdi tagging along to interpret, they toured the bridge and officers' wardroom. Then al-Afrit ordered that all the foreigners line up on the deck. He walked slowly down the line, ignoring the ten Filipinos but staring at the five Europeans.

His gaze lingered for a long while on the nineteen-year-old cadet, Ove Carlsson, neat in white tropical ducks. Through Abdi, he ordered the youth to take his cap off. He stared at the pale blue eyes, then reached up and fondled the corn blond hair. Carlsson blanched and pulled away. The Somali looked angry but took his hand away.

As the party left the deck for the ladder, al-Afrit finally uttered a stream of Somali. Four of the guards he had brought with him jumped forward, seized the cadet and hustled him to the ground.

Captain Eklund rushed out of the line to protest. Abdi grabbed his arm.

"Do nothing," he hissed. "It is all right, I am sure it will be all right. I know this man. Do not anger him."

The cadet was forced down the ladder into more waiting hands in the dhow.

"Captain, help me," he shouted.

Captain Eklund rounded on Abdi, the last man off his ship. He was red-faced with rage.

"I hold you responsible for this lad's safety," he snapped. "This is not civilized."

Abdi, with his legs already on the ladder, was pale with distress.

"I will intervene with the Sheikh," he said.

"I am going to inform London," said the captain.

"I cannot permit that, Captain Eklund. It is about our negotiations. They are very delicate. Let me handle this."

Then he was gone. On the way back across the swell to the beach, he sat in silence and cursed the old devil at his side. If he thought snatching the cadet would put pressure on London to raise the ransom price, he would ruin everything. He was the negotiator; he knew what he was doing. That apart, he feared for the boy. Al-Afrit had a reputation with the prisoners.

T hat evening, the Tracker called Ariel in his Centerville attic.

"You recall the short film I left with you."

"Yes, Colonel Jackson."

"I want you to screen it on the Jihadist Internet channel, the one the Preacher always uses."

It went worldwide an hour later. The Preacher sat in his usual chair, talking directly into the camcorder and thus to the Muslim world. With an hour of preannouncements, the entire fan base would be listening, plus millions who were not converted to extremism but were interested, and every counterterrorist agency in the world.

They were all surprised, then riveted. The figure they saw was a hard-looking man in his early to mid-thirties, but this time he wore no covering drawn from his headdress over his lower face. He had a full black beard, and his eyes were of a strange amber hue.

Only one man watching knew that the eyes were contact lenses and that the speaker was Tony Suárez, who lived in Malibu and could not comprehend a word of the Koranic inscriptions on the sheet behind him.

The voice was accent-perfect, the tones of the British mimic who had listened to only two hours of previous sermons before producing an identical replication of the voice. And the screening was in color, not black and white. But to the faithful, it was undoubtedly the Preacher.

"My friends, brothers and sisters in Allah, I have been missing from your lives for some time. But I have not wasted my time. I have been reading, and studying our beautiful faith, Islam, and contemplating many things. And I have changed, *inshallah*.

"I wonder how many of you have heard of the Muraja'at, the Revisions of the Salafist-Jihadist cause. These are what I have been studying.

"Many times in the past, I have urged upon you all to dedicate yourselves not simply to worship of Allah, may His name be praised, but also to hatred of others. But the Revisions teach us that this is wrong, that our beautiful Islam is truly not a creed of bitterness and hatred, even of those who think differently from us.

"The most famous of the Revisions are those of the Series for the Corrections of Concepts. Just as those who taught us hatred came out of Egypt, so also did the al-Gama'a al-Islamiyyas, who wrote the Corrections, and I now understand that it was they, not the teachers of bigotry and loathing, who were right."

The Tracker's phone in the embassy room rang. It was Gray Fox from Virginia.

"Am I hearing correctly or has something very weird happened?" he asked.

"Listen a while longer," said the Tracker, and hung up.

On the screen, the uncomprehending Tony Suárez carried on.

"I have read the Revisions now a score of times in English translation, which I recommend to you all who speak and read no Arabic and to those who do in the original tongue.

"For it is clear to me now that what our brothers the al-Gama'a say is true. The governmental system known as democracy is perfectly compatible with True Islam, and it is hatred and lust for blood that is alien to every word ever spoken by the Prophet Muhammad, may he rest in peace.

"Those who now claim to be the True Believers and who call for mass murder, cruelty, torture and the death of thousands are in truth like the Kharijite rebels who fought against the Prophet's Companions.

"We must now consider all Jihadists and Salafists like those Kharijites, and we who worship only the one true Allah and His blessed prophet Muhammad must destroy the heretics who have led His people astray these many years.

"And we True Believers must surely destroy these advocates of hatred and violence as the Companions once destroyed the Kharijites long ago.

"But now is my time come to declare who I really am. I was born Zulfiqar Ali Shah, in Islamabad, and raised as a good Muslim. But I fell and became Abu Azzam, a killer of men, women and children."

The phone rang again.

"Who the hell is this?" yelled Gray Fox.

"Hear him out," said the Tracker. "It's almost over."

"So, before the world, and especially before you, my brothers and sisters in Allah, I pronounce my *tawba*, my true repentance, for all that I have done and said in a false cause. And I declare my complete *bara'a*, my disavowal, of all that I said and preached against the true teachings of Allah the Merciful, the Compassionate.

"For I showed no mercy and no compassion, and must now beg you to show me that mercy, that compassion, which the Holy Koran teaches us may be extended to the sinner who truly repents his former sinful ways. May Allah bless you and be with you all."

The screen faded. The phone rang again. In fact, phones were ringing right across the *umma*, the world community of Islam, many of them to give vent to screams of rage.

"Tracker, what the hell have you done?" asked Gray Fox.

"I hope I have just destroyed him," said the Tracker.

He recalled what the wise old scholar at al-Azhar University had told him years ago when he was a student in Cairo: "The merchants of hatred have four levels of loathing. You may think you Christians are at the top level. Wrong, for you are also believers in the one true God and thus, with the Jews, also People of the Book.

"Above you come the atheists and idolaters, who have no god but only carved idols. That is why the Mujahideen of Afghanistan hated the communists more than you. They are atheists.

"But above even them, for the fanatics, come the moderate Muslims, who do not follow them, and that is why they seek to topple every Western-friendly Muslim government by exploding bombs in their marketplaces and killing fellow Muslims who have done no harm.

"But highest of all, a dog among the unforgivables, is the apostate, the one who abandons or denounces Jihadism, then recants and returns to the faith of his fathers. For him, forgiveness is out of the question and only death awaits."

And then he poured the tea and prayed.

M r. Abdi sat alone in his suite, a bedroom and office, in the fort behind Garacad, his knuckles white on the tabletop. The two-foot walls were soundproof but not the doors, and he could hear the sounds of the whipping down the corridor. He wondered which wretched servant had incurred the displeasure of his host.

There was no disguising the crack as the instrument of torture, probably a semirigid camel crop, rose and fell, nor did the rough timber doors mask the shrill screams following each lash.

Ali Abdi was not a brutal man, and although he was aware

of the distress of the mariners imprisoned in their anchored vessels out under the sun and would not be hurried if extra money could be extracted by delaying, he saw no reason for maltreatment—even of Somali servants. He was beginning to regret ever agreeing to negotiate for this pirate commander. The man was a brute.

He went ashen white when, in a pause in the flogging, the victim pleaded for mercy. He was speaking in Swedish.

The reaction of the Preacher to the broadcast worldwide of the devastating words of Tony Suárez was almost hysterical.

As he had not given a sermon online for three weeks, he was not watching the Jihadist post when it broadcast. He was alerted by one of his Pakistani bodyguards who spoke a smattering of English. He heard the end of it in stunned disbelief, then replayed it from the start.

He sat in front of his desktop computer and watched in horror. It was phoney—of course it was phony—but it was convincing. The likeness was uncanny, the beard, the face, the dress, the backcloth, even the eyes—he was looking at his own doppelgänger. And his voice.

But that was nothing compared to the words; the formal recantation was a death sentence. It would take many weeks to persuade the faithful that they had been deceived by a clever fraud. From outside the study, his servants could hear him screaming at the figure on the screen, that the *tawba* was a lie, his recantation a foul untruth.

When the face of the faraway American actor faded, he

sat, drained, for almost an hour. Then he made his mistake. Desperate to be believed by someone at least, he contacted his one true friend, his ally in London. By e-mail.

Cheltenham was listening, and Fort Meade. And a silent Marine colonel in an office in the U.S. embassy in London. And Gray Fox in Virginia, who had the Tracker's request on his desk. The Preacher might be destroyed now, Tracker had told him. But it was not enough. He had too much blood on his hands. Now he had to be killed, and he had laid out several options. Gray Fox would take it to the commander of J-SOC, personally, and he was confident it would go for discussion and judgment right up to the Oval Office. He didn't know what that judgment would be, however.

Within minutes of the e-mail out of Marka, the exact text and the precise location of each computer and the owner of each computer were proven genuine. The placing of the Preacher was completely beyond doubt, the complicity at every level of Mustafa Dardari the same.

Gray Fox was able to get back to the Tracker within twenty-four hours, on the secure line from TOSA to the embassy. The news was not good.

"I tried, Tracker, but the answer is no. There is a presidential veto on missiles on that compound. It's partly the dense civilian population all around it and partly the presence of Opal inside it."

"And the other proposal?"

"No to both. There will be no beach landing from the sea. Now that the al-Shabaab have reinfested Marka, we do not know how many there are or how well armed they are. The senior brass reckon he could slip away into that labyrinth of alleys and we'd lose him forever.

"And the same applies to a heli-borne drop on the roof, bin Laden style. Not the Rangers, not the SEALs, not even the Night Stalkers. It's too far from Djibouti and Kenya, too public in Mogadishu. And there is the danger of a shoot-down. The words 'Black Hawk Down' still cause nightmares.

"Sorry, Tracker. A great job. You've identified him, located him, discredited him. But I guess it's over. The bastard's inside Marka and unlikely to come out, unless you can find one helluva bait. And there's the problem of Opal. I guess you had better pack up and come home."

"He's not dead yet, Gray Fox. He has an ocean of blood on his hands. He may not preach anymore, but he is still a dangerous bastard. He could move west to Mali. Let me finish the job."

There was silence on the line. Then Gray Fox came back.

"OK, Tracker. One more week. Then you pack your kit."

As he replaced the phone, the Tracker realized he had miscalculated. In destroying the credibility of the Preacher throughout the entire world of Islamist fundamentalism, he had intended to force his target out of his bolt-hole and into the open. He wanted him on the run from his own people, devoid of cover, a refugee again. He had never intended his own superiors to call him off the chase.

He found himself facing a crisis of conscience. However he might vote as a citizen, as an officer and a U.S. Marine to boot, his commander in chief had his total loyalty. And that meant his obedience. Yet this he could not obey.

He had been given an assignment. It was not over. He had been tasked with a mission. It was not accomplished. And it had changed. It was now a personal vendetta. He owed a debt to a much-loved old man lying on a bed in an ICU ward in Virginia Beach and he intended to discharge it.

For the first time since cadet school, he contemplated resignation from the Corps. His career was saved a few days later by a dental technician he had never heard of.

Al-Afrit retained his horror picture for two days, but when it suddenly flashed up on the screen in the operations center at Chauncey Reynolds, it caused stunned shock. Gareth Evans had been talking to Mr. Abdi. The issues, of course, were ransom money and timescale.

Abdi had come down from twenty-five million dollars to twenty million, but the time was dragging—for the Europeans. It had been a week, to the Somalis a chronological fleabite. Al-Afrit was demanding all the money and he wanted it now. Abdi had explained that the Swedish owner would not contemplate twenty million. Evans was privately of the view that they would finally settle at about five million.

Then al-Afrit took over and sent his picture. By chance, Reynolds was also in the office, and Harry Andersson, who had been advised to fly home and wait in Stockholm. The picture made the three men sick and silent.

The cadet was held facedown over a rough wooden table by a big Somali, who had his wrists. His ankles were apart, each lashed to a table leg. His trousers and undershorts were missing.

His buttocks had been caned to a bloody mess. His face, turned sideways against the timber, was clearly screaming.

The reaction of Evans and Reynolds was to realize they were dealing with a sadistic madman. Nothing like this had ever happened before. The reaction of Harry Andersson was more extreme. He uttered a cry close to a scream and rushed to the bathroom. The others heard the retching as he knelt with his head over the pan. When he returned, his face was ashen save for two red patches, one on each cheek.

"That boy is my son!" he shouted. "My son!" He grabbed Gareth Evans by the lapels and hauled him out of his chair until they were face-to-face, inches apart.

"You get my son back, Gareth Evans, you get him back. Pay the swine what they want. Anything, you hear? You tell them, I pay fifty million dollars for my boy, you tell them."

He stormed out, leaving the two Britishers pale and shaken and the hideous picture still on the screen.

11

On the morning of his martyrdom, Tariq "Terry" Hussein rose long before dawn. Behind closed curtains, he purified his body according to the ancient rituals, seated himself in front of the bedsheet draped on the bedroom wall with the appropriate Koranic passages, switched on his camcorder and recorded his final words to the world. Then he logged on to the Jihadi channel and sent his message worldwide. Before the authorities noticed it, it would be far too late.

He drove through a lovely summer dawn to join the first of the morning's commuters, some coming from Maryland into Virginia, some going the opposite way, and many heading into the District of Columbia. He was in no hurry, but he wanted to time himself right.

To park in the nearside lane of a major commuter traffic artery could not be sustained for long. To be too early would mean that blocked commuters behind the stalled car would hammer their horns and attract attention. A state police car could well be summoned by one of the circling helicopters. It would have trouble penetrating the logjam but would duly arrive with two armed officers onboard. That was what Hussein intended, but not prematurely.

To be too late could mean the targets he had in mind might have passed by and he could not wait long for the next one. Just after ten past seven, he arrived at Key Bridge.

There are eight arches to this Washington landmark: five span the Potomac River, separating Virginia from Georgetown in D.C., two more on the Washington side cross the C&O Canal and K Street, and the eighth, on the Virginia side, spans the George Washington Memorial Parkway, another constantly in use commuter route.

Hussein, on U.S. Route 29, approached the bridge, hugging the nearside lane of the six-lane highway. At the center point above the GW Memorial, he broke down. His compact slowed to a halt. At once, angry cars behind began to swerve past him. He got out, went to the rear and opened the trunk. From it, he took two red "broken down" triangles and placed them on the road.

He opened both doors on the passenger side to create a small box between the car and the parapet. Reaching in, he withdrew the rifle, fully loaded with forty rounds in two switchover magazines, leaned over the parapet and squinted through the scope sight at the columns of steel passing beneath. If anyone coming up behind him could see what a man between the two open doors was doing, either they did not believe what they were seeing or they were too busy wrestling with their steering wheels and craning over their shoulders to avoid being rammed as they pulled out.

At that hour, a quarter after seven, almost every tenth vehicle below the bridge is a commuter bus. The D.C. Metro service runs several of them, some colored blue, some orange. The orange ones are on the 23C route, which runs from the Rosslyn Metro station right through to Langley, Virginia, where it terminates at the gates of the huge complex known simply as the CIA, or the Agency.

The traffic below the bridge was not logjammed, but it was moving sedately, nose to tail. Tariq Hussein's Internet research had told him which bus to look for and he had almost given up hope when he saw an orange roof in the distance. A helicopter wheeled and turned far out over the river. It would see the stalled vehicle in the middle of the bridge at any moment. He willed the orange bus to come closer.

The first four bullets, straight through the windshield, killed the driver. The coach swerved, hit a car alongside, stalled and stopped. There was a figure in a Metro service uniform slumped over the wheel quite dead. Reactions began.

Down below, the sideswiped car also stopped. The driver climbed out and began to harangue the bus that had hit him. Then he noticed the slumped driver, presumed a heart attack and produced his cell phone.

Horns behind the two stalled vehicles began to hoot. Some drivers also climbed out. One glanced upward, saw the figure on the parapet and yelled in alarm. The helicopter wheeled over Arlington and turned toward the Key Bridge. Hussein fired over and over again through the roof of the stationary bus. After twenty rounds, the firing pin met an empty chamber. He detached the magazine, reversed it and inserted the spare. Then he resumed firing.

Below him there was chaos. Word had spread. Drivers were leaping out of their cars to crouch behind them. Two at least were shouting into their cell phones.

On the bridge, two women back down the line were screaming. The roof of the 23C service bus was being torn apart. The interior was becoming a charnel house of blood, bodies and hysterical humanity. Then the second magazine ran out.

It was not the rifleman in the helicopter who brought closure but an off-duty patrolman ten cars down the line on Route 29 behind the stalled car. He had his window open to let the cigarette smoke out lest his wife later detected the odor. He heard the shots and recognized the crack of a high-powered rifle. He got out, unholstered his service automatic and started running, not away from the shots but toward them.

The first Tariq Hussein knew of him was when the window of the open door beside him shattered. He turned, saw the running man and raised his rifle. It was empty. The running officer could not know that. At twenty feet, he stopped, crouched, took the double-handed position and emptied his magazine into the door and the man behind it.

It was later established that three rounds hit the gunman and they were enough. When the officer reached the car, the gunman was on the verge of the road, gasping feebly. He died thirty seconds later.

For most of that day, there was chaos on Route 29, closed as forensic teams took away the body, the gun and finally the car. But it was nothing as to what was happening on the GW Memorial Parkway beneath.

The interior of the Rosslyn-to-Langley commuter coach was a butcher's shop. Later, figures released to the public told of seven dead, nine critically injured, with five major amputations and twenty flesh wounds, all inside the bus, there had simply been no cover from above.

At Langley, the shock among the thousands of staffers when the news came through was like a declaration of war— but from an enemy already dead.

The Virginia state police and the FBI wasted no time. The killer's car was easily traced through the vehicle-licensing bureau. SWAT teams raided the house outside Fairfax. It was empty, but forensic teams, muffled in their overalls, stripped it to the plasterwork—and then to the foundations.

Within twenty-four hours, the net of interrogators had spread far and wide. Counterterrorism experts pored over the laptop and the diary. The death declaration was played to rooms of silent men and women in the FBI's Hoover Building, with copies to the CIA.

Not everyone on the stricken bus worked for the Agency, since the bus served other stops. But most went to the end of the line—Langley/McLean.

Before sundown, the Director of the CIA exercised his prerogative and secured a private interview with the President in the Oval Office. Staffers in the corridors said he was still pale with anger.

I t is very rare for spymasters in one country to have any regard for their opponents among the enemy, but it happens. During the Cold War, many in the West had a grudging regard for the man who ran East Germany's spy service.

Markus "Misha" Wolf had a small budget and a big enemy—Germany and NATO. He did not even bother trying to traduce the cabinet ministers in the service of Bonn. He targeted those dowdy, scuttling, invisible mice in the offices of the high and mighty without whom no office can run: the confidential private secretaries to the ministers.

He studied their drab, spinsterly and often lonely private lives and targeted them with young, handsome lovers. These Romeos would start slow and patient, moving to warm embraces in chilly lives, promises of companionship for life in sunny places after retirement, and all just for a glance at those silly papers forever passing across the minister's desk.

And they did, those Ingrids and Waltrauds. They passed over the copies of everything confidential and classified that were left unattended when the minister stalked out to his four-course lunch. It reached a point where the Bonn government was so penetrated that the NATO allies did not dare tell Bonn what day of the week it was because within a day the information would go to East Berlin and then Moscow.

Eventually, the police would come, the Romeo would vanish and the office mouse, shrunken and in tears, would appear fleetingly between two hulking cops. Then she would exchange a lonely little flat for a lonely little cell in prison.

He was a ruthless bastard, was Misha Wolf, but after the

collapse of East Germany, he retired in obscurity, never charged with anything, and died in his bed of natural causes.

Forty years later, the British SIS would have loved to eavesdrop on what was said and done in the offices of Chauncey Reynolds, but Julian Reynolds regularly had his entire suite swept by a high-grade team of electronic wizards, some of them actually retired from government service.

So the Firm did not have state-of-the-art technology secreted in the private office of Gareth Evans that summer, but they did have Emily Bulstrode. She saw everything, read everything and heard everything, and no one noticed her with her tray of cups.

The day Harry Andersson screamed into the face of Gareth Evans, Mrs. Bulstrode bought her usual sandwich at the deli on the corner and went to her favorite telephone booth. She did not like those modern things that people kept in their pockets, always going off in conferences. She preferred to visit one of the few remaining red-painted, cast-iron kiosks where you put coins in a meter. She asked for a connection, spoke a few words and went back to her desk.

After work, she went on foot to St. James's Park, sat on the assigned bench and fed the ducks some crusts she had saved from her sandwich as she waited for her contact. Back in the day, she mused, her beloved Charlie had been the man in Moscow who every day went to Gorki Park and picked up top secret microfilm from the Soviet traitor Oleg Penkovsky. These state secrets, relayed to the desk of President Kennedy, enabled him to outwit Nikita Khrushchev and get those damn rockets removed from Cuba in the autumn of 1962.

A young man approached and sat down beside her.

The usual exchange of harmless chitchat assured true identity. She glanced at him and smiled. A youngster, she thought, probably a probationer, not even born when she used to slip through the Iron Curtain into East Germany for the Firm.

The young man pretended to read the *Evening Standard*. He took no notes because he had a recorder active but silent in his jacket pocket. Emily Bulstrode also had no notes; she had her two assets, a totally harmless air and a steel-trap memory.

So she told the probationer everything that had happened that morning in the law offices, detail by detail and word for word. Verbatim. Then she rose and walked to the station to catch her commuter train for her little house in Coulsdon. She sat alone, watching the southern suburbs drift by. Once she had dodged the dreadful Stasis; now she was seventy-five and made coffee for lawyers.

The young man from Vauxhall Cross went back in the dusk and filed his report. He noticed there was a flag attached, to the effect that the Chief had agreed that news concerning Somalia should be shared with the Cousins up at the U.S. embassy. He could not see what a brutal warlord in Garacad could have to do with a hunt for the Preacher, but a standing order is still a standing order, so he filed a copy for the CIA.

In his safe house half a mile from the embassy, the Tracker was almost finished packing when his BlackBerry throbbed discreetly. He looked at the message, scrolled down until the end, switched off and thought for a while. Then he unpacked. A benign deity had just given him his bait.

G areth Evans called a conference with Mr. Ali Abdi the next morning. The Somali, when he came on, was subdued.

"Mr. Abdi, my friend, I have always taken you for a civilized man," he began.

"I am, Mr. Evans, I am," said the negotiator in Garacad. Evans could tell his voice was tight with distress. He believed it was probably genuine. Of course, one could never tell one hundred percent. After all, Abdi and al-Afrit were of the same tribe, the Habar Gidir, or Abdi, would not have been trusted as a negotiator.

Evans recalled the advice he had been given years before when he was in Customs and Excise and had been posted in the Horn of Africa. His tutor was an old, parchment-skinned colonial *wallah* with eyes yellowed by malaria. The Somali, he was told, had six priorities, which never varied.

At the top was Self. Then came Family, then Clan, then Tribe. At the bottom were Nation, then Religion. The last two were only invoked to fight the foreigner. Left to themselves, they would simply fight each other, constantly shifting alliances and loyalties according to perceived advantage and waging vendetta according to perceived grievance.

The last thing he told the young Gareth Evans before he blew his brains out when the Colonial Service threatened to retire him back to rainy England was: "You cannot purchase the loyalty of a Somali, but you can usually rent it."

The idea at the back of Gareth Evans's mind that late-summer morning in Mayfair was to see whether Ali Abdi's loyalty to his fellow tribesman exceeded that of loyalty to himself.

"What has happened to one of the prisoners of your principal was disgraceful, unacceptable. It could derail our entire negotiation. And I must tell you I was so pleased before that that the matter was between you and me, because I believe we are both honorable men."

"I believe so, too, Mr. Gareth."

Evans could not know how secure the line was. He was not thinking of Fort Meade and Cheltenham—he knew that was a foregone conclusion—but whether any of the warlord's servants, listening in, was fluent in English. Nevertheless, he had to gamble on Abdi understanding even a single word.

"Because, you see, my friend, I think we may have reached the point of Thuraya."

There was a long pause. Evans's gamble was that if any other less educated Somali was listening in, he would not know what that was but that Abdi would.

Eventually, Abdi came back.

"I think I see what you mean, Mr. Gareth."

The Thuraya phone is a satellite-employing communicator. Four cell phone companies control the use of mobiles in Somalia, the others being NationLink, Hormud, and France Télécom. They all have masts. The Thuraya needs only the U.S. satellites, turning slowly in space.

What Evans was saying to Abdi was that if he had, or could get, a Thuraya phone, he should take a ride into the desert alone and, from behind a rock, call Evans so they could talk extremely privately. The reply indicated Abdi had understood and would try.

The two negotiators spun out another thirty minutes, bringing the ransom down to eighteen million dollars and each promising to be back in touch when they had consulted with their respective principals.

The lunch was on the American government; the Tracker had insisted on it. But his SIS contact, Adrian Herbert, had made the booking. He had chosen Shepherd's in Marsham Street and insisted on a booth for privacy.

It was affable, friendly, but both men realized the point of it all would come over coffee and mints. When the American made his pitch, Herbert put the coffee down in surprise.

"What do you mean lift?"

"Lift, as in abstract, pluck, sequester."

"You mean kidnap. From the streets of London? Without warrant or charge?"

"He is assisting a known terrorist who has motivated four murders in your country, Adrian."

"Yes, but a forcible snatch would create absolute havoc if it ever got out. We would need an authority to do it, and that would need the signature of the Home Secretary. She'd consult lawyers. They would demand a formal charge."

"You have helped us with extraordinary renditions before, Adrian."

"Yes, but they were snatched on the streets of places that were already completely lawless. Knightsbridge is not Karachi, you know. Dardari is, on the surface, a respectable businessman."

"You and I know different."

"Indeed we do. But only because we invaded his house, bugged his home and raped his computer. That would look wonderful coming out in open court. I'm sorry, Tracker, we try to be helpful, but that is as far as we can go."

He thought for a while, staring at the ceiling.

"No, it's just not on, old boy. We would have to work like Trojans to get permission for that sort of thing."

They settled up, and went different ways on the pavement. Adrian Herbert would walk back to the Office at Vauxhall. The Tracker hailed a cab. Sitting in the back, he mulled over that last sentence.

What on earth had classical allusions got to do with it? Back at his house, he consulted the Internet. It took a while but it was there. Trojan Horse Outcomes, a small, niche security company based outside Hamworthy in Dorset.

That, he knew, was Royal Marine territory. Their big base was at nearby Poole, and many men who had spent a working life in Special Forces retired and settled down near their old bases. Often they got a few mates together and formed a private security company—the usual rigmarole: bodyguards, asset protection, close escort work. If backer money was tight, they would work from home. Further research showed Trojan Outcomes was based in a residential district.

The Tracker called the given number and made an appointment for the next morning. Then he rang a Mayfair carhire company and booked a compact for three hours earlier. He explained he was an American tourist called Jackson, with a valid U.S. driver's license, and would need the car for a day to visit with a friend on the South Coast.

As he hung up, his BlackBerry pulsed. It was a text from

TOSA, secure from interception. Its identifier proclaimed it came from Gray Fox. What it could not reveal was that the four-star general commanding J-SOC had just left the Oval Office with fresh orders.

Gray Fox did not waste time. His message needed only four words. It said "The Preacher. No prisoners."

Gareth Evans had virtually taken up residence in the law offices. A truckle bed had been moved into the operations room. His bathroom had a shower, lavatory and basin. Cooked takeaways and salads from the corner deli provided sustenance. He had abandoned the usual procedure of conferences at fixed times with his opposite number in Somalia. He wanted to be in the ops room if Abdi followed his advice and rang from the desert. He might not have long unobserved. And just before midday the phone rang. It was Abdi.

"Mr. Evans? It is me. I have found a sat phone. But I do not have long."

"Then let us keep it short, my friend. What your principal did to the boy indicates to us one thing: He wants to pressure us to settle quickly. That is not usual. Normally, it is the Somalis who have all the time in the world. This time both parties are interested in a speedy conclusion. Not so?"

"Yes, I think so," said the voice from the desert.

"My principal takes the same view. But not because of the cadet. That was blackmail, but too crude to work. My principal wants his ship back at work. The key is the final release price and in this your advice to your principal will be crucial."

Evans knew it would be suicidal if he let slip that the boy was worth ten times the ship and cargo.

"What do you propose, Mr. Evans?"

"A final settlement at five million dollars. We both know that is very fair. We would probably have settled on that figure three months from now anyway. I think you know that."

Mr. Abdi, his phone to his ear, crouching in the desert a mile from the fortress behind Garacad, agreed, but said nothing. He sensed there was something coming for himself.

"What I propose is this. On five million, your share would be about one million. My offer is to pay that million into your private numbered account right now. A second million when the ship sails. No one need know anything about this but you and me. The key is a rapid conclusion. That is what I hope I am buying."

Abdi thought. The third million would still come from al-Afrit. Three times his usual fee. And he had other thoughts. This was a situation he wanted to get out of, regardless of any other factor.

The days of easy pickings and easy ransoms were over. It had taken a long time for the Western and maritime powers to get their act together, but they were turning much more aggressive.

There had already been two off-the-sea beach assaults by Western commandos. One anchored ship had been liberated by Marines descending on ropes from a hovering helicopter. The Somali guards had fought. Two seamen had died, but so had the Somalis—all but two, and these were now in prison in the Seychelles.

Ali Abdi was not a hero and had not the slightest intention of becoming one. He blanched with horror at the thought of these black-clad monsters with night vision goggles and blazing submachine guns storming the mud-brick fortress where he was presently in residence.

And, finally, he wanted to retire; with a large fortune and a long way from Somalia. Somewhere civilized and above all safe. He spoke into the sat phone.

"You have a deal, Mr. Gareth." And he dictated an account number. "Now I work for you, Mr. Gareth. But understand, I will press for a speedy settlement of five million dollars, but even then we have to look to four weeks."

It had been a fortnight already, thought Evans, but six weeks would be among the shortest on record between capture and release.

"Thank you, my friend. Let us get this dreadful business over with and go back to a civilized life . . ."

He hung up. Far away, Abdi did the same and went back to the fortress. The two men might not have been using the Somali phone network but that mattered not a jot to Fort Meade or Cheltenham who had captured every word.

According to orders, Fort Meade passed the text across the state line to TOSA, who fed a copy to the Tracker in London. A month, he thought. The clock is ticking. He pocketed his BlackBerry as the northern outskirts of Poole hove into view and kept his eyes peeled for a sign for Hamworthy.

T hat's a lot of money, boss."
Trojan Horse Outcomes was clearly a very small operation. The Tracker presumed it had been named after one

of the biggest deceptions in history, but what the man facing him could muster was a lot less than the Greek army.

It was run out of a modest suburban terrace house, and Tracker put the manpower at about two or three. The one facing him across the dining room table was clearly the mainspring, and Tracker put him down as a former Royal Marine and a senior NCO. It turned out he was right on both counts. His name was Brian Weller.

What Weller was referring to was a block of fifty-dollar bills the thickness of a firebrick.

"So what exactly do you want done?"

"I want a man lifted without fuss from the streets of London, taken to a quiet and isolated place, detained there for up to a month and then released back where he came from. No rough stuff—just a nice vacation far from London or any kind of telephone."

Weller thought it over. He had not the slightest doubt the snatch would be illegal, but his philosophy was simple and soldierly. There were good guys and bad guys, and the latter group got away with far too much.

Capital punishment was illegal, but he had two little girls at school, and if any swinish "nonce" interfered with them, he would unhesitatingly send him to another and maybe better world.

"How bad is this customer?"

"He helps terrorists. Quietly, with finances. The one he is helping right now has killed four Brits and seven Americans. A terrorist."

Weller grunted. He had done three tours in Helmand, Afghanistan, and seen some good mates die in front of him.

"Bodyguards?"

"No. Occasionally a rented limousine with a driver. More usually, black cabs right off the street."

"You have a place to take him?"

"Not yet. I will have."

"I would want to make a thorough recce before a decision."

"I'd walk right out of here if you didn't," said the Tracker.

Weller took his eyes off the block of dollars and assessed the American on the other side of the table. Nothing was said. Nothing needed to be. He was convinced the Yank had also seen combat, heard the incoming lead, seen mates go down. He nodded.

"I'll drive up to London. Tomorrow suit, boss?"

Tracker suppressed a smile. He recognized the address, what British Special Forces soldiers called an officer to his face. Behind his back was another matter. Usually Rupert, sometimes worse.

"Tomorrow will suit fine. A thousand dollars for your trouble. Keep the balance if you say yes. Give it back if you walk away."

"And how do you know I will? Give it back?"

The Tracker rose to leave.

"Mr. Weller, I think we both know the rules. We have been round the block a few times."

When he was gone, leaving a rendezvous and time well away from the embassy, Brian Weller went through the firebrick. Twenty-five thousand dollars. Five for outgoings; the Yank would provide the hideaway. He had two girls to educate, a wife to keep, food to put on the table and skills not really marketable at the vicarage tea party.

He made the rendezvous, brought a mate from the same commando unit and spent a week vetting the job. Then he said yes.

Ali Abdi screwed up his courage and went to see al-Afrit. "Things are going well," he reported. "We will secure a fine big ransom for the *Malmö*."

Then he broached another subject.

"The blond boy. If he dies, it will complicate matters, create delays, reduce the ransom."

He did not mention the prospect of European commandos storming ashore on a rescue mission, his personal nightmare. It might just provoke the man he faced.

"Why should he die?" growled the warlord.

Abdi shrugged.

"Who knows? Infection, blood poisoning."

He got his way. There was a doctor in Garacad with at least the knowledge of basic first aid. The cadet's welts were disinfected and bandaged. He was still being kept in the cellars, and there was nothing Abdi could or dared do about that.

That is deer-stalking country," said the man at the sporting agency. "But the stags are coming into rut, so the close of season is not far off."

The Tracker smiled. He was playing the harmless American tourist again.

"Aw, the stags are safe from me. No, I just want to write my book, and for that I need absolute peace and quiet. No phones, no roads, no callers, no interruptions. A nice cabin off the beaten track where I can write the Great American Novel."

The land agent knew a bit about authors. Weird people. He tapped his keyboard again and stared at the screen.

"There is a small stalking lodge on our books," he conceded. "Free until the shooting season starts again."

He rose and went to a wall map. He checked the grid reference and then tapped a pristine section of the map that was unmarked by towns, villages or even roads. A few spidery tracks ran across it, in northern Caithness, the last county of Scotland before the wild Pentland Firth.

"I have some pictures."

He led back to the computer screen and scrolled up a portfolio of pictures. It was a log cabin, all right, set in an endless sea of rolling heather, a huge glen framed by high hills; the sort of place where a city slicker, making a run for it with two Marines after him, might get five hundred yards before collapsing.

It had two bedrooms, a large main room, kitchen and shower room, a huge fireplace and a pile of logs.

"I surely think I have found my Shangri-la," said the tourist/writer. "I have not had time to set up a checking account. Will cash dollars do?"

Cash dollars did very well. Exact directions and keys would be sent within days, but to Hamworthy.

M ustafa Dardari chose not to have a car or drive himself in London. The parking was an abiding nightmare he could well do without. In his part of Knightsbridge, cruising cabs were constant and convenient, if expensive. Not a problem. But for the smart evening out, a black-tie dinner, he used a limousine company; always the same firm and usually the same driver.

He had been dining with friends a mile from his home, and as he made his farewells, he used his mobile to call the driver to come to the portico, where double yellow lines forbade all parking day or night. Around the corner, the driver responded, switched on the engine and touched the accelerator. The car moved a yard before one of the rear tires settled on its rim.

An examination revealed some rogue had slipped a small square of plywood pierced by a needle-sharp steel nail under the tread while the driver dozed at the wheel. The driver rang his client and explained. He would change the tire, but it was a big, heavy limo and would take a while.

As Mr. Dardari stood under the portico with the other guests departing around him, a cab came around the corner, light on. He raised his hand. It swerved toward him. Luck. He climbed aboard and gave his address. And the cab did indeed set off in that direction.

Cabbies in London are required to activate the rear door locks as soon as the client is seated. It prevents passengers from "doing a runner" without paying, but it also stops them being molested by troublemakers trying to climb in beside them. But this fool seemed to have forgotten.

They were barely out of sight of the limousine driver, crouched over his jack, than the cab swerved to the curb, and a burly figure pulled open the door and climbed in. Dardari protested that this cab was taken. But the burly figure slammed the door behind him and said:

"That's right, squire. By me."

The Pakistani tycoon was enveloped in a bear hug by one arm while the other arm jammed a large pad soaked in chloroform over his mouth and nose. In twenty seconds, he had stopped struggling.

The transfer to the minivan was made a mile later, where the third ex-commando was at the wheel. The cab, borrowed from a mate who had taken up cabs for a living, was parked as promised with the keys under the seat.

Two of the men sat behind the driver with their dozing guest propped between them, until they were well clear of north London. Then he was tucked in a single bed behind the seats. Twice he tried to wake up but each time was eased back into slumber.

It was a long drive, but they did it in fourteen hours, guided by a GPS locator and a SatNav guide. It took some pushing and shoving to get the minivan up the last section of track, but they arrived at sundown, and Brian Weller made a phone call. There were no masts up there, but he had brought a sat phone.

The Tracker called Ariel, but on his dedicated and secure line that not even Fort Meade or Cheltenham would be listening to. It was midafternoon in Centerville, Virginia.

"Ariel, you know that computer in London you gutted some time back? Could you now send e-mail messages that appear to be coming from it?"

"Of course, Colonel. I have its access right here."

"And you don't have to leave Virginia, right?"

Ariel was perplexed that anyone alive could be so naïve in the matters of cyberspace. With what he had at his fingertips, he could become Mustafa Dardari, transmitting from Pelham Crescent, London.

"And you recall the code based on fruit and vegetable prices that the user used to send in? Could you encrypt text in the same code?"

"Of course, sir. I broke it, I can re-create it."

"Just the way it was? As if the old user was back at the computer keys?"

"Identical."

"Great. I want you to send a message from the protocol in London to the receiver in Kismayo. Do you have pencil and paper?"

"Do I have what?"

"I know it's old-fashioned, but I want to stick to secure phone, not e-mail, just in case."

There was a pause while Ariel slithered down his ladder and returned with pieces of equipment he barely knew how to use. The Tracker dictated his message.

The message was encrypted in exactly the same code Dardari would have used, then it was sent. As everything from Dardari to Somalia was now taped, it was heard by Fort Meade and Cheltenham and decrypted again.

There were some raised eyebrows at both listening posts, but the orders were to eavesdrop but not interfere. According to standing orders, Fort Meade sent a copy to TOSA, which passed it on to the Tracker, who accepted it with a straight face.

In Kismayo it was not the Troll, now dead, who received it but his replacement, Jamma, the former secretary. He decoded it word by word, using the crib the Troll had left behind. But he was no expert, even if there had been a slip. But there was not. Even the required typos were in place.

Because it is cumbersome to send by e-mail in Urdu or Arabic, Dardari, the Troll and the Preacher had always used English. The new message was in English, which Jamma, a Somali, knew, but not with the same fluency. But he knew enough to know this was important and should be brought to the Preacher without delay.

He was one of the few who knew the Preacher's apparent appearance on the Internet to recant all his teachings was phony because his master had made no broadcasts for over three weeks. But he knew that across the great Muslim diaspora in the West, most of the fan base was disgusted. He had seen the posted comments, hour after hour. But his own loyalty was undimmed. He would make the long and wearisome journey back to Marka with the message from London.

Just as Jamma was convinced he had been listening to Dardari, Fort Meade and Cheltenham were convinced the pickle tycoon was at his desk in London, assisting his friend in Somalia.

The real Dardari was staring miserably out at the driving, early-September rain, while behind him, in front of a roaring fire, three former Marine commandos were having a laughter-filled ramble down memory lane and all the fights they had been in. Curtains of gray cloud swept down across the glen and hurled water onto the roof.

In the blistering heat of Kismayo, the loyal Jamma filled

the petrol tank of the pickup for that night's long haul to Marka.

In London, Gareth Evans transferred the first million of Harry Andersson's dollars to Abdi's secret account in Grand Cayman and reckoned that in three more weeks he would have the *Malmö*, cargo and crew back on the high seas with a NATO destroyer escort.

In an embassy safe house in London, the Tracker wondered if his fish would bite. As dusk settled on Virginia, he called TOSA headquarters.

"Gray Fox, I think I may need the Grumman. Could you send it back to Northolt for me?" he said.

12

The Preacher sat in his study inside his compound in Marka and thought about his enemy. He was no fool, and he knew he had one out there somewhere. The phony sermon on his website that had effectively destroyed his reputation proved it.

For ten years, he had deliberately made himself the most elusive of the al-Qaeda terrorists. He had moved from safe house to safe house in the mountains of North and South Waziristan. He had changed name and appearance. He had forbidden any camera to come near him.

Unlike a dozen, at least, now all dead, he had never used a mobile phone, for, unlike some of them, he knew the full scope of the American ability to pluck the tiniest whisper out of cyberspace, track the source to a single hut and blow both building and occupants to dust.

With one single exception, which he now bitterly regretted, he had never e-mailed anyone from the house in which he resided. He had always had his sermons of hate transmitted miles away from his residence.

Yet someone had penetrated. The actor on the phony sermon was too like him. The man who looked like him and spoke like him had announced to the world his real name and the pseudonym he had used as an executioner in the Khorosan.

He did not know how or why or who had betrayed him, but he had to accept that his pursuer could well have penetrated the real identity protocol of his computer in Kismayo. He did not understand how it could have been done, for the Troll had assured him it was impossible. But the Troll was dead.

He knew about drones. He had read volumes printed in the Western press about them and what they could do. He could presume that, even then, there were details that had never been divulged, even to the technical publications. He had to presume he had been traced and that, far above his head, invisible, inaudible, a circling machine was watching his town and even his compound.

All this had led him to the conviction that he would have to sever all contacts with his present life and disappear again. Then Jamma arrived from Kismayo with a message from his friend Mustafa in London that changed everything. It concerned fifty million dollars. He summoned his former secretary, now the Troll's replacement.

"Jamma, my brother, you are tired. It is a long journey. Rest, sleep, eat well. You will not be going back to Kismayo. It is abandoned. But there is another journey for you. Tomorrow, perhaps the next day."

G ray Fox was puzzled. His voice on the secure line from TOSA headquarters to the Tracker's operations room in the U.S. embassy in Grosvenor Square revealed it.

"Tracker, are you up to speed on the traffic between the helper in London and his pal in Marka?"

"Absolutely. Why?"

"The stuff he has been passing to the Preacher. He picked that up from a half-assed lawyer at a Belgravia dinner party."

The Tracker thought over his reply. There is a subtle difference between lying and being what a former British cabinet secretary once described as "economical with the truth."

"That's what Dardari seems to be saying."

"What do the Brits think?"

"They think," said the Tracker quite truthfully, "that the bastard is sitting in his London town house, passing scuttle-butt to his friend in the south. By the by, are my requests still getting a no-no from upstairs?"

He wanted to get the subject away from the issue of Mustafa Dardari, messaging out of London, when he was staring at the rain in Caithness with three former commandos for company.

"Absolutely, Tracker. No missiles because of Agent Opal and no beach assaults. And no heli-borne attacks from our compound in Mogadishu. One shoulder-fired rocket into a hovering helicopter full of Delta boys and we have another Somali catastrophe. You'll have to find another way."

"Yes, boss," said the Tracker as he put the phone down.

The Preacher was right about the uselessness of his Kis-mayo computer for secret transmissions, but he did not realize that his ally in London, his boyhood friend and secret supporter, had also been unmasked, and his encrypted mes-sages, shielded inside the vegetable price code, had also been broken. So he broke security again and sent Dardari a request from Marka. It was intercepted and deciphered.

Colonel Jackson?"

"Yes, Ariel."

"There's some very weird stuff going between Marka and London."

"You should know, Ariel. You're sending it in Dardari's name."

"Yeah, but Marka has just replied. He is asking his friend to lend him a million dollars."

He should have foreseen it. Certainly the budget could stand it. That sum was just a fraction of a single missile. But why waste tax dollars?

"Does he say how he wants it to be sent?"

"Something called Dahabshiil."

Tracker nodded, alone in his London office. He knew about it. Cunning and safe and almost untraceable. Based on the centuries-old figure of the hundi man.

Terrorism costs money, a lot of money. Behind the bomb-planting dupes, often no more than children, are the control-lers, usually mature men who have no intention of dying.

Somewhere behind them are the ring chieftans, and behind them are the financiers, often leading lives of apparent respectability.

For antiterrorist agencies, the money sources for terrorism have proved a fertile field for tracing the paper trail from operating account back to its source. For money movement leaves a paper trail. But the hundi man does not. In the Middle East, the system goes back many centuries.

It started because back then moving wealth through a landscape teeming with bandits was too dangerous without a small army. So the hundi man takes the money in country A and authorizes his cousin to disburse the same amount, minus commission, to the beneficiary in country B. No money moved across borders, just coded phone call or e-mail.

Dahabshiil was founded in Burco, Somalia, in 1970, presently headquartered in Dubai. In Somali, it just means "gold smelter," and mainly remits money earned by the hundreds of thousands of Somalis working abroad back to their families in the homeland. Many of the Somali diaspora are in Britain, accounting for a flourishing office in London.

"Could you break into Dardari's banking system?" asked the Tracker.

"I don't see why not, Colonel. Can you give me a day?"

Ariel went back to his glowing screen and into seventh heaven. He delved into the Pakistani tycoon's investments and his means of purchasing them, which led him to the offshore accounts, of which the principal was in Grand Cayman. It was protected by complex and sophisticated firewalls. The teenager with Asperger's syndrome in an attic in Virginia went through them in ten hours, transferred a million dollars to Dardari's personal London account and departed without leaving a trace, except confirmation that Dardari himself had done it legitimately.

The transfer from a London bank to the London office of Dahabshiil was a formality, along with details of the beneficiary, as listed by the Preacher in the e-mail that Ariel had intercepted and decoded. The Somali money brokerage warned that such a sum in U.S. dollars inside Somalia would take up to three days to assemble. And, yes, they had a branch in Marka.

Fort Meade and Cheltenham intercepted and logged the communications to and from the London computer but had no information other than the presumption it was Dardari sending and receiving. And their brief was to eavesdrop but not interfere.

J amma, I have a task for you of great delicacy. It can only be done by a Somali because it involves people who speak no other language."

With all its sophistication, Western technology can rarely intercept the personal emissary. For ten years, Osama bin Laden, not living in a cave at all but in a series of safe houses, communicated with supporters worldwide without once using a cell phone or being eavesdropped upon. He used personal messengers. It was the last of these, al-Kuwaiti, who was unmasked, tracked across the world and who finally led the followers to a compound in the town of Abbottabad.

The Preacher stood Jamma in front of him and recited the message in Arabic. Jamma translated it in his head into Somali and kept repeating it until he was word-perfect. He took one Pakistani bodyguard with him and departed.

He took the same pickup that had brought him from Kismayo two days earlier with the London message. From high above, foreign eyes watched the rear, filled with plastic jerrycans of extra fuel.

They were watching in the bunker outside Tampa as a tarpaulin was drawn over the fuel cans, but that was a normal precaution. Two men were seen to climb into the cab, but neither was the shrouded figure of the Preacher nor the slim young man in a red baseball cap. The pickup left and turned toward Kismayo and the south. When it passed out of view, the Global Hawk was instructed to resume its surveillance of the compound. Then the pickup stopped; the men in it removed the tarpaulin and painted the cab roof black. Thus disguised, it turned back, circled Marka to the west and headed north. At sundown, it skirted the Mogadishu enclave and pressed on toward Puntland and its numerous dens of pirates.

On pitted, rutted tracks, often driving over sharp-stoned deserts, with refuels and changes of tires, the journey to Garacad took two days.

M r. Gareth, it is I."
Ali Abdi was on the phone from Garacad. He seemed excited. Gareth Evans was both tired and strained. The relentless grind of trying to negotiate with people devoid of the simplest concept of haste or even the passage of time was always exhausting for a European. That was why the top hostage negotiators were few in number and highly paid.

Evans was also under constant pressure from Harry Andersson, who phoned daily, and sometimes more than that, seeking news of his son. Evans had tried to explain that even a hint of haste, let alone desperation, from the London end would make matters ten times worse than they already were. The Swedish billionaire was a businessman, and that half of him accepted the logic. But he was also a father, so the phone calls never stopped.

"Good morning to you, my friend," said Evans calmly. "What does your principal have to say this fine sunny day?"

"I think we are moving toward closure, Mr. Gareth. We would settle now for seven million dollars." Then he added, "I am doing my best."

It was a remark that, even if he were being overheard by an English-speaking Somali in the service of al-Afrit, would not be offensive. Evans realized it meant the negotiator in Garacad was trying to earn his second million-dollar bribe. But north and south of the Mediterranean Sea, the word "hurry" has two different meanings.

"That's very good, Mr. Abdi, but only so far," said Evans. The previous minimum offer acceptable to al-Afrit two days earlier had been ten million dollars. Evans had offered three. He knew Harry Andersson would have clinched at ten within a heartbeat. He also knew that would have triggered a forest of red flags in Somalia, where they knew that four to five million dollars would be about right.

A sudden collapse by the Europeans would have indicated panic and probably sent the price back up to fifteen.

"Look, Mr. Abdi, I have spent most of the night on the

phone to Stockholm, and my principals have agreed with extreme reluctance to release four million dollars into your principal's international account within the hour if the *Malmö* weighs anchor one hour later. It's a very good offer, Mr. Abdi. I think we both know that and your principal must surely see that."

"I will put the new offer to him immediately, Mr. Gareth."

When the line went dead, Gareth Evans mulled over the history of successful deals with Somali pirates. The uninitiated were always amazed that money would be paid into an account before the ship was released. What was to stop the pirates taking the money and not releasing their captives?

But here was the oddity. Of one hundred and eighty agreements written and exchanged by fax or e-mail between negotiators, all duly signed at each end, in only three cases had the Somalis broken their word.

Basically, throughout Puntland, the pirates realized they were into piracy for the money. They had no need or want of ships, cargoes or prisoners. To have broken deal after deal would have ruined their industry. Shifty and ruthless they might be, but self-interest was self-interest and it was supreme.

Normally. This was not normal. Of the three cases, two had been by al-Afrit. He was notorious, as was his clan. He was Sacad, a subclan of the Habar Gidir tribe. Mohamed Farrah Aideed, the brutal warlord whose thieving of aid supplies for the starving had brought the Americans into Somalia in 1993, and who had shot down the Black Hawk and slaughtered the U.S. Rangers, dragging their bodies through the streets, was also Sacad.

Speaking secretly on sat phones, Ali Abdi and Gareth Evans had agreed they would settle for five million dollars only if the old monster in the mud fort would agree and not suspect his own negotiator had been bought. Five million was, in any case, a perfectly acceptable figure for both sides. Harry Andersson's extra two-million-dollar bribe to Abdi was only to divide the delay by a figure of ten, if that were possible.

Out on the *Malmö*, under the scorching sun, things were becoming smelly. The European food was gone, either eaten or turned rotten when the freezers were turned off to save fuel. The Somali guards brought live goats onboard and slaughtered them out on the decks.

Captain Eklund would have had his decks hosed down, but the electric pumps were fuel based, like the air-conditioning, so he had the crew dip buckets into the sea and use brooms.

There was a mercy, in that the sea all around was teeming with fish, brought close by the goat offal thrown over the side. Both Europeans and Filipinos appreciated fresh fish, but it was becoming monotonous.

Washing facilities had been rigged with salt water when the showers went off, and fresh water was liquid gold, for drinking only, and even then made disgusting with purification tablets. Capt. Eklund was glad there had been no serious illness so far, just occasional diarrhea.

But he was not sure how long conditions would last. The Somalis often did not even bother to hoist their rears over the taffrail when they needed to defecate. The Filipinos, glaring with anger, had to broom it all through the scuppers in the pounding, enervating heat.

Captain Eklund could not even talk to Stockholm anymore. His satellite telephone had been disconnected on the orders of the one he called the little bastard in the suit. Ali Abdi did not want any interferences by amateurs in his delicate negotiations with the office of Chauncey Reynolds.

The Swedish skipper was thinking such thoughts when his Ukrainian deputy called out that a launch was coming. With binoculars, Capt. Eklund could make out the dhow and the neat little figure in the stern in a safari suit. He welcomed the visit. He would be able to ask yet again how fared the merchant marine cadet called Carlsson. In all that landscape, he was the only one who knew who the lad really was.

What he did not know was that the teenager had been beaten. Abdi would only tell him Ove Carlsson was well and detained within the fortress only as an earnest of the good behavior of the crew still onboard. Capt. Eklund had pleaded in vain for his return.

While Mr. Abdi was on the *Malmö*, a dusty pickup drove into the courtyard of the fortress behind the village. It contained one large and hulking Pakistani, who spoke neither English nor Somali, and one other.

The Pakistani stayed with the truck. The other was shown into the presence of al-Afrit, who recognized the man as from the Harti Darod clan, meaning "Kismayo." The Sacad warlord did not like the Harti, or indeed anyone from the south.

Though technically a Muslim, al-Afrit virtually never went to the mosque and rarely said any prayers. In his mind, the southerners were all al-Shabaab and insane. They tortured for Allah, he for pleasure.

The visitor introduced himself as Jamma and made the obeisances appropriate for a sheikh. He said he came as a personal emissary of a sheikh of Marka, with a proposal for the ears of the warlord of Garacad only.

Al-Afrit had never heard of any Jihadist preacher called Abu Azzam. He had a computer, which only the younger among his people really understood, but even if he had been thoroughly literate in its function, he would never have dreamed of watching the Jihadist website. But he listened with rising interest.

Jamma stood in front of him and recited the message he had memorized. It began with the usual lavish salutations and then moved to the burden of the message. When he lapsed into silence, the old Sacad stared at him for several minutes.

"He wants to kill him? Cut his throat? On camera? And then show the world?"

"Yes, Sheikh."

"And pay me a million dollars? Cash?"

"Yes, Sheikh."

Al-Afrit thought it over. Killing the white infidel, this he understood. But to show the Western world what he had done, this was madness. They, the infidel, the *kuffar*, would come take revenge, and they had many guns. He, al-Afrit, took their ships and their money, but he was not mad enough to trigger a blood feud between himself and the whole *kuffar* world.

Finally, he made his decision—which was to delay a decision. He instructed that his guests be taken to rooms, where they could rest, and be offered food and water. When Jamma was gone, he ordered that neither man retain the ignition key to his vehicle, nor any weapon he might have on him nor any kind of phone. He personally wore a curved *jambiya* dagger in a sash at his waist, but he did not like any other weapon to be near him.

Ali Abdi returned from the *Malmö* an hour later, but because he had been away, he did not see the truck arrive from the south, or the two visitors, one the bearer of a bizarre proposition.

He knew the times of his preagreed telephone talks with Gareth Evans, but because London was three time zones west of the Horn of Africa, they took place in midmorning in Garacad. So the next day he had no reason to leave his room early.

He was not present when al-Afrit lengthily briefed one of his most trusted clansmen, a one-eyed savage called Duale, just after dawn, nor did he see the pickup truck with the black roof drive out of the courtyard gate one hour later.

He had vaguely heard of a Jihadist fanatic who preached messages of death and hate over the worldwide web, but he had not heard of the man's utter discrediting, or his online protestations, that he had been foully defamed in a *kuffar* plot. But like al-Afrit, albeit for different reasons, he despised Salafists and Jihadists, and all other extremist maniacs, and observed Islam as little as he could get away with.

He was surprised and pleased to find his principal in a reasonably agreeable mood when he appeared for their morning conference. So much so that he suggested they could lower their demand from seven million to six million dollars and probably secure closure. And the clan chief agreed.

When he spoke to Gareth Evans, he exuded self-satisfaction. He was so tempted to say, "We are almost there," but realized that phrase could only mean that the pair of them were colluding on an agreed price. Privately, he thought: One more week, perhaps only five days, and the monster will let the *Malmö* sail.

With his second million dollars, added to his life savings, he felt a comfortable retirement in a civilized environment beckoning.

The Tracker was beginning to worry. In angling terms, he had dropped a heavily baited hook into the water and he was waiting for a monster to bite. But the floater was immobile on the surface. It did not even bob.

From his office in the embassy, he had a second-by-second patch through to the bunker outside Tampa, where a senior NCO from the Air Force sat silently, control column in hand, flying a Global Hawk high over a compound in Marka. He could see what the master sergeant could see—a silent collection of three houses inside a wall on a narrow cluttered street with a fruit market at one end of it.

But the compound showed no signs of life. No one came, no one left. The Hawk could not only watch, it could listen. It would hear the tiniest electronic whisper out of that compound; it would pluck a few syllables out of cyberspace, whether they were uttered, on computer or cell phone. The National Security Agency at Fort Meade, with its satellites in space, would do the same.

But all that technology was being defeated. He had not seen the pickup truck driven by Jamma change its configuration with a black cab roof, then double back and head north instead of south. He did not know it was on its way back. He could not know that his bait had been taken and a deal struck between a sadistic Sacad in Garacad and a desperate Pakistani in Marka. In Donald Rumsfeld's unusual terminology, he was facing "an unknown unknown."

He could only suspect, and he suspected he was losing, outwitted by barbarians cleverer than he. The secure phone rang.

It was Master Sergeant Orde from Tampa. "Colonel, sir, there's a technical approaching the target." Tracker resumed his study of the screen. The compound occupied the center of it, about a quarter of the space. There was a pickup at the gate. The cab had a black roof. He did not recognize it.

A figure in a white dishdash came out of the house at the side of the square, crossed the sandy space and opened the gate. The pickup drove in. The gate closed. Three tiny figures emerged from the truck and entered the main house. The Preacher had visitors.

The Preacher received the trio in his office. The bodyguard was dismissed. Opal introduced the emissary from the north. The Sacad Duale glared with his one good eye. He, too, had memorized his brief. With a gesture, the Preacher indicated that he could begin. The terms of al-Afrit were terse and clear.

He was prepared to trade his Swedish captive for one million dollars cash. His servant Duale should see and count the money and alert his master that he had actually seen it.

For the rest, al-Afrit would not enter al-Shabaab land. There would be an exchange at the border. Duale knew the place of the exchange and would guide the vehicles bearing the money and guards to it. The delegation from the north would make the rendezvous and bring the prisoner.

"And where is this meeting place?" asked the Preacher. Duale simply stared and shook his head.

The Preacher had seen tribesmen like this in the Pakistani border territories, among the Pathan. He could pull out all the man's nails, both fingers and toes, but he would die before he spoke. He nodded and smiled.

He knew there was no real border between north and south on any map. But maps were for the *kuffars*. The tribesmen had their maps in their heads. They knew exactly where, a generation earlier, clan had fought clan for the ownership of a camel and men had died. The spot marked the place where the vendetta had begun. They knew if a man from the wrong clan crossed the line, he would die. They needed no white man's map.

He also knew he could be ambushed for the money. But to what end? The clan chief from Garacad would get his money anyway, and what use to him was the Swedish boy?

Only he, the Preacher, knew the true, staggering value of the merchant marine cadet from Stockholm, because his good friend in London had told him. And that immense sum would restore all his fortunes, even among the supposedly pious al-Shabaad. North or south, money not only talked, it shouted.

There was a tap on the door.

There was a new vehicle at the compound site, a small sedan this time. At 50,000 feet, the Hawk wheeled and turned, watching and listening. The same white-clad figure crossed the sand and conferred with the car's driver. In Tampa and London, Americans watched.

The car did not enter the yard. A large attaché case was handed over and signed for. The figure in white headed for the main building.

"Follow the car," said the Tracker. The outlines of the compound slid out of screen as the camera suite high in the stratosphere followed the car. It did not go far; under a mile. Then it stopped outside a small office block.

"Close up. Let me have a look at that building."

The office block came closer and closer. The sun in Marka was overhead, so there were no shadows. These would come, long and black, as the sun set over the western desert. Pale green and dark green; a logo, and a word beginning with D in roman script: "Dahabshiil." The money had arrived and been delivered. The overhead scrutiny returned to the Preacher's compound.

B lock after block of hundred-dollar bills were removed from the case and placed on the long polished table. The Preacher might be many miles from his origins in Rawal-pindi, but he liked his furnishings traditional.

Duale had already announced he had to count the ran-som. Jamma continued to interpret from Arabic to Swahili, Duale's only language. Opal, who had brought the attaché case, stayed in case he was needed, the junior of two private secretaries. Seeing Duale fumbling with the bundles, Opal asked him in Somali: "Can I help you?"

"Ethiopian dog," snarled the Sacad, "I will finish the task."

It took him two hours. Then he grunted.

"I have to make a call," he said. Jamma translated. The Preacher nodded. Duale produced a cell phone from his robes and tried to make a call. Inside the thick-walled building, he could get no tone. He was escorted outside to the open yard.

"There's a guy in the yard on a cell phone," said M.Sgt. Orde in Tampa.

"Grab it, I need to know," snapped the Tracker.

The call trilled in a mud-brick fort in Garacad and was answered. The conversation was extremely brief. Four words from Marka and a reply of two. Then the connection was severed.

"Well?" asked the Tracker.

"It was in Somali."

"Ask NSA."

Nearly a thousand miles north in Maryland, an American Somali lifted the headphones off his ears.

"One man said, 'The dollars have arrived.' The other replied, 'Tomorrow night,'" he said.

Tampa called the Tracker in London.

"We got the two messages, all right," the communications intercept people told him. "But they were using a local cell phone network called Hormud. We know where the first speaker was—in Marka. We don't know who replied or from where."

Don't worry, thought the Tracker. I do.

13

C olonel, sir, they're moving."

The Tracker had been dozing at his desk in front of the screen in the London embassy that showed him what the drone over Marka could see. The voice was from the speakerphone linked to the control bunker outside Tampa. The voice belonged to M.Sgt. Orde, back on shift.

He jerked awake and checked his watch. Three a.m. London time, six in Marka, the darkness before dawn.

The Global Hawk had been replaced by one with full tanks and hours of loiter time before it, too, would run dry. On the Somali coast, there was the tiniest pink blush across the eastern horizon. The Indian Ocean was still black, as was the end of the night over the alleys of Marka.

But lights had come on in the Preacher's compound, and small red blobs were moving about—the heat sources caught by the drone's body sensors. Its cameras were still on infrared mode, enabling it to see in the dark what was going on ten miles beneath it.

As the Tracker watched, the level of daylight rose with the sun; the red blobs became dark shapes moving across the courtyard far below. Thirty minutes later, a garage door was opened and a vehicle rolled out.

It was not a dusty, dented pickup truck, the all-purpose personnel-and-load carrier of Somalia. This was a smart Toyota Land Cruiser with black windows, the vehicle of choice of al-Qaeda right back to bin Laden's first appearance in Afghanistan. The Tracker knew it could hold ten people.

The watchers, four thousand miles apart in London and Florida, watched just eight dark shapes board the SUV. They were not close enough to see that in the front were two of the Pakistani bodyguards, one to drive, the other heavily armed in the passenger seat.

Behind them sat the Preacher, shapeless in Somali robes with head covered, and Jamma, his Somali secretary. The third seat went to Opal and the other two Pakistani guards, making up the only four the Preacher could really trust. He had brought them all from his days in the Khorosan killer group.

The last was squatting in the baggage area behind the rows of seats. He was the Sacad Duale.

At seven Marka time, other servants hauled the gate open and the Land Cruiser rolled. The Tracker faced a quandary: Was this a red herring? Was the target still in the house, preparing to slip away, while the drone he must now know was above him went elsewhere?

"Sir?"

The man with the control column in the Tampa bunker needed to know.

"Follow the truck," said the Tracker.

It led through the labyrinth of streets and alleys to the outskirts of town, then turned off and drove under the cover of a large, asbestos-roofed warehouse. Once in there, it was out of sight.

Fighting to control the panic, the Tracker ordered the drone to return to the residence, but the compound and its yard were wreathed in shadows and quiet. Nothing moved. The drone returned to the warehouse. Twenty minutes later, the large black SUV emerged. It drove slowly back to the compound.

Somewhere down there, it must have sounded its horn, for a single servant emerged from the house and opened the gate. The Toyota rolled inside and stopped. No one got out. Why? wondered the Tracker. Then he caught it. No one got out because no one was in it except the driver.

"Get back to the warehouse fast," he ordered M.Sgt. Orde. In reply, the controller in Florida simply widened the camera lens from close-up to wide-angle, capturing the whole town but in lesser detail. They were just in time.

From the warehouse, not one but four half-body pick-ups, the so-called technicals, were rolling out one after the other. The Tracker had almost fallen for the basic switch.

"Follow the convoy," he told Tampa. "Wherever it goes. I may have to leave, but I'll stay on my cell."

In Garacad, Mr. Ali Abdi was woken by the growling of engines below his window. He checked his watch. Seven a.m. Four hours until his regular morning conference with

London. He peered through the shutters and watched two technicals leave the courtyard of the fort.

It was of no matter. He was a very contented man. The previous evening, he had secured the final concurrence of al-Afrit to his mediations. The pirate would settle with Chauncey Reynolds and the insurers for a ransom of five million U.S. dollars for the *Malmö*, including cargo and crew.

Despite the one minor fly in the ointment, Abdi was sure Mr. Gareth would also be happy when he learned that two hours after the pirate's Dubai bank confirmed lodging of the dollars the *Malmö* would be allowed to sail. By then, a Western destroyer would surely be offshore to escort her to safety. Several rival clans had already sent skiffs to prowl around the Swedish merchantman in case she was ill guarded and could be snatched again.

Abdi thought of the future. The second of his million-dollar bribes would be assured. Gareth Evans would not cheat him lest they ever had to deal again. But only he, Abdi, could know that he was retiring and emigrating to a lovely villa in Tunisia, where he could live in peace and safety miles from the chaos and killing of his native land. He checked his watch again and rolled over for an extended snooze.

The Tracker was still in his office, considering a limited range of options. He knew a lot, but he could not know everything.

He had an agent inside the enemy camp, probably riding a few feet away from the Preacher in one of the four technicals rolling through the desert six miles below the Global Hawk. But he could not communicate with his man nor the reverse. Opal's transceiver was still buried beneath a shack on the beach outside Kismayo. It would have been suicidal for him to have attempted to bring anything with him to Marka save the harmless-looking item he had been given by the casuarina trees.

The Tracker presumed there would be a meeting somewhere and a handover of money for the Swedish prisoner. He had no qualms about what he had done, reasoning that the cadet from Stockholm was in greater danger with the man even his own clansmen nicknamed Devil than with the Preacher, who would keep him alive and well for the money.

After the swap, the Preacher would presumably return to Marka, where he was untouchable. The only chance of destroying him had been to lure him out into the Somali desert, to those wide-open spaces where there were no civilians to hurt.

But missiles were forbidden anyway. Gray Fox had made that plain yet again the previous evening. As the sun that now blazed down on Somalia brought the first light to London, he considered his options. Despite all his pleadings, they were not generous.

The SEALs' Team 6 was on base at Dam Neck, Virginia, and there was no time to bring them across half the world. The Night Stalkers, with their long-range helicopters, were at

Fort Campbell, Kentucky. That apart, he suspected choppers would be too noisy. He had been in jungle and desert. He knew that at night the jungle is an infernal din of frogs and insects while the desert is eerily silent, the creatures who live in it have the hearing of the bat-eared foxes that share the sand with them. The thump of helicopter rotors, carried on the night breeze, can be heard for miles.

There was one unit he had heard of but never seen in action or even met. But he knew their reputation and specialty. They were not even American. There were two American units that, by repute, could match them; but the SEALs and the Delta boys were across the Atlantic.

He was roused from his thoughts by M.Sgt. Orde.

"Colonel, they seem to be separating."

He went back to the screen, and again incipient panic was like a punch in the gut. Down on the desert floor, the four technicals were in column but widely spaced. They had four hundred yards between each of them.

This was the Preacher's precaution to ensure the Americans would not dare use a missile for fear it would miss the truck he was traveling in. He was not to know he was safe because of the young Ethiopian behind him. But now they were not just separated in a line, they were all diverging.

The convoy was north of the soldier-guarded enclave of Mogadishu, heading northwest into the valley of the She-belle. To cross the river, there were half a dozen usable bridges between Ethiopia and the sea. Now the four technicals were parting company as if heading for different bridges. His one drone could not follow them all.

Even at full maximum screen width, it could only observe

two. But, by then, each truck would have become too tiny to see. From Tampa, the controller's voice was urgent.

"Which one, sir?"

G areth Evans came into the office just after eight. Lawyers are rarely early risers, and he was always the first to appear in the office. The night watchman was by now accustomed to emerging from his box behind the reception desk to unlock the plate-glass doors and admit the negotiator—and that was when he was not spending the night on his cot in the office upstairs.

He had brought his vacuum flask of coffee from the nearby hotel where Chauncey Reynolds had billeted him for the duration. Later, dear Mrs. Bulstrode would appear, then go to the deli to secure him a real breakfast and be back before it went cold. He had no idea that every stage of his negotiations was faithfully reported to the Secret Intelligence Service.

A pulsing red light at half past eight told him Mr. Abdi was on the line. Gareth Evans never liked to permit himself a rush of optimism; he had been disappointed before. But he thought he and the Somali go-between were close to the agreed-upon ransom of five million dollars, for which he had full clearance. The money transfer was not his problem; others would handle that. And he knew there was a British frigate not far offshore to escort the *Malmö* to safety when the moment came.

"Yes, Mr. Abdi, Gareth Evans here. You have news for me? You are earlier than usual."

"Indeed news, Mr. Gareth. And very good news. The best. My principal has agreed to settle on five million dollars only."

"That's excellent, my friend." He tried to keep the exultation out of his voice. This is the fastest release he had ever secured. "I think I can get the transfer made this day. Are all the crew well?"

"Yes, very well. There is . . . how do you English say . . . a wasp in the ointment, but not important."

"I think it's a fly. A problem. But, never mind, a wasp will do. How big a wasp, Mr. Abdi?"

"The Swedish boy, the cadet . . ."

Evans froze. He held up a hand to stop Mrs. Bulstrode in her tracks, breakfast in hand.

"You mean Ove Carlsson. What problem, Mr. Abdi?"

"He cannot be coming, Mr. Gareth. My principal, I'm afraid . . . It was nothing to do with me . . . He received an offer . . ."

"What has happened to Mr. Carlsson?" Evans's voice had lost all its good humor.

"I'm afraid he has been sold to the al-Shabaab in the south. But do not worry, Mr. Gareth. He was only the cadet."

Gareth Evans replaced the receiver, leaned forward and buried his face in his hands. Mrs. Bulstrode put down his breakfast and left.

Agent Opal sat between Jamma and the door. The Preacher was on the far side. The technical, which did not have the suspension of the Land Cruiser, bucked, rocked and shuddered with every stone and pothole. They had been motoring for five hours; it was nearly midday, and the heat was stifling. Any air-conditioning the vehicle had once had was long for the archives.

The Preacher and Jamma were both dozing. Had it not been for the jolting, Opal might have fallen into a fitful sleep and missed it.

The Preacher awoke, leaned forward, tapped the driver on the shoulder and said something. It was in Urdu, but the meaning became clear only moments later. They had been driving in line since leaving Marka, and their vehicle was the second of four. Just after the tap on the shoulder, the driver turned off the track of the one in front and took another.

He glanced out and back. Trucks three and four were doing the same. The seating arrangements were different from the Land Cruiser. There was just the driver up front, with the Preacher, Jamma and himself along the seat behind. The three bodyguards were out in the open behind the cab with Duale the Sacad.

From above, all four technicals would look the same, and like eighty percent of other pickup trucks in Somalia. Three of the technicals were local hirelings from Marka. Opal knew about drones; they had featured large in his training at the Mossad agent school. He began to retch.

Jamma looked at him in alarm.

"Are you all right?"

"It's the jolting," he said. The Preacher looked across.

"If you are going to be ill, go ride outside," he said.

Opal opened the door next to him and hauled his torso outside. The desert wind blew his hair about his face. He reached a hand toward the open bed of the truck, and a hefty Pakistani grabbed it. After a wild second dangling over the rear wheel, he was pulled into the rear. Jamma leaned across and slammed the door from the inside.

Opal smiled wanly at the three Pakistani bodyguards and the one-eyed Duale. They all ignored him. From inside his dishdash, he took out what he had been given under the casuarinas and had already used once. He pulled it on.

Which one do we follow, sir?" The question was becoming very urgent. As the Global Hawk widened its aperture, the desert moved farther away, with all four trucks at the periphery of the picture. The Tracker noticed a disturbance in one of the technicals.

"What's that guy doing?" he asked. "Truck number two."

"He seems to have climbed out for air," said M.Sgt. Orde. "He's pulling something on. A baseball cap, sir. Bright red."

"Close in on truck two," snapped the Tracker, "ignore the others. They are decoys. Follow truck two."

The camera moved to truck two at the center of the frame, then closed in. The five men in the back became bigger and bigger. One had a red cap. Very faintly, the watchers could make out the insignia "New York."

"God bless you, Opal," breathed the Tracker.

The Tracker caught his colleague, the defense attaché, as the man came back from his morning five-mile run through the country lanes around Ickenham, where he lived.

It was eight a.m. The attaché was a full colonel, drawn from the 101st Airborne, the Screaming Eagles. The Tracker's question was brief and simple.

"Sure, I know him. He's a good guy."

"Do you have his private line?"

The attaché scrolled through his BlackBerry and dictated the number. Seconds later, the Tracker had the man he sought, a British major general, and asked for the meeting.

"My office. Nine o'clock."

"I'll be there," said the Tracker.

The office of the director of Special Forces of the British army is in Albany Barracks, Albany Street, in the elegant residential district of Regent's Park. A ten-foot-high wall shields the cluster of buildings from the road, and the double gates are sentry guarded and seldom opened to strangers.

The Tracker was in civilian clothes and arrived by cab, which he dismissed. The sentry studied his embassy pass, which gave his army rank, made a phone call and then ushered him through. Another soldier led him into the main building, up two floors and to the office of the DSF at the back.

The two men were around the same age and there were other similarities. Both looked hard and fit. The Britisher was two ranks higher than a lieutenant colonel, and though he was in shirtsleeves, a jacket on a peg in the corner bore the red lapel tabs of the General Staff. Both men had the indefinable air of those who had seen hard combat and rather a lot of it.

Will Chamney had started in the Guards then transferred to the Special Air Service Regiment. He had survived the grueling selection course and spent three years as a troop commander with D Squadron, 16 Troop—the free fallers.

In the regiment, as it is simply called, an officer, or "Rupert," cannot opt to come back for a second tour; he has to be invited. Chamney went back as a squadron commander just in time to take part in the liberation of Kosovo, and then the Sierra Leone affair.

He was with the SAS team that, with the paras, rescued a group of Irish soldiers captured alive by a mob of limb-chopping rebels at their base deep in the jungle. The West Side Boyz, as the drug-fueled insurgents called themselves, took over a hundred casualties in under an hour before fading into the bush. On his third tour at SAS base, Hereford, he had commanded the regiment with the rank of colonel.

At the time of the meeting, he controlled the four declared units of Special Forces: the SAS, the Special Boat Service, the Special Forces Support Group and the Special Reconnaissance Regiment.

Due to the extreme flexibility of officer deployments in the Special Forces, he had, between three assignments at Hereford, commanded Air Assault (paratrooper) units in the UK and in Helmand, Afghanistan.

He had heard of the Tracker, knew that he was in town and knew why. Though TOSA was in the lead, destroying the Preacher had long been a joint op. The man had provoked at least four murders on British soil.

"What can I do for you?" he asked after handshakes and the usual greetings.

The Tracker explained at some length. He wanted a favor,

and security clearance was not an issue. The DSF listened in silence. When he spoke, he went straight to the core.

"How long have you got?"

"I suspect until dawn tomorrow, and there are three time zones between here and Somalia. It is just past midday there. We take him out tonight or we miss him again, and probably forever."

"You're tracking him by drone?"

"As we speak. A Global Hawk is right over him. When he stops, I believe he will overnight. They have twelve hours of darkness down there. Six to six."

"And a missile is out?"

"Absolutely. Riding with him in his entourage is an Israeli agent. He has to be extracted alive. If he is wasted, the Mossad are going to be displeased. Putting it mildly."

"Not surprised. And you don't want to upset that lot. So what do you want from us?"

"Pathfinders."

General Chamney slowly raised an eyebrow.

"HALO?"

"I figure it's the only thing that might work. Do you have any Pathfinders presently within that theater?"

Probably the least known or heard-of unit in the British armed forces, the Pathfinders are, with just thirty-six badged operatives, also the smallest. They are drawn mainly from the Parachute Regiment, already rigorously trained, then re-trained almost to destruction.

They operate in six teams of six. Even with their support unit, they are no more than sixty, and no one ever sees them.

They can operate miles out ahead of the conventional forces—in the 2003 invasion of Iraq, they were sixty miles ahead of the American point units.

When on land, they use stripped-down, strengthened Land Rovers, in desert pink camouflage, called pinkies. A fighting unit is just two pinkies, three men per vehicle. Their specialty is to drop in by parachute, high altitude, low opening, hence HALO.

Or they can enter a war zone by HAHO (high altitude, high opening) deploying the chutes just after leaving the aircraft and flying the canopy mile after mile into enemy territory; silent, invisible, landing like an alighting sparrow.

General Chamney turned a computer screen toward him and tapped for several seconds at the keyboard. Then he studied the screen.

"By chance, we have a unit at Thumrait. Desert familiarization course."

The Tracker knew of Thumrait, an air base in the desert of Oman. It had figured as a staging post in the 1990/91 first invasion of Saddam Hussein's Iraq. He did a mental calculation. In a C-130 Hercules, the Special Forces aircraft of choice, about four hours to Djibouti. A huge American air base.

"What kind of authority would you need to lend them to Uncle Sam?"

"High," said the DSF, "way up there. My best guess, our Prime Minister. If he says go, it's go. But everyone else would simply pass it upward."

"And who could best persuade the PM?"

"Your President," said the general.

"And if he could persuade the PM?"

"Then the order would come down the chain. To the defence secretary, to the chief of the defence staff, to the chief of the general staff, to the director of military operations, then to me. And I do the necessary."

"That could take all day. I don't have all day."

The DSF thought for a while.

"Look, the boys are heading home anyway. Via Bahrain and Cyprus. I could divert them via Djibouti to Cyprus." He glanced at his watch. "It's about one p.m. in Somalia. If they take off in two hours, they could land in Djibouti around sundown. Can you fix for them to be made welcome and refueled?"

"Absolutely."

"On the house?"

"Our tab."

"Can you be there to brief them? Pictures and targets?"

"Personally. I have a company Grumman out at Northolt."

General Chamney grinned.

"It's the only way to fly." Both men had spent many hours on rock-hard seats in the back of pitching transport planes. The Tracker rose.

"I must go. I have a lot of calls to make."

"I'll divert the Hercules," said the DSF. "And I won't leave the office. Good luck."

The Tracker was back at the embassy thirty minutes later. He raced to his office and studied the screen showing the pictures being recorded at Tampa. The Preacher's technical was still bucking and rolling over the ocher/brown desert. The five men still sat in the back, one with a scarlet baseball cap. He checked his watch. Eleven a.m. in London, two p.m.

in Somalia, but only six a.m. in Washington. To hell with
Gray Fox's beauty sleep. He put through his call. A sleepy
voice answered on the seventh ring.

"You want what?" he yelled when the morning's events in
London were explained.

"Please, just ask the President to ask the British Prime
Minister for this little favor. And authorize our base in Djibouti to cooperate in full."

"I'll have to rouse the admiral," said Gray Fox. He was
referring to the commanding officer of J-SOC.

"He's been roused before. It'll soon be seven a.m. with
you. The commander in chief rises early for his fitness regi-
men. He'll take the call. Just ask him to speak with his friend
in London and grant the favor. It's what friends are for."

The Tracker had more calls to make. He told the pilot of
the Grumman at Northolt to draw up a flight plan for Djibouti. From the car pool in the embassy basement under
Grosvenor Square, he required a car for Northolt within
thirty minutes.

His last call was to Tampa, Florida. Though he was no
master of electronics, he knew what he wanted and that it
could be done. From the cabin of the Grumman, he wanted
a patch through to the bunker controlling the Global Hawk
over the Somali desert. He would not get a picture, but he
needed constant updating on the passage of that pickup truck
across the desert and its final stopping place.

In the communications center at Djibouti base, he wanted
direct communication, sound and picture, with the Tampa
bunker. And he wanted Djibouti's complete cooperation with

himself and the incoming British paratroopers. Thanks to the clout of J-SOC right across the U.S. armed forces, he got the lot.

T he President of the United States took the call from the commander of J-SOC after he showered after his morning fitness session.

"Why do we need them?" was his query after listening to the request.

"The target is one you designated in the spring, sir. The one designated back then simply as the Preacher. He has inspired seven assassinations on U.S. soil, plus the slaughter of the CIA staff on the bus. We now know who he is and where he is. But he will probably light out at dawn."

"I recall him, Admiral. But dawn is almost twenty-four hours away. We can't get our own people there in time?"

"It's not dawn in Somalia, Mr. President. It's almost sundown. The British team happens to be in the theater. They were on a training mission nearby."

"We can't use a missile?"

"There's an agent from a friendly agency in his entourage."

"So it's up close and personal?"

"The only way, sir. So says our man on the spot."

The President hesitated. As a politician, he knew that a favor creates a marker and markers can later be called in.

"All right," he said, "I'll make the call."

The British Prime Minister was in his office in Downing Street. It was one o'clock. It was his habit to take a light salad lunch before going across Parliament Square to the House of Commons. After that, he would be out of contact. His private secretary took the call from the Downing Street switchboard, put his hand over the receiver and said, "It's the U.S. President."

Both men knew each other well and got on at a personal level, which is not vital but extremely useful. Both had stylish wives and young families. There was the usual exchange of greetings and inquiries after the near and dear. Unseen operators in London and Washington recorded every word.

"David, I have a favor to ask."

"Ask away."

The President took no more than five sentences. It was a strange request and took the Prime Minister by surprise. The call was on speakerphone; the cabinet secretary, the senior professional civil servant in the country, looked askance at his boss. Bureaucrats hate surprises. There were possible consequences to be thought through. Dropping Pathfinders into a foreign country could be regarded as an act of war. But who governed the Somali wilderness? No one worth the name. He wagged an admonitory finger.

"I'll have to check with our people. I'll call you back in twenty minutes. Scout's honor."

"This could be very dangerous, Prime Minister," said the cabinet secretary. He did not mean dangerous for the men involved but for international repercussions.

"Get me, in order, the chief of the defence staff and the chief of Six."

The professional soldier came on first.

"Yes, I know the problem and I know about the request," he said. "Will Chamney told me an hour ago."

He just assumed the Prime Minister would know who the director of Special Forces was.

"Well, can we do it?"

"Of course we can. Providing they get a damn accurate briefing before they go in. That's down to the Cousins. But if they have a drone overhead, they should be able to see the target clear as day."

"Where are the Pathfinders now?"

"Over Yemen. Two hours short of the U.S. base at Djibouti. That's where they'll land and refuel. Then they'll be fully briefed. If the young officer in charge is satisfied, he'll tell Will at Albany Barracks and ask for a green light. That can only come from you, Prime Minister."

"I can give you that in the next hour. That is, I can give you the political decision. The technical one is up to you professionals. I have two more calls, then I'll be back in touch."

The man who came on from the SIS, or MI6, or just 6, was not the Chief but Adrian Herbert.

"The Chief is out of the country, Prime Minister. But I have been handling this case with our friends for some months now. How can I help?"

"You know what the Americans are asking for? To borrow a unit of our Pathfinders?"

"Yes," said Herbert, "I know."

"How?"

"We do a lot of listening, Prime Minister."

"Did you know the Americans cannot use a missile because there is a Western agent inside the bastard's entourage?"

"Yes."

"Is he one of ours?"

"No."

"Anything else I should know?"

"By sundown there will probably be a Swedish merchant marine officer, a hostage, a few yards away as well."

"How the hell do you know that?"

"It's what we do, Prime Minister," said Herbert. Mentally, he made a note to put in for a bonus for Mrs. Bulstrode.

"Can it be done? Extraction of both men? Wipeout of the target?"

"That's a military question. We leave that sort of thing to them."

The British premier was not a politician without having a keen eye for benefit. If British Pathfinders could pull the Swedish officer out of there, the Swedes would be rather grateful. The appreciation might go right up to King Carl Gustaf, who might mention it to Queen Elizabeth. No harm done, no harm at all.

"I'm giving the green light, subject to the military's overriding judgment on feasibility," he told the chief of the defence staff ten minutes later. Then he called the Oval Office back.

"You got it," he told the President. "If the military say it can be done, the Pathfinders are yours."

"Thanks, I won't forget it," said the man in the White House.

———

As the phones went down in London and Washington, the Grumman twin jet entered Egyptian airspace. Egypt, Sudan, then the descent toward Djibouti.

Outside, at 33,000 feet, the sky was still blue, but the sun was a blazing red ball above the western horizon. In Somalia, and at ground level, it would be about to set. Through the Tracker's headphones, a voice came from Tampa.

"They've stopped, Colonel. The technical has pulled into a tiny hamlet miles from anywhere, on a track between the coast and the Ethiopian border. It's just a cluster of a dozen, maybe twenty, mud-brick houses, with some scrubby trees and a goat pen. We don't even have a name for it."

"Are you sure they are not moving on?"

"Looks like no. They are climbing out and stretching. I am zooming in close. I can see one of the target party, talking with a couple of villagers. And the guy with the red baseball cap. He's taking it off. Wait, there are two more technicals approaching from the north. And the sun's about to go down."

"Get the GPS fix on the village. Before you go to infrared, get me a series of vari-scaled pictures by last daylight from as many angles as possible. Then patch them through to the comms room at Djibouti base."

"You got it, sir. Will do."

The copilot came through from the flight deck.

"Colonel, we just had a call from Djibouti control. A British C-130 Hercules in RAF livery just landed from Oman."

"Tell Djibouti take good care of them and refuel the Herc.

Tell the Brits I'll be there momentarily. By the by, how long to ETA?"

"Just cleared Cairo, sir. About ninety minutes to runway threshold."

And, outside, the sun went down. Within minutes, South Sudan, eastern Ethiopia and all Somalia were enveloped in moonless night.

14

eserts can be furnace hot by day yet freezing at night, but Djibouti is on the warm Gulf of Aden and remains balmy. The Tracker was met at the foot of the steps of the parked Grumman by a USAF colonel sent by the base commander to welcome him to the command. He was in light, tropical-weight desert camouflage, and the Tracker was surprised by the balminess of the night as he followed the colonel across the tarmac to the two rooms in the operations block that had been set aside for him.

The base commander had been told very little by Air Force HQ in the U.S. except that this was a J-SOC black operation and that he was to offer every cooperation to the TOSA officer, whom he would only know as Colonel Jamie Jackson. It was the name the Tracker had elected to use because he had all the supporting paperwork.

They passed the British RAF C-130 Hercules. It had the standard roundels on the tail fin but no other insignia. Tracker knew it came from the 47th Squadron of the Special Forces Wing. There was a glimmer of light from the flight deck, where the crew had elected to stay onboard and brew up real tea rather than the American version of it.

They walked under the wing, past a hangar buzzing with ground crew and into the ops building. Part of the "every cooperation" instruction included welcoming the six scruffy-looking British free fallers who were gathered inside, staring at an array of still pictures on the wall.

A rather relieved-looking American master sergeant, whose shoulder flash indicated he was a comms specialist, turned and threw up a salute. He returned it.

The first thing the Tracker noticed of the six Brits was that they were in desert cammo, but without either rank or unit insignia. They were deeply suntanned on their faces and hands, stubbled around the jaw and with tousled hair, except for the one who was bald as a billiard ball.

One of them, the Tracker knew, must be the junior officer commanding the unit. He thought it better to cut straight to the matter in hand.

"Gentlemen, I am Lieutenant Colonel Jamie Jackson of the U.S. Marine Corps. Your government, in the form of your Prime Minister, has been kind enough to allow me to borrow you and your services for this night. Which of you is in command?"

If he thought the mention of the Prime Minister was going to start any genuflecting, he had the wrong unit. One of the six stepped forward. When he spoke, the Tracker recognized the kind of voice derived from years at a private boarding school that the British, with their talent for saying the opposite, call public school.

"That's me, Colonel. I am a captain, name of David. In our unit we never use surnames or ranks, or throw salutes. Except to the Queen, of course."

The Tracker recognized that he was never going to match the white-haired Queen, so he just said, "OK, so long as you can do what is required this night. And my name is Jamie. Would you introduce me, David?"

Among the other five were two sergeants, two corporals and a trooper, although the Pathfinders rank is never mentioned. Each had a specialty. Pete was a sergeant and the medic, with skills way beyond mere first aid. Barry was the other sergeant, expert in weapons of all kinds. He looked like the product of a loving union between a rhino and a battle tank. He was huge, and it was all very hard. The corporals were Dai, the Welsh Wizard, who was in charge of communications and would carry the various pieces of wizardry that would enable the Pathfinders, once on the ground, to remain in touch with Djibouti and Tampa, and provide the video downlink that would enable them to see what the drone overhead could see. The bald one, of course, was Curly, who was a vehicle mechanic of near-genius level.

The youngest, in age and rank, was Tim, who had started in the Logistics Corps and has trained in explosives of all kinds, along with bomb dismantlement.

The Tracker turned to the American master sergeant.

"Talk me through it," he said, gesturing at the wall display. There was a large screen showing exactly what the drone controller in MacDill Air Force Base outside Tampa was seeing. He passed the Tracker an earpiece with a mic attached.

"This is Colonel Jackson in Djibouti base," he said. "Is that Tampa?"

On the flight down, he had been in constant contact with Tampa, and the speaker had been M.Sgt. Orde. But the shift had changed eight time zones to the west. The voice was female, a Deep South drawl, molasses over cane sugar.

"Tampa here, sir. Specialist Jane Allbright on the control stick."

"What have we got, Jane?"

"Just before the sun went down, the target vehicle arrived at a tiny hamlet in the middle of nowhere. We counted the occupants climbing out. Five from the open back, including one in a red baseball cap. And three from the front cab.

"Their leader was greeted by some kind of village headman, then the light faded and human shapes went to heat blobs on infrared.

"But at the very last light, two more open-backed pickups arrived from a northern direction. They provided eight bodies, of which one was being half dragged by two others. The prisoner seemed to have blond hair. Darkness came in seconds, and one of the men from the south joined the northern group. The blond prisoner stayed with the northern group.

"Judging by the red heat signals, they were housed in two of the residences either side of the central clearing, where the three vehicles are parked. The engine heat faded, and they are now in darkness. No one seems to have emerged from either house. The only heat signals remaining are from a goat pen to one side of the open square and a few smaller, wandering ones we believe to be dogs."

The Tracker thanked her and went to the display wall. The village, in real time, was being studied by a new-on-shift Global Hawk. This RQ-4 would have thirty-five hours of endurance, more than enough, and with its synthetic-aperture radar and electro-optical infrared camera would see anything move down there.

The Tracker spent some minutes watching the red blobs of the pye-dogs, ranging between the dark squares of the houses.

"Do you have anything for alarm dogs, David?"

"We shoot 'em."

"Too noisy."

"We don't miss."

"One squeal and the rest will scatter, barking."

He turned to the master sergeant.

"Will you send someone to the med center? Ask for the strongest and fastest-acting edible anesthetic they have. And from the commissary, some packs of raw beefsteak."

The sergeant got on the phone. The Pathfinders exchanged glances. Tracker moved to the still photos, the last taken in natural daylight.

The hamlet was so crusted with desert sand that, being built of local sandstone the same color, it had virtually disappeared. There were a number of scrubby trees around it, and in the center of the square, its life-source: a well.

The shadows were long and black, thrown from west to

east by the setting sun. The three technicals were still clear, parked next to one another near the well. There were figures around them, but not sixteen. Some must have gone straight inside. There were eight photos from different angles, but they all told the same story. What was of most use was to learn the angle from which the attack should come—the south.

The house to which the Marka party had gone was on that side, and there was an alley that led from it into the desert. He moved to the large-scale map pinned to the wall beside the photos. Someone had helpfully marked with a small red cross the speck in the desert on which they would be dropping. He gathered the six Pathfinders around him and spent thirty minutes pointing out what he had deduced. They had seen most of it for themselves before he arrived.

But he realized they would all have to sandwich into three hours the sort of detail absorption that could take days of study. He glanced at his watch. It was nine p.m. Wheels-up time could not be delayed beyond midnight.

"I advise we aim to drop five clicks due south of the target and tab the rest."

He knew enough to use British army slang: *click* for "kilometer" and *tab* for "forced march." The captain raised an eyebrow.

"You said 'we,' Jamie."

"That's right. I did not fly down here just to brief you. The leadership is yours, but I'm jumping with you."

"We don't usually jump with passengers. Unless, of course, the passenger is in tandem, strapped to Barry here."

Tracker glanced at the giant towering over him. He did

not fancy plunging five miles through freezing blackness harnessed to this human mastodon.

"David, I am not a passenger. I am a U.S. Recon Marine. I have seen combat in Iraq and Afghanistan. I have done deep-dive scuba and free falling. You can put me where you like in the stick, but I'll go in with my own canopy. Are we clear?"

"Clear."

"How high do you want to exit the plane?"

"Twenty-five thousand."

It made sense. At that height, the four roaring Allison turboprops would be almost inaudible, and to any alert listener it would still sound like a passing airliner. Half that height might sound alarm bells. He had only ever dived from 15,000 feet, and there was a difference. At fifteen, you do not need thermal clothing or an oxygen bottle; at twenty-five, you do.

"Well, that's all right, then," he said.

David asked the youngest, Tim, to go to the Hercules outside and come back with various pieces of extra kit. They always carried spare equipment, and because they were returning home from a fortnight in Oman, the hull of the Hercules was stacked with things that might otherwise remain on the ground. A few minutes later, Tim came back with three extra men in army fatigue overalls; one of them was carrying a spare BT80, the French-made canopy the Pathfinders always insisted on using. Like all British Special Forces, they had the privilege of picking their own stuff on a worldwide spectrum.

In this manner, apart from a French chute, they chose the

American M4 assault rifle, the Belgian Browning thirteen-shot sidearm and the British SAS combat knife, the K-bar.

Dai, the comms man, would be packing the American PRC-152 TacSat (tactical satellite) handheld radio and the British FireStorm video-downlink optical sensor.

Two hours to wheels up. In the operations room, the seven men dressed themselves, piece by piece, in the equipment that would finally leave them, like medieval knights in armor, hardly able to move unaided.

A pair of jump boots were found for the Tracker. Fortunately, he was of medium build, and the rest of the clothing fit without a problem. Then came the Bergen haversack that would contain night vision goggles, water, ammunition, sidearm and more.

They were assisted in this, and most of all the Tracker, by the three new men, the PDs, or parachute dispatchers. These, like squires in the days of old, would escort their Pathfinders to the very edge of the ramp, locked to tether lines in case they slipped, and see them launch into the void.

In dummy runs, they pulled on both BT80 and Bergen, one on the back side, the other on the chest, and tightened the straps of both until they hurt. Then the carbines, muzzle pointing downward, gloves, oxygen bottles and helmets. The Tracker was surprised to see how similar to his motorcycle helmet was the Pathfinder's, except that this version had a black rubber oxygen mask dangling beneath it, and the goggles were more like the scuba version. Then they undressed again.

It was ten-thirty. Wheels up could be no later than midnight, for there were almost exactly five hundred miles to cover between Djibouti and the speck in the Somali desert that they intended to attack. Two hours' flying time, the Tracker had calculated, and two hours' tab to target. Going in at four a.m. ought to catch their enemies at the deepest depth of sleep and at slowest reaction time. He gave his six companions the last mission briefing.

"This man is the target," he said and handed around a postcard-sized portrait. They all studied the face, memorizing it, aware that in six hours it might show up in the glow of their night vision goggles inside a stinking Somali shack. The face staring out of the postcard was that of Tony Suárez, presumably enjoying the Californian sun eleven time zones to the west. But it was as good as they were going to get.

"He is a very high-value al-Qaeda target, a practiced murderer with a passionate hatred of both our countries."

He moved over to the photos on the wall.

"He arrived from Marka in the south, al-Shabaab territory, in a single pickup truck, or technical. This one. He had with him seven men, including a guide who went off to rejoin his own group—of that, more later. That leaves seven in the target's party. But one won't fight. Inside the bastard's group is a foreign agent working for us. He looks like this."

He produced another photo, bigger, a blowup, of the face of Opal in the Marka compound, gazing up at the sky, straight into the Hawk's camera lens. He wore the red baseball cap.

"With luck, he will hear the shooting and dive for cover, and, hopefully, he will think to pull on the red cap you see here. He will not fight us. Under no circumstances shoot him. That leaves six in all and they will fight."

The Pathfinders stared at the black Ethiopian face and memorized it.

"What about the other group, boss?" asked the shaven Curly, the motor vehicles man.

"Right. The drone watched our target and his team billeted in this house here, on the south side of the village square. Across the square is the group they came to meet. These are pirates from the north. They are all of the Sacad clan and fight like hell. They have brought with them a hostage in the person of a young Swedish merchant marine cadet. This one."

The Tracker produced his last photo. He had got it from Adrian Herbert of the SIS, who had obtained it from Mrs. Bulstrode. It was taken from his merchant marine ID card application form, delivered by his father Harry Andersson. It showed a handsome blond boy in a company uniform, staring innocently at the camera.

"What's he doing there?" asked David.

"He is the bait that lured the target to this spot. He wants to buy the kid and has brought with him a million dollars for the purchase. They may have made the swap already, in which case the boy will be in the target's house and the million dollars across the square. Or the swap may be scheduled for the morning before departure. Whatever, keep all eyes peeled for a blond head and do not shoot."

"What does the target want with a Swedish cadet?" It was Barry, the giant. The Tracker framed his answer carefully. No need to lie, just observe the rule of need to know.

"The Sacads from the north who captured him at sea

some weeks ago have been told the target intends to hack his head off on camera. A treat for us in the West."

The room went very quiet.

"And these pirates, they'll fight as well?" David, the captain, again.

"Absolutely. But I figure when they are woken by shooting, they will be bleary from the aftereffects of a gut full of *khat*. We know it makes them dopey or ultra-violent.

"If we can put a long stream of bullets through their windows, they will presume not that some free fallers have arrived from the West but that they are under attack from their business partners, trying to get the boy for free or their money back. I would like them to charge across the open square."

"How many, boss? The pirates?"

"We counted eight climbing out of these two technicals just before sundown."

"So fourteen hostiles in all?"

"Yes, and I'd like half of them dead before they are vertical. And no prisoners."

The six Brits gathered around the photos and maps. There was a murmured conference. The Tracker heard phrases like "shaped charge" and "frag." He knew enough to know the first referred to a device to blow off a stout door lock and the second to a high-fragmentation grenade. Fingers tapped various points on the blown-up photo of the village by last daylight. After ten minutes, they broke up, and the young captain came over with a grin.

"It's a go," he said. "Let's kit up."

The Tracker realized they had been agreeing to proceed

with an operation that had been requested by the President of the United States and authorized by their own Prime Minister.

"Great," was all he could think to say. They left the operations room and went outside, where the air was still balmy. While they had been studying the mission, the three PDs had been busy. Bathed in the light from the open door of the hangar were seven piles of kit in a line. This was the line (in reverse) in which they would march into the belly of the Hercules and the order in which they would hurl themselves into the night at 25,000 feet.

Assisted by the PDs, they began to climb into their equipment. The senior PD, a veteran sergeant known only as Jonah, paid special attention to the Tracker.

The Tracker, who had arrived in the tropical-weight uniform of a U.S. Marine colonel, into which he had changed in the Grumman, was instructed to pull on the spare desert cammo jumpsuit that the other six already wore. Then came the weight, burden by burden.

Jonah hoisted the thirty kilos of parachute onto his back and buckled the array of broad canvas straps that keep it in place. When he had the straps in place, he tightened them until the Tracker felt he was being crushed. Two of them went around each side of the groin.

"Just keep the nuts free of these, sir," Jonah murmured. A faller with his family furniture inside these straps will find life very unfunny when the chute jerks open.

"I surely will," he said, feeling down below to make sure nothing was trapped behind the straps.

Next came the Bergen haversack, hung on the chest. This

was forty kilos and pulled him into a forward stoop. The straps of this were also tightened to chest-crushing levels. But from his U.S. Marine parachuting school, he knew there was a point to all this.

With the Bergen on the front, the faller would have to be diving chest first. When the chute finally streamed, it would be out the back and away above him. A faller on his back could go straight through his opening chute, which would literally wrap around him like a shroud as he died on the ground below.

The Bergen's weight was mainly made up of food, water and ammunition—the latter being extra clips for his carbine and for grenades. But also in there was his personal sidearm and night vision goggles. It was out of the question to wear these while diving; they would be ripped away by the slipstream.

Jonah attached his oxygen canister and the array of hoses that would bring the life-giving gas to the mask on his face.

Finally, he was given his helmet and tight-fitting visor that would protect his eyes from being blasted out by the 150 mph airstream he would experience in the dive. Then they took off the Bergens until jump time.

The seven men had been transformed into extraterrestrials from the special effects department. They did not walk; they waddled, slowly and carefully. On a nod from the captain, David, they made their way across the concrete pan to the gaping rear of the Hercules, which waited, doors open and ramp down.

The captain had decreed the order of jumps. First out would be Barry, the giant, simply because he was the most experienced among them. Then would come the Tracker, and right behind him the captain. Of the remaining four, the last man out would be one of the corporals, Curly, also a veteran, because he would have no one to watch his back.

One by one, the seven jumpers, helped by the three PDs, stumbled up the ramp and into the hull of the C-130. Twenty to midnight.

They sat in a line of red canvas seats along one side of the hull while the PDs continued to run through the various tests. Jonah took personal care of the captain and the Tracker.

He noticed it was now much darker inside the aircraft, with only reflected lights from the arcs above the hangar doors, and he knew when the ramp came up, they would be seated in utter blackness. He also noted crates of the unit's other equipment lashed down for the journey back home to England and two shadowy figures up near the wall between the cargo and the flight deck. These were the two parachute packers who traveled with the unit wherever they went, packing and repacking the chutes. The Tracker hoped that the fellow who had packed what he now wore on his back knew exactly what he was doing. There is an old adage among free fallers: Never quarrel with your packer.

Jonah reached over him and flipped up the top of his para rucksack to check that the two wires in red cotton were present and correct. Seals unbroken. The veteran RAF sergeant clipped his oxygen mask into the aircraft supply and nodded. The Tracker checked his mask was a snug and airtight fit, and took a breath.

A rush of near-pure oxygen. They would be breathing this all the way to altitude to flush the last traces of nitrogen out of the blood. This prevents diver's bends (nitrogen bubbling in the blood) when they hurtled back down through the pressure zones. Jonah switched off the oxygen and moved on to the captain to do the same for him.

From outside came a high-pitched whine, as the four Allisons turned on starter motor and then coughed to life. Jonah stepped forward and buckled the safety strap across the Tracker's knees. The last thing he did for him was to plug the oxygen mask into the C-130's onboard supply.

The engine noise increased to a roar as the rear ramp rose to shut out the last of the lights of Djibouti air base and closed with a clunk as the air seal locked in. It was now pitch-dark inside the hull. Jonah broke out Cyalume light sticks to help him and his two fellow PDs take their seats, backs to the wall, as the Herc began to roll.

The seated men, leaning back into their chute packs, forty-kilo Bergens on their laps, seemed to be slumbering in a nightmare of pounding noise, plus the whine of hydraulics, as the aircrew tested the flaps, and the scream of fuel injectors.

They could not see, but only feel, as the four-engined workhorse turned onto the main runway, paused, crouched, then leapt forward. Despite its deceptive bulk, the Herc accelerated fast, tilted its nose up and left the tarmac after five hundred yards. Then it climbed steeply.

The most frills-free airliner cannot compare with the rear of a C-130. No soundproofing, no heating, no pressurization and certainly no beverage service. The Tracker knew it would never get quieter, but it would become savagely cold as the air thinned. Nor is the rear leakproof. Despite the oxygen-delivering mask on his face, the place was by now redolent with the odors of aviation gas and oil.

Beside him, the captain unhooked his helmet, took it off and pulled a pair of earphones over his head. There was a spare pair hanging from the same socket, and he offered them to the Tracker.

Jonah, up against the forward wall, was already on earphones. He needed to listen to the cockpit to learn when to start preparing for P-hour—*P* for "parachute"—the jump time. The Tracker and the captain could hear the commentary from the cockpit, the voice of the British squadron leader, a veteran of the 47th Squadron, who had flown and landed his "bird" into some of the roughest and most dangerous airstrips on Earth.

"Climbing through ten thousand," he said, then "P-hour minus one hundred." One hour and forty minutes to jump. Later came: "Leveling at twenty-five thousand." Eighty minutes passed.

The headphones helped muffle the engine roar, but the temperature had dropped to near zero. Jonah unbelted himself and came over, holding on to a rail running down the side of the hull. There was no chance of conversation; everything was hand signals.

In front of the face of each of the seven, he went through his pantomime. Right hand high, forefinger and thumb forming an O. Like scuba divers. You OK? The Pathfinders replied in kind. Hand held up, fist clenched, then a puff from the lips to blow the fingers open, then five raised fingers. Wind speed at touchdown point, estimated five knots. Finally, fist held high with five fingers splayed, four times. Twenty minutes to P-hour.

Before he finished his odyssey, David grabbed his arm and thrust into his hand a flat packet. Jonah nodded and grinned. He took the packet and disappeared into the flight-deck area. When he came back, he was still grinning in the darkness and resumed his seat.

Ten minutes later, he was back. This time, ten fingers held up in front of each of the seven men. Seven nods. All seven rose with their Bergens, turned and placed the haversacks on the seats. Then they hefted the forty-kilo burdens onto their chests and tightened the straps.

Jonah came forward to help the Tracker, then tightened the straps until the American thought his chest was being crushed. But the speed in the dive would be up to 150 mph, and nothing must shift by even an inch. Then the switch from the onboard oxygen to personal canister.

At this moment, the Tracker heard a new noise. Over the roar of engines, the aircraft's speaker system was booming out music, fortissimo. The Tracker realized what David had given to Jonah to be passed to the flight deck. It was a CD. The cavernous hull of the C-130 was being drowned in the pounding clamor of Wagner's "Ride of the Valkyries." The start of his personal chant was the signal: three minutes to P-hour.

The seven men were standing along the starboard side of the fuselage when the dull clunk of a breaking seal meant the ramp was coming down. Jonah and his two assistant PDs had attached their tether lines to ensure they could not slide out.

As the sinking ramp revealed a barn-door-sized opening to the sky, an icy blast of wind roared in, accompanied by the stench of aviation fuel and burning oil.

The Tracker, standing second in line behind Barry, the giant, looked past the lead jumper toward the void. Nothing out there, just swirling darkness, freezing cold, pounding noise, and inside the fuselage the raging brass of the Valkyries on their insane ride to Valhalla.

There was one last check. The Tracker saw Jonah's mouth open but heard not a word. Down the line, Curly, the last out, checked Tim, the trooper, in front of him to ensure his chute and oxygen had no tangles. Then he shouted, "Seven OK."

Jonah must have heard it because he nodded at Tim, who then did the same for Pete, the medic, in front of him. The mutual checking rippled down the line. The Tracker felt the clap on his shoulder and did the same for Barry in front of him.

Jonah was standing in front of the giant, facing him. He nodded as the Tracker made the last check and stepped aside. There was nothing left to do. After all the pushing and shoving and grunting, the seven free fallers could only hurl themselves into the night five miles above the Somali desert.

Barry took one step forward, lowered his torso into a dive and was gone. The reason for the line being tightly bunched was that wide separation in the air could be disastrous. A three-second gap in the blackness, and two fallers could be so far apart they would never see or find each other. As briefed, the Tracker went out within a second of Barry's heels disappearing.

The sensations were immediate. In half a second, the noise was gone; the roar of the C-130's four Allisons, the Wagner—all gone, to be replaced by the silence of the night, broken only by a gentle and rising wind hiss as his falling body accelerated past 100 mph.

He felt the slipstream of the departing Hercules try to flip him over, ankles above head, then onto his back, and fought against it. Though there was no moon, the desert stars, hard and bright, cold and constant, unmarred by any pollution for two thousand miles, gave a low illumination to the sky.

Looking down, he saw a dark shape far below. He knew that close behind his shoulder would be the para captain, David, with the other four strung out upward to the sky.

David appeared beside him, arms by his sides, adopting the arrow position to increase speed and close up on Barry. The Tracker did the same. Slowly the big black form ahead came closer. Barry was in the starfish shape, gloved fists clenched ahead of him, arms and legs half spread, to slow the fall to 120 mph. When they came level with him, the Tracker and the captain did the same.

They fell in a rough echelon formation, joined one by one by the other four. He saw the captain check his wrist altimeter, adjusted for the ambient air pressure above the desert.

Although he could not see it, the altimeter said the troop was passing through 15,000 feet. They would open chutes at 5,000. As the lead jumper, it was Barry's job to ease ahead and, using experience and the dim light of the stars, try to pick a landing zone as smooth and rock-free as possible. The

Tracker's concern was to stay with the para captain and do whatever he did.

Even from 25,000 feet, the free fall only lasted ninety seconds. Barry was by now slightly below the other six, scanning the ground rushing toward him. The others gently moved into staggered line formation, never losing eye contact with each other.

The Tracker reached for the pocket in his chute pack to make sure he had contact with the chute release mechanism. Pathfinders do not use the D ring rip to open the chute. They can opt for aneroid pressure-triggered release, but things mechanical can and do go wrong. Coming down at 120 mph is no time to discover the gizmo has not worked. David and the rest preferred manual release.

This is what the Tracker was reaching for. It is a parachute-shaped piece of cloth attached to a twine and stored in an easy-access pocket on the top. When thrown into the slipstream, it will pull the entire BT80 out of its pack and deploy it.

Below him, the Tracker saw Barry hit the 5,000-foot mark and the flash of the canopy, gray in the surrounding blackness. Out of the corner of his eye, he saw David toss his release drogue into the air and then disappear upward.

The Tracker did the same and almost instantaneously felt the jerk of the huge chute pulling him backward and upward—or so it seemed. It was, in fact, simply slowing him down. The sensation was of driving a car fast into a wall and the air bag going off. But it lasted just three seconds; then he was floating.

The BT80 is nothing like the domed parachutes of paratroopers jumping on a military exercise. It is a colossal oblong of silk, mattress-shaped, a flying wing that, on a high-altitude opening, can let the trooper glide mile after mile behind the enemy lines unseen by radar or the human eye.

The Pathfinders liked it for that, and another reason. It opens silently as opposed to the whip-crack of others, which can alert a sentry below.

At 800 feet, the para captain released his Bergen, which dropped on its lanyard to hang twelve feet beneath him. The Tracker did the same. A few feet above them, the remaining four followed suit.

The U.S. Marine watched the ground, now clear in the starlight, rushing toward him, heard the plop of the Bergen hitting the sand and performed the final braking maneuver. He reached upward, grabbing the two toggles controlling the canopy, and pulled down. The chute flared and slowed, permitting him to hit the deck at a brisk run. Then the chute lost its shape, folded and flopped to the ground as a tangled mess of silk and nylon cords. He unclipped the chest and leg harnesses, and the remainder of the para pack fell to the sand. It had served its purpose. All around him, six Pathfinders were doing the same.

He checked his watch. Four minutes after two a.m. Good scheduling. But it took time to clear up and form a line of march.

The seven chutes had to be collected, along with the no-further-use helmets and oxygen masks, plus the oxygen canisters. They were all piled together, and three Pathfinders covered them with rocks.

Out of the Bergens came the sidearms and night vision

goggles, the NVGs. There was enough starlight for them not to be needed on the march, but they would certainly give an unmatchable edge when attacking the village, turning pitch-black night into green and watery day.

Dai, the Welsh Wizard, was poring over his equipment. Thanks to modern technology, their task was simpler than it would have been before the drone.

Somewhere high above them was a Global Hawk RQ-4, operated by J-SOC out of MacDill Air Force Base, Tampa. It was gazing down at them, and at the village, and could see them both. It could also detect any living creature by body heat, showing up as a pale blob of light on the landscape.

J-SOC headquarters had patched through an image of everything Tampa saw to the communications room at Djibouti, with sound and picture. Dai was setting up and testing his direct radio link with Djibouti, which could tell him exactly where he was, where the village was, the line of march between the two and whether there was any activity in the target area.

After a murmured conversation with Djibouti, Dai reported to the rest. Both controllers could see them as seven pale blobs on the desert. The village was motionless, seemingly fast asleep. There were no human beings outside the cluster of houses, inside which they could not be detected. But all the village's wealth, a flock of goats, four donkeys and two camels, was in a corral or tethered out in the open and showed up clearly.

There were a few smaller blobs that moved about—the pye-dogs. The distance was 4.8 kilometers and the optimum line of march on a compass heading of 020 true.

The para captain had his own Silva compass and his own SOPHIE thermal imaging system. Despite the assurances of Tampa, he switched it on and ran its beam in a circle around them. They froze when a small blob showed up on top of a ridge along the edge of the sandy basin Barry had chosen as a good place to land.

Too small for a human but big enough for a watching head. Then it gave a low whine and disappeared. A desert jackal. At 02.22, they set off in Indian file to the north.

15

They tabbed in a loose line astern, with Curly as the lead scout to give warning of the first sign of opposition. There was none. David the captain was second. He swung his imaging system from side to side, but no other warm-blooded creatures showed themselves.

Dai had his comm set in his rucksack at the top of his Bergen, behind his head, and a plug in one ear to listen to anything from Tampa via Djibouti, which were watching them from the stratosphere. At ten to four, he advanced to David's side and whispered: "Half a mile, boss."

They advanced the next eight hundred yards at a crouch, each man bowed by the forty kilos on his back. While they marched, high above them clouds appeared in the sky, lowering the light level.

The captain stopped and made a gentle wave-down motion with one arm. The rest sank toward the sand. David produced a monocular night vision scope and peered ahead.

Then he saw it, the first of the squat cuboidal houses of the village. The Silva compass had brought them to the threshold of the target.

He stowed the monocular and pulled on the goggles. The other six followed. For each man, the vision changed from slowly diminishing starlight to a brighter, almost sub-aqua-green tunnel. All the NVG does is to capture every scintilla of ambient light and concentrate it into one forward tunnel. The wearer loses spatial awareness and must turn his head to see anything left or right.

With the target in sight, the men had no need of the Bergens but great need of the ammunition and grenades inside them. They lowered the packs to the ground, slipped out of the shoulder straps and filled every pocket on their jumpsuits with ordnance. Their M4 rifles and sidearms already had full chambers.

David and the Tracker crawled forward together. They were staring at exactly what one of the angled shots from the Global Hawk had freeze-framed for them back at Djibouti. There was an alley that led from the village center to the desert where they crouched. Somewhere up it, on the left side, was the larger house identified as that of the headman, now taken over by the Preacher's party.

A small pye-dog trotted down the alley, stopped and sniffed. Another joined it. They were both mangy, possibly rabid, accustomed to foraging amid the garbage, eating excrement or, on feast days, the entrails of a slaughtered goat. They sniffed again, suspecting there was something out there but not yet alarmed enough to bark and trigger a multi-dog alarm.

The Tracker took something from a breast pocket and

threw it like a baseball pitcher toward the dogs. It landed with a soft phut in the sand. Both dogs jumped, then sniffed again before barking. Raw beefsteak. They approached, sniffed again, and the lead dog swallowed the tidbit in a single gulp. Another followed for his friend. The second treat disappeared.

The Tracker sent a salvo of meat chunks into the mouth of the alley. More dogs appeared, nine in all, saw their leaders gulping down the treats and did the same. There were twenty morsels, more than two each. Every cur got at least one. Then they sniffed around to see if there were more.

The original eaters began to stumble. Then their legs failed and they fell over, lying on their sides, kicking feebly. Finally, they ceased to move. The remaining seven did the same. Within ten minutes of the first throw, they were all unconscious.

David rose to a crouch and gestured forward, rifle at the port, finger on trigger. Five followed him. Barry remained to scan the exteriors of the houses. A donkey brayed from deep inside the hamlet. Nothing moved. The enemies ahead of them either slept or waited in ambush. The Tracker believed it was the former. The men from Marka were also strangers, and the dogs would have barked at them also. He was right.

The attack group entered the alley and approached the house on the left. It was the third up, facing the square. The masked men could make out a door on the alley, thick old timber, brought once from somewhere else, for only scrubby camel thorn bushes grew nearby. The plank door had two ring handles but no lock with keyhole. David tested it with fingertips. It did not budge. Barred from the inside, crude but effective. It would take a battering ram. He beckoned to Tim, the munitions man, pointed at the door and withdrew.

Tim was holding what looked like a small wreath. He applied this to the crack between the left- and right-hand halves of the double door. Had it been metal, magnets or putty would have worked. Being timber, he used thumbtacks. There was no hammering, just pressure from his thumb. When the wreath was fixed, he set the short fuse and waved the others back.

They withdrew fifteen feet and crouched. Because it was a shaped charge, there would be no outward explosive force. The fury of the PETN plastic explosive would all be forward, cutting the wood like a chain saw in a fraction of a second.

When it came, the Tracker was surprised how low the noise was: a muted crack like a twig snapping. Then the first four were through the door, which swung weakly to the touch, its inner crossbar splintered and broken. Tim and Dai remained outside, covering the square with its three pickup trucks, tethered donkeys and corralled goats.

The para captain was first in, the Tracker at his shoulder. There were three men rising, half asleep, from the floor. The hitherto silent night was ripped by two M4 carbine on automatic mode. All three were from the Marka party. They were the Preacher's bodyguards. They were dead before they got upright. Yells came from an inner room beyond a farther door.

The captain paused a moment to ensure all three were very dead; Pete and Curly came in from the alley; the Tracker kicked the inner door and went through. He prayed Opal, wherever he was, would have responded to the first fusillade by diving for the floor, preferably under a bed.

There were two men in the room. Unlike their companions in the hall, they had requisitioned two of the family's beds, rough charpoys with camel's hair blankets. They were up but sightless in the pitch-blackness. The burly one, the fourth bodyguard, had been perhaps dozing but not fast asleep; clearly he was the night watch, supposed to stay awake. He was up, with a handgun, and he fired.

The bullet went past the Tracker's head, but what really hurt was the blaze of light from the muzzle, magnified many times by the goggles. It was like a searchlight in the face. He fired blind but on auto, sweeping right to left. His bullet stream took both men, the fourth Pakistani and the one who turned out to be Jamma, the private secretary.

Outside at the entrance to the square, as agreed, Tim and Dai raked the house across the square, the one sheltering the Sacad clansmen from Garacad. The paras fired long streams through each window. There was no glass in them, just nailed-up blankets. They knew their bullets would be above bed height, so they slammed in fresh magazines and waited for the reaction. It was not long.

In the headman's house there was a low scuffling noise and a hint of movement. The Tracker swung toward it. A third truckle bed, tucked away in the corner. Someone beneath it, a hint of baseball cap.

"Stay there," he shouted. "Don't move. Don't come out." The scuffling stopped, the cap was withdrawn.

He swung around to the three men behind him.

"Clear in here. Go help with the northern gang."

Out on the square, six from Garacad, convinced they were betrayed by those from Marka, came across the square in a charge, Kalashnikovs held low, dodging between the donkeys, which screamed and reared on their halters, and the three parked vehicles.

But they were in darkness. The clouds now covered the stars. Tim and Dai picked out one each and "slotted" them. The muzzle flashes were enough for the other four. They brought up their Russian guns. Tim and Dai went facedown fast. Behind them, Pete, Curly and their captain came into the alley, saw the muzzle flashes from the Kalashnikovs and also went down.

From prone positions, the five paras took out two more of the running men. The fifth, firing on empty when his magazine ran out, paused to slot in a fresh one. He was clearly visible beside the goat pen, and two M4 rounds took his head off.

The last was crouching behind one of the technicals, out of sight. The firing died and stopped. Trying to find a target in the darkness, he popped his head around the front of the engine block. He was unaware his enemies had NVGs; his head was like a green football. Another round blew his brains out.

Then there really was silence. There was no more response from the house with the pirates, but the paras were two short. They needed eight; they had taken down six. They prepared to charge and risk taking casualties, but there was no need. From way behind the village, they heard more shots, three in all, spaced a second apart.

Seeing the village well roused, Barry had abandoned his useless vigil outside the alley and raced around to the back. With his NVGs, he saw three figures running out of the back of the pirate house. Two were in robes, the third, stumbling and pleading, being hustled along with the two Somalis, had a thatch of blond hair.

Barry did not even challenge the runners. He rose from the camel thorn scrub when they were twenty yards away and fired. The one with the Kalashnikov, Duale, of the one eye, went first; the older man, later identified as al-Afrit, the Devil, took two spaced bullets in the chest.

The huge para walked over to his kills. The blond lad was between them, on his side, in the fetal position, crying softly.

"That's all right, son," said the veteran sergeant. "It's over. Time to take you home."

He tried to raise the teenager to his feet, but his legs had given way. So he picked the lad up like a doll, put him over his shoulder and began to stride back to the village.

The Tracker stared through his goggles at the room where the last of the Marka party had died. All but one. There was a doorway to one side; not a door but a hanging blanket covering the aperture.

He went through it on a rolling dive, staying below the likely firing line of a shooter in the room. Inside, he jumped to one side of the doorway and brought his M4 to bear. There was no shot.

He stared around the room, the last of the house, the best, the headman's room. There was a bed with a coverlet, but it was empty, the blanket thrown to one side.

There was a fireplace and a cluster of still-glowing embers, painfully white through the goggles. A large armchair, and sitting in it, watching him, an old man. They stared at each other for several seconds. The old man spoke quite calmly.

"You may shoot me. I am old and my time has come." He spoke in Somali, but, with his Arabic, the Tracker could just understand it. He replied in Arabic.

"I do not want to shoot you, Sheikh. You are not he whom I seek."

The old man gazed at him without fear. What he saw, of course, was a cammo-uniformed monster with frog's eyes.

"You are of the *kuffar*, but you speak the language of the Holy Koran."

"It is true, and I seek a man. A very bad man. He has killed many. Also Muslims, women and even children."

"Have I seen him?"

"You have seen him, Sheikh. He was here. He has"—the old man would never have seen amber—"eyes the color of fresh-drawn honey."

"Ah." The old man waved a hand dismissively, as one gesturing away something he did not like. "He has gone with the woman's clothes."

For a second, the Tracker felt a punch of disappointment. Escaped, swathed in a burqa and hijab, hiding in the desert, impossible to find. Then he noticed the old man was glancing upward, and he understood.

When the women of the hamlet washed their clothes in water from the well, they dared not hang them to dry in the square for the goats, who could feast off camel thorn spines, would tear them to shreds. So they erected frames on the flat roofs.

The Tracker went out the door across the room. There was a set of steps running up the side of the house. He leaned his M4 against the wall and drew his sidearm. His rubber-cleated jump boots made no sound going up the brick steps. He emerged on the roof and looked around. There were six drying frames.

In the half-light, he examined them all. For the women, dishdashas; for the men, white cotton *lungis*, the sarongs of the Somalis, draped over twig frames to dry. One seemed taller and narrower. It had a long white Pakistani *shalwar kameez* shirt, a head, a bushy beard, and it moved. Then three things happened so fast they almost cost the Tracker his life.

The moon came out from behind the clouds at last. It was full and dazzlingly white. It destroyed his night vision in a second, blinding him through the light-concentrating NVGs.

The man ahead of him was charging, and the Tracker tore off his goggles and raised his Browning thirteen-shot. The assailant had his right arm raised, and there was something in it that glinted.

He squeezed the Browning's trigger. The hammer fell—on an empty chamber. A misfire, and, on a second squeeze, another. Very rare but possible. He knew he had a full magazine in there but nothing in the chamber.

With his free left hand, he seized a cotton dishdasha, bunched it into a ball and threw it at the descending blade. The steel hit the fluttering cloth, but the material wrapped itself around the metal so that when it hit his shoulder, it was blunted. With his right hand, he threw down the Browning and from a sheath on his right thigh he drew his U.S. Marine fighting knife, almost the one thing he still had that he had brought from London.

The bearded man was not using a *jambiya*, the short, curved but mainly ornamental knife of Yemen, but a *billao*— a big, razor-sharp knife used only by Somalis. Two slashes from a *billao* will take off an arm; a lunge with the needle point will go through a torso from front to back.

The attacker changed grip, twisting his wrist so the blade was held low for an upward thrust, as a street fighter would hold it. The Tracker had his vision back. He noted the man in front of him was barefoot, which would give him a good grip on the clay-brick roof. But so would his own rubber soles.

The next attack from the *billao* came fast and low to his left side, rising for the entrails, but that was where he expected it. His own left hand came down on the rising wrist, blocking it, the steel tip three inches from his body. He felt his own right wrist also gripped.

The Preacher was twelve years younger and hard from a life of asceticism in the mountains. In a trial of brute strength, he might win. The *billao* point advanced an inch toward his midriff. He remembered his parachute instructor at Fort Bragg, a seasoned fighting man apart from teaching free fall.

"East of Suez and south of Tripoli, they're not good street fighters," he explained once over a beer or three at the sergeants' club. "They rely on their blades. They ignore the balls and the bridge."

He meant the bridge of the nose. The Tracker pulled back his head and snapped it forward. He took his own pain on the top of the forehead and knew he would have a bump; but he felt the crack as the other man's septum shattered.

So also did the grip of the hand holding his wrist. He tore his hand free, drew back and lunged. His blade went clear between the fifth and sixth ribs on the left side. A few inches away from his face, he saw the hate-filled amber eyes, the slow expression of disbelief as his steel drove into the heart, the light of life fading away.

He saw the amber fade away to black under the moon and felt the weight sag against his knife. He thought of his father on the bed in the ICU and leaned forward until his lips were just above the full dark beard. And he whispered: "Semper Fi, Preacher."

The Pathfinders formed a defensive ring to wait out the hour until dawn, but the watchers in Tampa were able to reassure them there was no hostile intervention heading their way. The desert was the province of only the jackal.

All the Bergens were recovered from the desert, including Pete's medical pack. He tended the rescued cadet Ove Carlsson. The lad was infected with parasites from his weeks in the dungeon in Garacad, undernourished and traumatized. Pete attended to what he could, including a shot of morphine. The cadet went into a deep sleep, his first in weeks, on a bed in front of the stoked-up fire.

Curly examined all three technicals in the square by torch light. One was riddled with M4 and Kalashnikov fire and would clearly not roll again. The other two were roadworthy when he had finished with them and contained petrol-filled jerrycans, enough for several hundred miles.

At first light, David talked with Djibouti and assured them the patrol could use the two technicals to drive west to the Ethiopian border. Just across it was the desert airstrip they had designated as their best extraction point, if they could make it. Curly estimated two hundred miles, or ten hours' driving, accounting for fuel stops, some tire changes and presuming no hostile action. They were assured the C-130 Hercules, long back at Djibouti, would be waiting for them.

Agent Opal, the jet-black Ethiopian, was hugely relieved to be free of his increasingly dangerous masquerade. The paras broke open their food packs and made a passable breakfast, of which the highlight and center point was a blazing fire in the grate and several mugs of strong, sweet milky tea.

The bodies were dragged out to the square and left for the villagers to bury. A large wad of local Somali currency was found on the body of the Preacher and donated to the headman for all his trouble.

The case containing one million dollars in cash was found under the bed from which the Preacher had fled to the roof. The para captain made the point that, as they had abandoned half a million dollars of parachutes and para packs in the desert, and as going back in the wrong direction to look for them would not be a good idea, could they not reimburse the regiment from the booty? Point conceded.

At dawn they rigged a truckle bed in the open rear of one of the technicals for the still-sleeping Ove Carlsson, hefted their seven Bergens into the other, bade farewell to the headman and left.

Curly's estimate was pretty accurate. Eight hours from that speck of a hamlet brought them to the invisible Ethiopian border. Tampa told them when they crossed it and gave them a steer toward the airstrip. It was not much of a place. No concrete runway, but a thousand yards of dead-flat, rock-hard gravel. No control tower, no hangars; just a wind sock, fluttering fitfully in the breeze, of a baking day about to die.

At one end stood the comforting bulk of a C-130 Hercules, in the RAF livery of the 47th Squadron. It was the first thing they saw, a mile away, across the Ogaden sand. As they approached, the rear ramp came down, and Jonah trotted out to greet them, along with his two co-dispatchers and the two packers. There would be no work for them: The seven parachutes, at £50,000 a pop, were gone.

Standing beside the Herc was a surprise: a white Beech King Air, in the livery of the United Nations World Food Programme. Two deeply tanned men in desert camouflage stood next to it. Each soldier on each shoulder wore a flash bearing a six-pointed star.

As the two-truck convoy came to a halt, Opal, who was riding in the back of the lead pickup, jumped out and ran over to them. Both embraced him in fervent man hugs. Curious, the Tracker walked across.

The Israeli major did not introduce himself as Benny, but he knew exactly who the American was.

"Just one short question," said the Tracker. "Then I'll say good-bye. How do you get an Ethiopian to work for you?"

The major looked surprised, as if it was obvious.

"He's Falasha," he said. "He's as Jewish as I am."

The Tracker vaguely recalled the story of the small tribe of Ethiopian Jews who, a generation ago, was spirited in its entirety out of Ethiopia and the grip of its brutal dictator. He turned to the young agent and threw a salute.

"Well, thank you, Opal. *Todah rabah* . . . and *mazel tov.*"

The Beech went first, with just enough fuel to make Eilat. The Hercules followed, leaving the two battered pickups for the next party of desert nomads that might happen along.

Sitting in a bunker under AFB MacDill, Tampa, M.Sgt. Orde watched them go. He also saw a convoy of four vehicles, well to the east, heading for the border. An al-Shabaab pursuit party, but far too late.

At Djibouti, Ove Carlsson was taken into the state-of-the-art American base hospital until his father's executive jet arrived with the tycoon onboard to collect him.

The Tracker said good-bye to the six Pathfinders before boarding his own Grumman for Northolt, London, and Andrews, Washington. The RAF crew had slept through the day. They were fit to fly when refueling was complete.

"If I ever have to do anything that insane again, can I ask you guys to come with me?" he asked.

"No problem, mate," said Tim. The U.S. colonel did not recall when he was last called mate by a private soldier and found he quite liked it.

His Grumman took off just after midnight. He slept until it crossed the Libyan coast and chased ahead of the rising sun to London. It was autumn. There would be red and gold leaves in northern Virginia, and he would be dearly glad to see them again.

EPILOGUE

When the news of the death of their clan chief came through to Garacad, the Sacad tribesmen on the *Malmö* simply left for the shore. Captain Eklund took advantage of the—to him—unexplained chance, raised anchor and headed for the open sea. Two war skiffs from a rival clan tried to intercept him but shied away when a helicopter from a British destroyer on the horizon loudspeakered them to think again. The destroyer escorted the *Malmö* to the safety of Djibouti port, where she could refuel and then resume her journey, but in a convoy.

Mr. Abdi also heard of the death of the pirate chief and told Gareth Evans. News of the rescue of the boy was already through; then came news of the escape of the *Malmö*. Evans at once stopped payment of the five million dollars, just in time.

Mr. Abdi had already received his second gratuity of a million. He retired to a pleasant villa on the coast of Tunisia.

Six months later, some burglars broke in and, when he disturbed them, killed him.

Mustafa Dardari was released from his sojourn in Caithness. He was taken back, blindfolded and released on the streets of London, where he met two things. One was a polite official refusal to believe he had not been in his town house all along because he could not prove otherwise. His explanation of what had happened to him was regarded as quite ludicrous. The other thing was a deportation order.

The Pathfinders went back to their base at Colchester and resumed their careers.

Ove Carlsson made a complete recovery and studied for a master's degree in business administration. He joined his father's company, but he never went back to sea.

Ariel became famous in his tiny and, to most people, incomprehensible world when he invented a firewall that even he could not penetrate. His system was widely adopted by banks, defense contractors and government departments. On the Tracker's advice, he acquired a shrewd and honest business manager, who secured him royalty contracts that made him comfortably off.

His parents were able to move to a bigger house set in its own grounds, but he still lived with them and hated going out.

Colonel Christopher "Kit" Carson, aka Jamie Jackson, aka the Tracker, served out his time, retired from the Corps, married a very comely widow and set up a company delivering personal security for the ultra-wealthy traveling abroad. It made him a good living, but he never went back to Somalia.

ABOUT THE AUTHOR

Frederick Forsyth is the author of sixteen novels and short story collections, from *The Day of the Jackal*, *The Odessa File*, and *The Dogs of War* to, most recently, *The Afghan* and *The Cobra*. A former pilot and print and television reporter for Reuters and the BBC, he has had five movies and a television miniseries made from his works, and in 2012 he won the Diamond Dagger Award from the Crime Writers' Association for a career of sustained excellence. He lives in Buckinghamshire, England.